Since 2004, internationally bestselling author **Sherrilyn Kenyon** has placed over sixty novels on the *New York Times* bestseller list; in the past three years alone, she has claimed the No.1 spot seventeen times. This extraordinary bestseller continues to top every genre she writes within.

Proclaimed the pre-eminent voice in paranormal fiction by critics, Kenyon has helped pioneer – and define – the current paranormal trend that has captivated the world and continues to blaze new trails that blur traditional genre lines.

With more than 25 million copies of her books in print in over 100 countries, her current series include: The Dark-Hunters, League, Lords of Avalon, Chronicles of Nick, and Belador Code.

Visit Sherrilyn Kenyon online:

www.darkhunter.com
www.sherrilynkenyon.co.uk
www.facebook.com/AuthorSherrilynKenyon
www.twitter.com/KenyonSherrilyn

Praise for Sherrilyn Kenyon:

'A publishing phenomenon . . . [Sherrilyn Kenyon] is the reigning queen of the wildly successful paranormal scene'
Publishers Weekly

'Kenyon's writing is brisk, ironic and relentlessly imaginative. These are not your mother's vampire novels'
Boston Globe

'Whether writing as Sherrilyn Kenyon or Kinley MacGregor, this author delivers great romantic fantasy!'
New York Times bestselling author Elizabeth Lowell

Dragonbane

SHERRILYN KENYON

piatkus

PIATKUS

First published in the US in 2015 by St Martin's Press, New York
First published in Great Britain in 2015 by Piatkus

1 3 5 7 9 10 8 6 4 2

A CIP catalogue record for this book
is available from the British Library.

ISBN {HB} 978-0-349-40070-9
ISBN {TPB} 978-0-349-40071-6

Printed and bound by Clays Ltd, St Ives plc

Papers used by Piatkus are from well-managed forests
and other responsible sources.

MIX
Paper from
responsible sources
FSC® C104740

Piatkus
An imprint of
Little, Brown Book Group
Carmelite House
50 Victoria Embankment
London EC4Y 0DZ

An Hachette UK Company
www.hachette.co.uk

www.piatkus.co.uk

In memory of Vanessa Delagarza, and to all we have loved, who have left us too soon. We miss you, but you will forever live in our hearts.

For my friends and readers who have filled my heart with love and joy. Thank you for being part of my life . . . the very best part.

For my publisher, editor, agent, and the staff at Macmillan and Trident for all the hard work you do on my behalf. Thank you so very much!

And as always, a special thank-you to my family for tolerating me and my absentminded ways when I'm on deadline. Especially for being so understanding when I tend to drift off mid conversation because I just "had a thought." Love you all!

DRAGONBANE

PROLOGUE

Arcadia, 2986 BCE

Is this dead or hell?

Maxis growled at his brother as he struggled to carry Illarion out of the filthy dungeon where he'd been held for more weeks than he could count. Damn, his little brother was heavy for a creature who made his meals mostly off field mice and wheat.

Shut it, Max snapped at him with his thoughts. *If you can't help, then don't distract me while I'm trying to save your scaly, worthless hide from the human vermin.*

I don't know why you're complaining so. Humans aren't so bad. I rather like them, myself. . . . They taste like chicken.

In spite of the danger surrounding them and his bitter rage over their latest "lovely" predicament and the betrayal that had put them here, Max had to bite back his laughter. Leave it to Illarion to find humor at the worst time imaginable. But then, that was why he was risking life, scale, and claw to save Illarion when all dragon-sense he possessed told him to abandon his brother and worry about his own cursed arse.

You're not making this any easier on me, you know.

Sorry. Illarion tried to use his human legs to walk, but the weak, unfamiliar appendages buckled beneath him. *How do they balance on these spindly things, anyway?* He scowled at Max. *How are* you *doing it?*

Sheer piss and vinegar . . . and the resolute need to live long enough to get to the ones who'd done this to them and kill them all.

And after those poor demons went to all that trouble to cave-break you. They'd be so disappointed to see their efforts go for naught.

Max let out a frustrated breath. *I swear by all the gods, Illy, if you don't stop your nonsense, I will leave you here.*

His expression sobering, Illarion fisted his hand in Max's long, matted blond hair and forced him to meet his gaze. *Go, brother. Like this, I'm nothing but an anchor to you and your freedom, and we both know it. Together, we're caught. Alone you stand a chance at daylight again.*

Tightening his arms around his brother's frail human body, Max locked gazes with Illarion. It was so eerie to see blue human eyes staring up at him and not his brother's normal yellow serpentine ones. To stare into the face of a man and not a dragon. What had been done to them against their will was all kinds of wrong.

Without their permission, they'd been bespelled, captured, and merged with a human soul that neither of them understood, or comfortably wore.

One day, they'd been fully Drakos, the next . . .

Human.

But though they weren't the same in form, they were still the same in heart and spirit. And one thing would never, *ever* change.

We are drakomai! And we do not abandon our kinikoi. You know this!

They might not cluster together in living communities, or share domiciles, once they reached their majority, but when the Bane-Cry sounded, they were honor bound to heed it and fight together until they defeated all threats. . . .

Or death separated them.

Illarion winced as he stumbled and fell, dragging Max down with him. *Why did they do this to us? Isn't it enough that they hunt and kill us for sport? That they've enslaved us for centuries? What more do the human vermin want of our kind?*

Max didn't speak as he helped his brother regain his feet and staggered with him toward the narrow opening he prayed led to the forest where they might find shelter. The answer wouldn't comfort Illarion any more than it'd comforted him. Rather, it pissed him off to no end.

They'd been a merciless experiment so that King Lycaon could save his worthless, whiny sons who'd been cursed by the god Apollo to die at age twenty-seven. While Max could respect the man for not wanting to lose his children over a curse that had nothing to do with the king's family, but over an ancient grudge the god bore the queen's bloodline, Max didn't appreciate being the means by which Lycaon hoped to accomplish the cure.

Even now, he remembered the sight of the fierce Akkadian god Dagon in his blackened armor as Dagon had trapped him with his arcane powers.

"Easy, *Drakos,*" the god had breathed as Maxis had struggled against him and done his damnedest to fight him off. "You'll thank me for what I do. I'm going to make you better. Stronger."

But this was neither of those things. Never had he felt so weak or vulnerable.

So lost.

And the worst had been to awaken in front of his "twin." A human male identical to this body whose soul had somehow been merged with his. Unlike Max, the human hadn't been strong enough to survive the spell that Dagon had used on them. Probably because Dagon hadn't bothered to learn what type of drakomai Maxis was before he cast his magick.

Magick had never played well with Max's accursed breed. It was why they'd been originally conceived and charged with their sacred duties.

The weak human had died howling in agony a few hours after the spell-casting, as his body attempted to become a dragon's form. While Max hadn't enjoyed the transition to human, he'd survived it.

Barely.

He just wished he could control the impulse that threw him from human to dragon and back again. Those horrid transitions came at random intervals without warning. Something that kept him grounded for the time being, since the last thing he wanted was to be airborne when his wings turned to arms and sent him plummeting.

"There they are!"

Max hissed as he heard the humans behind them. He tried to use his powers on them, but like this . . .

Useless.

Illarion's eyes widened in panic. *Go! Leave me.*

Never! Better I die by your side trying, than sacrifice your life to save mine. I will not leave you, little brother.

A single tear ran down Illarion's bloodied cheek as they were overrun by the humans, retaken, and chained like the animals they were. Max fought as best he could. But since he didn't really know how to use his human body, it did him no good.

In a matter of minutes, they were dragged back to their dark, filthy cage where other species awaited the same horrid fate.

Experiments for gods and man.

Disgusted and furious, he held his brother in his arms and protected him as best he could while the pitiful creatures around them howled for mercy and death.

What's to become of us, Maxis?

Honestly? He had no idea. But one thing was absolutely clear to him. *We are drakomai. We are kinikoi. And if I have to kill every human and god in this universe, above and below, my oath to you, little brother, you will fly again in blue skies as we were born to, and we will both live free of them and their wretched curses. No one will stop us.*

Yet even as he spoke those words, he knew what Illarion did. Some things were much easier said than done.

And no matter the intent or heartfelt emotion, not all promises could be kept. A jealous goddess herself, Fate was a cruel, bitter bitch who often made liars of man and beast. Never one for mercy, she'd never shown any to either of them or his breed.

"Does it live?"

Max froze at the sound of the king of Arcadia's voice as the old man neared their rusty cage. It was a gruff tone Max had learned to recognize, to his deepest regret.

"Aye, Majesty. Both of the animals that were merged with the princes survived and are intact. Should we kill them now?"

Max went cold at that.

"No!" the king roared. "Those are my sons, too. Even if they are born of beasts, they are still of my royal bloodline, whether their hearts are those of my sons or of a mindless creature who was merged with them. They are all that remain of my precious

Mysene, and I will never dishonor her. Fetch them to me so that I can embrace my blood and that of my fallen queen. I want to meet my wolfson and my dragonson and welcome them to this world."

1

Sanctuary
New Orleans, 2015

"You know, really, someone should just drop a razor-wire fence around this entire place, and declare it an insane asylum."

Max snorted at Dev Peltier's dry wit as he set the plastic rack of clean glasses on the mat for Aimee Kattalakis to put away. With blond hair a few shades lighter than Max's, Dev was one of the rare males at Sanctuary who was also more muscular.

Pausing behind the counter next to Dev, Aimee draped one long, graceful arm around her brother's waist, and wrinkled her nose at him. "The correct term is mental health facility. Get with the times, you old knuckle-dragging cave-bear."

Max laughed at the female werebear's quick humor. One thing about the prickly bar owner, Aimee always kept her brothers and employees on their toes. She stepped away to pick up two glasses from the crate and placed them on the shelf under the bar while she sang along to the jukebox metal song. For a bear, she had the voice of an angel.

And that snarky, long-legged blonde had been one of Max's favorite members of the Peltier bear clan since the day he'd sought refuge in the famed Sanctuary bar and grill her family had founded in the heart of New Orleans.

Wounded and barely alive after a nasty encounter with an ancient enemy, Max had collapsed on the third floor of this very building, at Aimee's feet. When he'd awakened a week later, she'd been sitting on the floor of their attic next to him, petting the scales of his head, completely unafraid of his dragon form, and humming a soft French lullaby. She, alone, had nursed him back to health and made sure that he survived. The true depth of her kindness and compassion for others had never failed to amaze him.

There wasn't a shapeshifter in this building or the one adjoining it who wouldn't give his life to save hers.

But none more so than the lucky dark-haired bastard who called her his.

Fang Kattalakis came up to the front of the bar and passed around the specially brewed long-neck beers reserved for their "unique" shapeshifter metabolisms to let them know he'd locked the front door. A ritual that signified Sanctuary was now closed to the humans for a few hours of Were-Hunter respite. He angled his fortified beer at Max. "So many village idiots, brother. So few fire-breathing dragons."

Dev burst out laughing.

Taking his beer, Max arched a brow at the strange remark, curious as to what prompted it. "Pardon?"

Fang released a long-suffering sigh as he glanced to his mate. "How attached are you to Cody? Can I offer him up as a sacrifice to Max? Please?" He glanced at Max. "I know he's not a female or a virgin, but exactly how picky are you dragons about those things?"

Not wanting to go there for several personal reasons, Max moved to break down and clean the soda dispensers while Dev prepped the beer taps. "Depends on the dragon."

Aimee tsked at them. "Please don't kill and eat my little brother. I don't want to listen to you bitch about the indigestion he'd give you, and I doubt Carson has enough Rolaids to cure *that* burn. Probably take half the firefighters in Orleans Parish to put it out."

"Damn." Fang sighed again. Then he looked up hopefully. "Hey, if I accidentally blew pepper in your face, Max, and you happened to sneeze, what are the odds you'd spew fire all over him?"

Running carbonated water into a metal bin, Max shook his head at the wolf. "Doesn't work that way."

"Then what good is having a fire-breathing dragon on hand?"

"There's always Simi," Dev said. "With enough barbecue sauce, she'll eat anything. Even obnoxious bear kin."

"Y'all are so bad." Frowning, Aimee placed her hand to her distended stomach and sucked her breath in sharply.

Fang immediately teleported to the backside of the counter to support her. "You okay?"

Leaning back against him, she smiled up at her husband. "Your sons are frolicking like cubs on a picnic-honey high."

A proud smile spread across his face. "The little she-wolves are nocturnal. . . . Like their father."

She snorted at that. "I swear, if I have puppies, I'm turning you into a wolf rug for my floor."

Fang laughed, then kissed her cheek. "Why don't you go on up and rest? I'll finish closing and prepping the bar."

Aimee hesitated.

"Don't worry. I won't even attempt the paperwork. After the gnarled mess I made of it last time, I have learned my lesson to keep my paws off it." Fang motioned for the tall, blond Amazon who was sweeping the floor to join them. A former Dark-Hunter, Samia was Dev's better, much more attractive half. In spite of the Greek goddess Samia had once been enslaved to that Max couldn't stand, Max liked Sam a great deal, especially since she didn't talk much. And she never asked him questions about his guarded past—something he appreciated even more.

Like Aimee, Sam was compassionate and kind when it came to others, whether they were people, animals, or a mixture of the two.

As soon as Aimee's pregnancy had been made public, Sam and Dev had moved back into Dev's old room in Peltier House next door to soothe Dev's fears, as he worried like an old woman over the health and well-being of his only sister. Not that Aimee needed it. With eleven blood-related brothers and even more in-laws and close friends, she had more than her share of males wanting to help her lift any object in the place, and carve body parts off her husband for risking her life with a complicated hybrid pregnancy.

"Sam?" Fang asked as the Amazon paused at the counter. "Will you please take Aimee up to bed for me and make sure she's tucked in?"

"Sure. Be glad to." Sam held her gloved hand out to Aimee. "C'mon, hon. You don't want to overtax yourself. You need to take care of those Chow Chows you're carrying."

Aimee groaned at her worst fear of what her hybrid bear-wolf children might look like. "You're off my Christmas list, Sam. Anyone else?"

Dev held his hands up and shook his head.

The bearswan glared at him, then turned toward her husband as Dev's identical brother sauntered up to grab a fortified beer from Fang. The fierce, bloodthirsty grimace on his face would have sent small children screaming for their mothers and made seasoned gladiators wet their armor in terror.

Aimee tsked at his expression. "Fang, make sure Dev doesn't kill Rémi while I'm gone."

Popping the top off the beer, the bearswain looked at her with an even fiercer scowl. "Not Rémi . . . Cherif. Damn, Aims, you're usually the only one who can tell us apart. Has the pregnancy knocked loose your brain cells?"

Aimee bit her lip. "Sorry, Boo. The way you've been scowling all night, I could have sworn you were Rémi."

Dev, Rémi, and Cherif were part of a set of identical quadruplets, with their brother Quinn rounding out their number. Alone, the bears were badass. Together, they were damn near invincible.

Unless you happened to be a fire-breathing dragon. Then there wasn't much in this world that provided a threat to your health or well-being.

Cherif snorted. "Yeah, well, what do you expect? Y'all threw me upstairs with Etienne all night. He's been dry humping my last nerve like it's the only female he's seen for a hundred years. I swear, Maman should have done us all a favor and eaten that cub at birth. At least it would have saved my humor . . . and sanity. You're all lucky they're not hauling me away for murder right about now."

"Here, here." Dev clanked bottles with him. "Where is the little prick?"

"Finishing up a hand of poker with Eros. I'm hoping he wins

and the god splinters him on the wall in anger. That's one mess I'd volunteer to clean."

Aimee met Max's amused gaze. "Oh my God, they're awful! I'm so glad you love your brother."

Max shrugged as he rinsed off the soda nozzles and put them back in place. "What can I say? Absence does indeed make the heart grow fonder, and the guilt of having him locked away in a hell realm for a thousand years means I have to tolerate any annoying habit Illarion possesses with utmost patience."

She popped Dev in the stomach. "See how great dragons are? You should be taking notes."

"Fine. Lock Etienne and Rémi in a hell realm for a thousand years and I promise I'll be nice to them when they get out."

Fang laughed. "Give it up, Aimee. You're not going to win this one."

"Are you seriously taking his side?"

Fang went pale. "Uh, no. Never. I'm not a dumb wolf and I have no desire to sleep in a doghouse tonight."

Playfully, she wagged her finger at him before she tapped his nose and kissed him.

All of a sudden, there was a loud crash upstairs that said Cherif might have gotten his wish that Eros had killed Etienne for winning. But it wasn't the unexpected noise that made the hair on the back of Max's neck rise. It was a fissure in the air he hadn't felt in centuries. One that went down his spine like a shredder.

Every sense he possessed was on high alert.

No. There was no way it was possible . . .

It couldn't be.

His breath caught as he saw a bleeding Serre scrambling down the stairs, leading a small group of women dressed in the ancient war garb and armor of a long-dead race. While Sanctuary closed to humans at four thirty in the morning, it remained open around the clock to any preternatural creature who needed a safe haven to rest from battle. Limani such as this had always been few and far between, and in the twenty-first century, there were only a handful left intact and operating.

As a precaution to keep humans from accidentally discovering their supernatural breed and freaking out, the Peltier bear family had the entire building shielded. Anyone coming here by way of magick was confined to do so on the third floor only, where a shapeshifting bouncer was always posted.

Tonight, Serre Peltier had pulled that duty. As blond as his brothers and sister, he was a slightly smaller version of the quads, which meant he was still bigger than most creatures. But even so, it hadn't kept him from getting his ass kicked by the Arcadian newcomers who beat him down in front of their group.

So much for abiding by the eirini, or so-called peace laws, that Savitar and the Omegrion had set down for their species to follow.

Blond and built for murder, the leader of the small group of women grabbed Serre by his short hair and wrenched his head up to show his battered face to their group. She held an old-fashioned Greek kopis to his throat. "Who owns this place?"

When Aimee started forward, Max, her brothers, and her

husband cut her off to protect her and the unborn babies she carried. It was obvious this preter group was here for war and not to make peace or truce.

Fang moved to meet the warrior bitch face-to-face while Max covered Aimee. "That's my brother you hold. I suggest you release him or lose your head."

She raked a scathing glare down Fang's body. "I am Drakaina Arcadia and we don't deal with inferior species. Stand aside, *animal.*"

Sam stepped to Fang's side. Gloved hands on hips, she met the women with the open hostility of someone ready to battle. "And I am Samia, Basilinna of the Thurian Riders, granddaughter of Hippolyte—who was the daughter of Ares. Declare yourself."

"Nala, Basilinna of the Drakaina, most favored of Ares, Artemis, and Athena."

Samia scoffed. "Color me unimpressed. Now release my most beloved brother or suffer my full wrath and battle-tested blade."

Nala tightened her grip on his hair. The pain of it must have been severe, since a moment later, Serre involuntarily shifted into his native bear form. Something that only happened when the Katagaria were in severe pain or suffered an electrical shock.

Sam manifested her staff. The men moved forward to engage their group as Aimee shot past him to cover Serre.

"Wait!"

All eyes went to the stairs and for a full minute, Max stood completely motionless as the mark on his hand heated and burned in response to her appearance. Every part of his body came alive in a way it hadn't for more centuries than he could recall.

The dragon inside salivated and it was devouring the human in him so fast, he could barely hold his form.

He struggled to breathe. If he broke dragon right now, he'd take out half the bar. He was far too large in his native body to shift here and now.

But it wasn't easy to remain human. . . .

Not when the beast inside him was stirred to this level. Not when it wanted blood.

Her blood.

Like a grand queen wrapped in a mantle of red, brown, and gold feathers, a lush, full-figured, Titian-haired beauty descended the stairs. Her red helm fell over her face to form a sharp beak that shaded her eyes.

But he knew their color. Searing, haunting green that was salted with gold. Filled with bold intelligence. They had a way of looking at him with ball-shriveling scorn.

Seraphina of the Drakaina-Scythian Riders. Voluptuous. Passionate.

How he hated every breath she drew.

The Amazons parted to make way for her to pass through them, to reach their queen. To the baretos humans, her armor would appear as painted, scaled bronze. Yet it wasn't. Those were the tanned and preserved scales of Katagaria dragons she'd slain, and marked her as one of the most vicious dragonslayers of her tribe.

Her queen's champion rider.

Seraphina struck her chest in salute and lowered her head. "Forgive my interruption, Basilinna, but perhaps I can be of assistance?"

Nala hesitated. "Is he here?"

"No, my basilinna. I fear your informant lied to you. I would know if my mate were here."

Nala cursed and kicked Serre in the ribs. With a flick of her vibrant red cloak, she faced Seraphina. "I'm going to gut that demon." And with that, she led her warriors back upstairs.

Seraphina stayed behind as they left. It was all kinds of stupid to lie to her queen. She knew that and yet . . .

She swept her gaze over the gathered men. The raven-haired one was definitely not the Drakos she sought. By his fetid stench, she knew him to be wolfborn Katagari. The rest were all blonds. All exceptionally handsome and well built. Two were twins. They couldn't be her Maxis. They, like the one wheezing as he turned human again and pushed himself to his feet, were bears.

That only left the one.

Like the others, he wore strange clothing—not that of a warrior or traditional Drakos. His dark blond hair was cropped *very* short, but as their eyes met, she recognized those perfectly chiseled masculine features. That strong, rigid, and unyielding jaw. That look of fiery defiance that pierced her with its proud arrogance. A pride that had always dared her against their traditions and culture.

Her hand heated up with that familiar burn. Something that only happened when two mates were brought together again after a long separation.

Determined, she headed toward him, only to have her path blocked by the other Amazon in the room.

Samia gestured toward the stairs. "You need to leave with your tribe."

Seraphina shook her head. "You have something that belongs to me."

Samia stood fast and solid. "There's nothing here for you."

"Oh yes, there is." She held her hand up for Samia to see the dragon mark on her palm. "I'm here for my mate."

2

Max cursed while those words cut through the immediate and echoing silence of the room. All attention went straight to him as jaws dropped in comical unison.

Before Max could think to leave, Dev took his hand in his own and checked to see the matching mark. Tsking, he shook his head in chiding condescension. "Maxy! You got some 'splaining to do!"

He shoved at Dev over his bad Ricky Ricardo

impression. Dev laughed it off good-naturedly. Nothing ever really fazed that huge bastard.

Aimee stepped away from where she'd been checking on Serre's busted nose and bleeding lip. "Is this true, Max? Are you really mated to . . . *her*?" By the way she hesitated, it was obvious she had to struggle to use a more polite term.

Releasing a tired sigh, Max nodded slowly. "Yes, the gods hate my guts. And they have a sick sense of humor." Hence the living proof before them.

They'd mated him to *her*.

A natural-born dragon to an Arcadian-born dragonslayer.

Cherif snorted. "Well that explains the mystery about your lack of interest in women all these years. We just assumed you were gay."

Max passed him a droll, irritated smirk.

Actually, he'd have much rather been gay than forced to his involuntary celibacy. The worst curse of their species was that mated males were physically incapable of sleeping with anyone other than their mated females. Once the Fates assigned them a partner, they could take no other so long as that mate lived. The ultimate pair-bond.

On the day he'd walked away from his wife, he'd known exactly what he was giving up. The steep price he'd be paying for his freedom and sanity . . . which said it all about the utter travesty and hell of their marriage.

Making sure to keep his expression blank, he crossed his arms over his chest. "What are you doing here, Sera?"

"We need to talk. . . . Alone."

Yeah, right. I went to war to train for my marriage. . . . Alone for the two of them had never worked out all that well for either party.

Unless they were naked and she was in heat.

Unfortunately, that only happened twice a year, and he could tell by her pissed-off stance he wasn't getting lucky tonight.

Unless she happened to gut him. That might be construed as a step up for his current celibate situation.

Max shook his head. "I said everything I had to say to you a long time ago."

"Things have changed."

"I haven't, and I seriously doubt you have. Hell, you're even wearing the same clothes you had on the last time I saw you. And that's been what? Three thousand years? Give or take?"

She glared at him.

He laughed bitterly. "And there's that ball-shriveling glare of hatred I remember so well. Point taken. It's all the same. Now there's the stairs." He started for the door that led to the kitchen.

Seraphina teleported across the room to catch his arm and keep him in place. Those golden-green eyes enchanted him and weakened his will more than he wanted to cop to. "No, Maxis. It's very different. Please. I must speak with you."

He arched a brow at that. "Wow, that is a new word for you. I had no idea it was even in your vocabulary." In the past, she'd always treated him like a brainless animal to be ordered about. One she had to train not to piss on her rug or chew her furniture.

A little more curious about whatever had brought her to this time period, he glanced to Fang. "If I'm dead by dawn's light, wolf, hunt her down and tear her throat out."

"I don't think I want to know what kind of kinky sex dragons have if they come with *that* kind of warning. So glad I'm a bear mated to a beautiful woman."

Max ignored Dev's dry comment. He also knew better than to take Seraphina near his younger brother, who was currently sleeping in Max's attic apartment . . . in full dragon form. The last thing he'd ever do was bring more harm to Illarion. His little brother had been through enough.

His job was to protect his family.

Even against his own mate. And having been mated to her and forced to live with her breed, he knew exactly what dragonslayers did to dragons. What they thought of them. Her armor paid a gory tribute to what her people thought of his kind.

They were better off dead and their remains used solely as decoration, or ingredients for their candles and beauty ointments.

So instead, he teleported her to the special room on the second floor that Dev and his brothers had built for their more unruly clientele. Completely soundproof, it would give them total privacy. It was also shielded to keep her from using magick against him. Given what she'd done to him the last time he'd made the mistake of being alone with her, it was an appropriate precaution, too.

He waited until she was inside before he turned the light on and shut the door to the small, spartan room.

What he didn't count on was the involuntary reaction of his

hormones to her close proximity. The sweet rose scent of her skin made his blood burn and his mouth water. Before he could stop himself, he began circling her as she stood in the center of the room, under the light that reflected off her armor and tawny skin like a majestic halo.

Damn it to Hades. He'd forgotten just how beautiful his mate could be when she wasn't trying to kill him and mount his hide to her tent wall. She had that lush, full body that was made for countless hours of marathon sex. And a heated Amazon passion that any male would kill to taste.

Worse? All the memories of the hours they'd spent together when they weren't fighting, and insulting each other, and their heritage came flooding back to him. The hours of the two of them sequestered in her tent, laughing and teasing.

Curse his mind and its inability to forget. . . .

Seraphina tried to focus on why she was here. Why she was so desperate to speak to her enemy. But Maxis wasn't making this easy on her. How could she have ever buried the memory of how incredibly handsome and sensual Maxis was? How much his presence affected her?

How fierce and lethal. Compelling. Seductive. Forbidden. Overwhelmingly masculine and primal, he possessed a raw Drakos magnetism that was impossible for any female to resist. Even small girls had been reduced to unintelligible fits of giggles in his presence.

Worse, he had his head bent low and was circling her like prey he wanted to devour. And it was making her breathless and hot against her will.

She scowled at him. "Could you stop that?"

"Stop what?" His rumbling deep baritone was challenging. No one had an accent like he did. Words rolled off his tongue like poetry.

Refusing to let him beguile her, she answered his challenge with the same amount of ferocity. "You know what you're doing."

A sexy, insidious grin spread over his lips. "Is it bothering you?"

Yes. Of course it was. It was what all Drakos males did to spread their irresistible pheromones and intoxicate any female they hungered for. That fierce predator's lope was every bit as mesmerizing, and he knew that, too. No creature born had ever held a seductive lure akin to that of a full-grown dragon male. It was part of what made them so incredibly dangerous. "I need to talk to you."

He approached her then. Pressing the front of his muscular body against her back, he lowered his head to lay his cheek against hers. Those prickly whiskers teased her flesh as he began the slow, rhythmic Drakos swaying that was its own form of foreplay. She could feel every single muscle in his body taut and ripped as it wrapped around her and held her against him.

Oh dear gods . . .

How did they do this? Was it something dragons were born with or did they take them aside as young males and teach them? Her entire body came alive as if she were in the heat of battle. Or lying naked in his bed. It was so intense that she couldn't even protest when he removed her helm and dropped it to the floor. Or when he freed her hair to fall around her shoulders. All she could do was lean back against him and surrender her weight to his hypnotic, primal dance.

Breathless, she felt his hardness against her hip as he encircled her waist with his arm and dipped his head to brush his lips against her neck. Her throat went dry and every part of her ached to feel his hands on her body. "I have needs too, Sera."

Closing her eyes, she trembled and hated the part of her that responded instinctively to his touch as he slowly caressed her. But then that was the nature of the beast. While she and Maxis were different species of dragon, they were still dragons.

Not human.

A different breed entirely.

More passionate.

Fiery . . .

In all things.

She should have known he wasn't human the first time they had met. Normally she would have, but, as was the biggest weakness with all of her kind, she'd been in the height of her spawning cycle. Like humans, dragons could have sex anytime they wanted, and many did, especially since they couldn't become pregnant until they found their mates.

But every six months, females entered a fertile period where they were driven to mate against all reason and sanity. The urge was so strong that it was impossible for them to think of anything else. It was what had led to many of the myths regarding Amazons. A time when they came into town for no other purpose than to find men to satiate their bestial cravings. A time when the lack of eligible, fertile males in their clans would drive them to war on their neighbors with a berserker's fury.

It was bad for them before the Fates created a mated bond. Once that mate was selected and ordained, the craving to spawn during their fertile period was even worse.

Tonight, it was unbearable.

Unable to resist him, she sank her hand in his soft hair and pressed his lips closer.

And when he lowered his hand to cup her through her armor, she cried out, needing him with an unbearable madness.

"Tell me what you want," he whispered in her ear.

Biting her lip, she cupped his hand and pressed him harder against her. "I need you inside me."

He took her earlobe into his teeth to nip it gently as he rubbed his swollen groin against her hip. Then he placed a precious kiss to her cheek. . . . His breath tormented her flesh with its heat.

Then he released her and coldly stepped away.

Those golden fair eyes pierced her with icy loathing. "I'm not your whore or your chattel. Most of all, I'm not your pet dog to come at your command."

Stunned and breathless, she glared at him. "Excuse me?"

His own breathing ragged, he put more room between them. "I told you what my terms for marriage were. A partnership. Not slavery and servitude to your capricious whims and arbitrary rules of unreasonable, Amazonian law. And what did you do? You ruthlessly chose your tribe over me. And I still bear those scars."

Seraphina winced as that long-ago night replayed through her mind. Nala had almost killed him. "I was young and stupid, and I'm dragonswan enough to admit it."

"It's too late. I would rather live out eternity in monastic celibacy than suffer one more day with any of you. Now go! Your sisters are waiting."

His rejection stung her more than she would have ever thought possible. Not that it mattered. She wasn't here to beg him back to her bed. She was here to plead for his help. "It's not that simple."

"It is that simple. You and I are finished. I accept the fact that I can't take another lover, but you're free to find whatever fool you can to satiate your hunger. Now go. Bother me no more."

Seraphina choked as she remembered the last words he'd spoken to her so long ago as he glared up at her with eyes haunted by betrayal—*I told you when we mated that I would gladly give you my heart, my life, and my love, but that when I did so they came with one condition. Never abuse me. Love is not abuse. And you have harmed me for the last time, my lady. I am done with you. Forever.*

But Fate had forced her back to him.

And she had no choice. She needed his help.

Her throat tightened as she thought of the best way to tell him what she needed to. He would hate her even more for the secret she'd kept. And she couldn't blame him for it. She'd been so wrong for what they'd done to him.

What she'd personally done.

Arcadian. Katagari. In retrospect, it all seemed so stupid. And the bitter agony in his eyes tonight told her exactly how much damage their cruelty had wrought—the lingering scars they'd engraved on his loyal soul.

You have to tell him.

But how? The human race had already done so much to him and his brothers before she'd even met him, and by way of her own cruel hands, they'd done him even more harm. He had every right to despise them all.

Stop being a coward. You have to let him know. He has a right to hear it from your own lips.

Honestly, there was no easy way to do this.

No quick or easy, or even gentle method.

And as he headed for the door to leave, she had no choice except to blurt it out for him.

"Your children need you, Maxis. If I don't hand you over, they'll kill them both."

3

Max blinked slowly as Seraphina's words hit him like a sledgehammer. For a full minute, he couldn't breathe as they sank in and he realized their full implication. "Children?"

"Son and daughter."

The room tilted. Yeah, that really was what she'd meant. He hadn't misunderstood her.

Max reached out and braced his hand against the wall as he struggled to comprehend everything she was telling him.

He was a father.

"I don't understand."

"It was the night before your rebellion . . ."

His rebellion. Nice word choice, there. Screw the truth and what had actually happened. Skew everything out of proportion. Sure. Let him be the bad guy in all of this.

Why not?

Nothing ever changes. And that right there was why he'd walked away and left behind the only real home he'd ever known. Why he'd had no choice. To them, to *her,* he was nothing but a mindless animal that needed to be controlled and collared. Something to be placed in a cage and fed table scraps.

Or viciously put down.

He'd been forced to leave before they'd taken the last vestige of his sanity, along with what had been left of his shattered pride.

He'd stupidly thought all this time that she'd already taken everything from him.

Now this. She'd hidden his children from him. Hated him and his heritage so much that she'd purposefully kept him out of their lives where he couldn't even be there to participate in the raising of his own dragonets.

Max clenched his teeth as pain racked him. "Why didn't you tell me?"

"I was going to . . . that night . . . you know. . . . Then afterward, you were long gone. I had no way of tracking you."

Because a pregnant dragonswan couldn't time travel and he'd left her Amazon village far behind, vowing to never, ever return to her or her world again. She was the only reason he'd ever stayed in ancient Greece.

And he'd only ventured there because of his brother's Bane-Cry that had summoned him to war from his own home and time period.

After Hadyn's brutal death, his intent had been to leave that time period and country far behind . . . but in Max's darkest hour, she'd found him. There for a little while, he'd mistakenly thought that she'd been divinely sent to comfort his pain. . . .

He couldn't have been more wrong. Seraphina had never been anything but his own personal hell.

"You could have sent one of your sisters," he spat that hated word out, "after me."

"I did. You covered your trail admirably. No one was ever able to find any trace of you."

It was just as well. As pissed as he'd been back then, he'd have most likely slaughtered them before they could speak. Only time and distance—and absolute shock—had allowed him to spare them on their arrival here tonight.

She swallowed hard before she spoke again. "You would be proud of your children, Maxis. They are an honor to us both."

Those words were a dagger through his heart. "Their names?"

"Hadyn and Edena."

He repeated the names silently in his head and let the warmth of fatherly love spread over him as he tried to imagine what they would look like. Be like.

If they would hate him as much as he hated his own father.

But in Max's defense, his absence had been lack of knowledge. Not the hatred and disgust for his young that his father had borne for him.

"Named for your mother?" he whispered.

She nodded. "And Hadyn in honor of your brother who died the day before we met."

He couldn't believe she'd remembered his brother's name. He'd only mentioned Hadyn to her once, in an hour of extreme weakness on the first anniversary of Hadyn's death. Never before and never since.

"Where are they now?"

"Nala has them in hiding. She's in league with a demon who has demanded the Dragonbane be delivered to him. If I fail to bring you to them, they'll kill the children."

Max cursed under his breath. The only reason Nala knew of his dragonbane mark that betrayed his wretched heritage and curse was from the night Sera had handed him over to her queen for public discipline and ridicule.

He involuntarily flinched as he remembered the bitter details of something he did his best to never think about. "Why didn't you tell her who I was when she was here?"

"I didn't realize it was you until after she was gone. Not that it matters. I still wouldn't have turned you over to her. Not after last time."

Yeah, right. Her loyalty to those bitches was absolute. A lesson learned the hardest way imaginable. "Forgive me if I find that difficult to believe."

At least she had the decency to look away. "You were warned, repeatedly, what would happen if you didn't stop rebelling against our laws. I begged you to bow down to them."

"I am drakomai!" he snarled. "Born in the sacred hallow of gods, and nursed on the breastmilk of demons! I'm not a dog to be leashed and taught to heel. Not even for a queen."

"No, that you most certainly aren't." She walked into his arms and he felt his resolve weaken.

Worse? His self-preservation crashed even faster.

Damn it.

Standing up on her tiptoes, she pressed her breasts against his chest and sank her graceful hand in his hair. Those long, finely shaped nails scraped against his skin, making him even harder and more desperate for the last thing he could do with her.

He wanted to curse her and pull back, but she had him captured in her siren's lure.

And he was helpless in her arms. He'd always been helpless before her wiles.

"I never wanted you hurt, Maxis. If I could take back my actions, I would have gone with you when you asked me to leave my tribe. And you're right. I should have fought for you. You would have fought for me."

Yes, he would have. With every ounce of lifeblood he possessed.

If only she'd been so loyal to him.

Even now, he struggled not to touch her. To remain perfectly still and wrapped in the hatred he needed to feel in order to protect himself from allowing her to hurt him any worse. She hadn't just carved out his heart, she'd hand-fed it to him. "I would have died for you."

A sad frown lined her brow as she brushed her fingers through the hair at the nape of his neck. It raised chills all along his body and fired every hormone he possessed. "I miss your braids and feathers. You look so foreign with this short hair and odd clothing. But no less fierce or handsome."

He missed the days when he'd foolishly thought they could have a future together. When he'd stupidly believed that she loved him and was as committed to their mated-union as he was. "Tell me of this demon who holds my dragonets. Why is it after me?"

"Because you are drakomai, they believe you're guarding some object the demon needs for vengeance against a Daimon named Stryker. The demon stole something called the Smaragdine Tablet and—"

"You mean the Emerald Tablet?"

She shrugged. "I don't know. It is green. Is that important?"

Was it important? He couldn't believe she'd asked that.

He gave her a droll stare. "Since it contains the words to undo the creation of the world . . . Little bit."

The color drained from her face. "You're serious?"

"I would never joke about the end of all existence, or something that could open the sacred gates and unleash all manner of hell onto this earth. . . . That tablet was what my brother protected. What Hadyn gave his life for."

She dropped her hand. "So you know this object?"

"I know of it. Hadyn would never allow me to view it. That

is the curse of *my* race. We keep our secrets from all. Even blood kin."

Seraphina silently winced as those words reminded her of her betrayal against him. Sadly, it wasn't the nature of her species. But he was right. The drakomai were bred to be the sentinels and protectors of sacred objects for the gods and fey. It was hardwired into their DNA to savagely defend whatever fell under their protection. To let no one take it from them so long as they had breath in their bodies. The need to keep that pact was so strong that they'd been known to regenerate limbs and even heads to continue their fight against any enemy who tried to take their charges from them.

There was nothing like their will to survive and to protect. They were truly the most vicious and loyal creatures ever born.

And she had callously thrown that away for a group of bitches who lacked all understanding of real loyalty.

I am all kinds of stupid.

Wishing she could change what had happened between them, she brushed her hand against the area of his thigh where he'd been branded as a young drakomas.

He caught her wrist to stop her from touching him. Those golden hazel eyes seared her with the fiery beauty that had always been her Maxis. How could she have ever chosen someone else over him?

"Where are my dragonets?" By his tone, she knew he intended to go after them. Alone. But then, that was the nature of the beast.

"They'll kill you."

He scoffed. "Let them try."

Ever brave.

Ever stupid.

"You are one. They are many."

And still that old light burned deep in his fearlessly ferocious eyes. Nothing could ever deter a dragonswain when he was set on his course.

Even one of suicide.

"Draki don't scare me. I was a natural-born drakomas long before they were created or birthed. Not half-bred. Fully blooded and vested, spawned from the egg of my demon mother. If they think they can stop me, I defy them to bring the best they have and I shall roast them over a pit of their own arrogant stupidity."

Reaching up, she cupped his cheek in her palm. "And you were merged with an Apollite prince. That blood and form weakens you. They know how to force your change and lock you in this frail body where you can't fight with your full drakomas power." Tears choked her as the past came back with a vengeance and she remembered what they'd done to her proud mate. "I can't watch them do that to you again. I barely survived your last harrowing."

He stiffened as the fury returned to his eyes and his cheeks darkened, warning her that he was barely holding on to his human form. "That makes two of us."

A tear slid from her eye as her memories surged again. For a moment, she saw him as he'd been when they met. Wrapped in the furs and hides of the Arcadian Were-Hunters he'd vanquished who had foolishly tried to slay him, he had been sitting in the rear of the small kapeleia, drinking alone. His long, dark blond hair had held tiny braids in the front like many Thracians, and Gerakian feathers had been braided into it. His beautiful face had been painted like a thousand other barbarians' with a spiraling Celtic or Pictish pattern.

At the time, she'd thought nothing of it because she knew naught of his breed. She hadn't realized that the feathers in his hair were trophies from Were-Hunter Sentinels who'd once hunted him for sport and found him a far worthier adversary than their advanced martial skills had been prepared to handle. Rather, she'd assumed he was of some human nomadic steppe tribe that was passing through Scythian territory.

Her Amazonian sisters had spread out through the crowded drinking den to find partners, who'd eagerly greeted them with drunken revelry.

Grief-stricken, Maxis hadn't even looked up at their approach. His golden gaze haunted, he'd been lacing a silver chain through his fingers. One that still bore the bloodstains of his slaughtered brother.

When she'd neared his small table, he'd given her a look of warning that said he wanted to be left alone. She should have listened.

Rather, that aloof arrogance had beckoned her toward him against all common sense. And of course, it hadn't hurt that he'd possessed the best body and handsomest face of any male there.

Even better, those long legs and arms had told her he was much taller than the average man. Something that she'd always found desirable and sexy. Irresistible.

Best of all, he held the aura of a savage, bloodthirsty warrior. A barbarian warlord. A fact the dragon sword on the table next to his hand had borne testament to. Had she not been in the throes of her spawning cycle, she might have resisted him.

Instead, she'd walked up with full Amazon temerity, pushed him back in his chair, and boldly straddled that long, muscular body.

As she slid herself up his thighs and into his lap, he'd gasped audibly and she'd taken advantage of that to ravage his open mouth. To sink her hands into his lush, soft, feather-laced hair and taste every bit of those amazing lips and skilled tongue. Now fully vested in her embrace and attention, Maxis had only broken from her kiss long enough to pay the kapeleia owner for his drink and to rent one of their oikemata—small rooms—for privacy.

That had been the most amazing night of her life. She should have known by his stamina, dexterity, skills, and scars that he wasn't human. But truthfully, she'd been too grateful to find a male who could finally satiate the aching hunger inside her to question it.

Naked, breathing raggedly, and still entwined, they'd finally paused for a small repast just after dawn. Right as the room began to lighten, both of them had pulled back as the burning in their palms began and their mating marks appeared.

Shocked and horrified, she'd looked from her hand to his to verify her worst fear. "You're a Were-Hunter?"

He'd hesitated before he responded. "Not exactly."

She'd frowned and prayed silently that they were at least the same branch of her species and that that was what he'd meant by his cryptic response. Because they were born humans who learned to shapeshift during puberty, many of her breed disavowed their animal natures. "Arcadian?"

"No."

Her fear had tripled with that simple denial. *Dear gods, don't let it be true.* She'd almost choked on the next, bitterly despised word. "Katagaria?"

"No."

No? Even sicker to her stomach, she could only think of one other grisly possibility. "Human?" she'd tried again.

He'd shaken his head.

What the hell was left? He didn't have fangs so there was no way he could be a Daimon or Apollite.

No Were-Hunter had ever mated to a god or demon to her knowledge. . . .

Even more terrified, she'd stared at him. "I don't understand." She compared their marks again and they were identical. Neither one had been there earlier. They were definitely the unique mating marks of the Draki. "If you're not Arcadian, Katagari, or human, what are you? How are we mated together?"

"By a trio of vicious bitches who hate us both and begrudge the very air we breathe."

It was then he'd explained that he was a rare, true-born dragon who'd been captured and deformed by an ancient god and the king who'd begun her race to save his sons so that they wouldn't die horribly as his wife had done.

That *he* was the very first dragon Were-Hunter ever made of man and beast. And that he knew exactly what the mark meant.

They either accepted the mating they'd had no say in, or he'd be left impotent, and both would be sterile for the rest of their lives.

Which was no choice at all since he was an immortal drakomas born from the forbidden and cursed union of a demon and an arel.

Now here, centuries later, they stood as eternal bitter enemies.

He a natural-born drakomas.

She a born Arcadian dragonswan who was pledged to hunt down and kill all the Katagaria Draki she could find.

That was just the beginning of their differences—with the largest being that he was the dragon who'd founded her race. *The* Dragonbane—the one creature every Were-Hunter would sell their soul to kill.

Another mark on his body she hadn't seen until after they'd consummated their mating, and Maxis was dressing. The moment her eyes had fallen to the branded shape of a dragon crawling from its egg that was hidden beneath the hairs on his left thigh, she'd known its significance instantly.

Maxis was the branded Drakos—the first of their breed who had killed another Were-Hunter in cold-blooded savagery. Killed, it was rumored, for no reason whatsoever.

The one beast all Were-Hunters wanted to skin alive and claim the bounty for. His life had been the first one the Omegrion—the council that governed her people—had come together to denounce and demand a death sentence for.

And he was her mate.

The father of her children.

The originator of her race.

Wincing over the cruelty of the Fates who'd seriously screwed her, Seraphina swallowed before she spoke again. "I know that while it is the nature of my species to congregate and stay together, to fight as a group, that your kind is solitary. But—"

A sudden knock at the door interrupted her.

She growled in frustration as Maxis moved to answer it.

He opened the door to show her the wolf from downstairs. "Given what you said earlier when you left to sequester yourself with your mate, I wanted to make sure you were still alive, and . . ." He stepped aside to show the last thing she'd ever thought to see.

A ghostly pale and rare mandrake.

4

Max let out an irritated sigh as he saw Blaise standing outside the room, behind Fang. While his long, braided hair was white as snow, his skin was as darkly olive as Max's, in spite of Blaise's Albinism. At first glance, there was little that denoted them as family—something that had served them all well, as it kept their enemies from using them against each other. "Brother, you've always had the shittiest timing."

Though Blaise was supposed to be virtually

blind in his human incarnation, the slow smile that spread across his face said he knew Max wasn't alone. "Is that the scent of a prime spawning dragonswan I smell? You lucky dragon, you. No wonder you wanted to be alone."

Agitated all the more at the vulgar insinuation, Max rumbled a low growl that was unique to their breed. A sign of warning parents used to correct their errant children, it usually preceded a sound thrashing. "That is my mate you insult. Apologize."

Even though it wasn't in his nature, Blaise immediately backed down. But only because they were family and Max was the eldest.

Otherwise, they'd be fighting right now.

"Forgive me, Strah Draga." Blaise used the formal term for a dragonswain's mate. "It appears my brother didn't share his good news with me." Blaise tsked in Max's direction. "I would have sent a wedding present had I known."

"Since we were mated centuries before you were born, I'd have paid money to see you do that."

Blaise's jaw dropped. "And you failed to mention this to me? Seriously?"

Fang clapped him on the back. "Told you you were in for a surprise. Didn't I?"

"Nice." Blaise passed a vengeful glare in Fang's direction. "Remember, wolf. Payback's a bitch."

Fang snorted. "What can I say? My wife's always complaining that I'm the worst behaved of all her children. And given the fact that Dev's one of her unruly brood, that says it all." His grin widened to an irritating level. "And on that note, I'm drifting back downstairs to give you guys space to hash out this fresh hell. Let me know if any bodies need to be hidden later, or if there are any blood splatters I have to clean . . . try not to get the hemoglobin on anything that stains. I don't want to listen to Quinn bitch about repainting."

Seraphina glanced black and forth between the two different species of dragon before she slowly neared Blaise and sniffed him. Strange. He smelled more human than dragon.

"Hey! I bathed," Blaise said in a playfully offended tone as he stepped away from her.

"You really *are* related."

Max smirked at her stunned disbelief. "Our mother was as discriminating as an Amazon in heat, and had the morals of one to boot."

She glared at him. "Which is the only way *you* could have ever been deemed worthy of one of us."

Blaise sucked his breath in sharply. "Ouch, Max, she's quick. I like her."

He ignored the comment. "Why are you here, Blaise?"

"I was coming to warn you about something fairly significant . . . am thinking now that I might be too late."

"For?"

"Someone accessed the power of the Emerald Tablet. It fractured a part of Merlin's spell around Terre Derrière le Voile and almost unleashed the great evil back into the Myddangeard."

Seraphina scowled as Max cursed under his breath over that potentially fatal near miss. "Back into what?"

"Midden-guard," Max repeated the Old English word slowly. "You'd know it as Oecumene . . . the world inhabited by mankind. This realm."

"And Merlin?"

"My boss in Avalon," Blaise explained.

Max knew that would be meaningless to her, too, since she long predated Arthur and all the legends that surrounded the medieval fey king and his court. "It's an alternate dimension, similar to the one you were banished to."

Her jaw dropped as indignation darkened her cheeks. Her eyes telegraphed that familiar disdain that had once cut him to the core of his soul. "You bastard! You knew I was trapped and yet you left me there to rot for all eternity?"

The irony of her righteous anger amused him. "Again, I remind you of how we parted ways. I begged you to come with me to start our family in peace, together, away from the corrupted politics of your tribe that *you* knew and agreed were wrong, and what did you do? You collared me for your queen and handed me over to her *tender loving* care. So tell me why I should have defied your gods who punished you for *her* rebellion and risked my life to free you after what all of you did to me?"

Seraphina wanted to remind him that she was his mate, but that cut both ways. How could she expect him to defy the gods to protect her when she'd refused to defy her own basilinna, who had far less reaching power?

He was right. She should have stood by him, instead of surrendering him for something she'd known even then was wrong.

And that just made her all the angrier. Not at him, but at

herself . . . which she took out on him for making her feel this way, for reminding her of the shame she bore for her own part in the travesty of his wrongful trial and punishment.

"I hate you! If not for my children, I wouldn't be here."

Max gave her a cold, dry sneer. "If not for my dragonets, I'd have already killed you."

The saddest part was, she didn't doubt that. He was, after all, an animal. A reptilian serpent. His cold-blooded, merciless nature was what had caused him to be branded the Dragonbane.

Mistaking him for human was what had gotten her into this mess. She couldn't let herself ever forget again that at the end of the day, there was no real human in him. Though he might wear the skin of a man, his heart was and would forever be that of a winged dragon serpent.

One born not of a mother's warm, nurturing womb, but from a cold, empty egg.

He hadn't been held and nursed as an infant. Never protected or loved. Within minutes of his solitary birth, he'd clawed his way from his egg and made his first kill so that he could live. Had crawled into the corpse of his prey so that he could be warm for a bit as he gnawed on its entrails.

Maxis had been spawned with no understanding of love, compassion, or decency. Only pecking order, and where creatures fell on his food chain—a food chain where he reigned supreme. Every creature that walked this planet was on his menu, and subject to his invincible martial skills. Nothing and no one was sacred to him. And he'd left a bloody trail of human and Arcadian bodies in his wake.

Trying not to think about that or else she'd be sick, she looked to the newcomer who appeared to have somewhat more humanity in him than Maxis. While his species of dracokyn was familiar to her, she didn't know much about the mandrakes. Yet the aura of magick he could command was unmistakable. He, like Maxis, was a sorcerer of supreme skill. "What is this great evil that you spoke of?"

"Morgen le Fey. You know her?"

She shook her head.

"Lucky you," Blaise said under his breath, then louder, "She's related to the Tuatha Dé Danann, and is a dark sidhe queen."

"Should you ever cross her path, you will want to avoid her." Maxis's tone was flat and dry. "Even though you're Arcadian, she'll take your heart same as ours and use it for her spells."

"Speaking of . . . where's Illarion?"

Maxis cut a chilling sideways glare to her before he answered Blaise's question. "Resting. And since you're here, can I ask a favor?"

"Of course."

"Will you watch over him while I attend a matter with my dragonswan?"

Blaise frowned. "What matter is this?"

"A personal one I'd rather not involve my brothers in."

Seraphina saw the dragon light flash in Blaise's lavender gaze as he realized Max was about to do something extremely dangerous. Alone.

"Max—"

"No lip. This is something I need to do without either of you getting in my way and annoying me in the process. Illarion is still adjusting to this world and time. He doesn't need to be left on his own right now."

Blaise screwed his face up. "With the exception of Monty Python and a few other movie franchises, I'm not real fond of this time period, either, you know."

"I know."

As Maxis turned back toward her, she hesitated. *Don't do it. He won't forgive you.*

Then again, he already hates me. What's the difference?

And in her mind, she saw him down in the pit as she'd left him the last time she'd seen him in her village. Nearly dead. Bleeding because of her and what she'd done.

Yes, he was immortal, but he could be killed.

That was what they'd almost done to him then and it was what they intended to do now. To take his powers and his dragon's heart and to use them against this Stryker.

He's an animal. Sacrifice him for your children and be done with it.

Cold-blooded. Ruthless.

Like him and all of his kind.

Yet in her mind, that wasn't what she remembered of her mate. It wasn't the dragon beast who haunted her dreams and brought tears to her eyes whenever she remembered their past together. It was the bashful male who'd been so curious about her world. So kind to her and thoughtful in spite of his cold beginning. The one who'd tried to fit in with her tribe and please her. To that end, he'd shed his clothes and dragon customs, and had adopted their style of dress and manner of doing things. For three years, he'd laid aside his claws and wild ways, and done his best to suppress everything he knew and was so that he wouldn't anger her sister tribeswomen.

And they had been merciless to him. Goading and insulting. Demeaning. Even their men had rejected him and made sure that he wasn't included in anything they did.

You're incapable of understanding. You're just a dumb animal. They'd even thrown rocks or sticks at him to drive him away whenever he came near them, as if he were a crow or some other vermin nuisance they didn't want around.

Never once did he complain to her over it. He'd merely walked away in silence, head high. Eyes haunted.

It was why he'd done his best to never show them his real form. Rather, he'd stayed in his human body as long as he could physically do so. Until he'd been so weak and ill that he couldn't stand it anymore. Then he'd seek privacy to shift for a brief respite and to sleep. Someplace dark and secluded so that no one in her tribe would see his real body, as if what he did, what he really was, was innately wrong and grotesque.

Forbidden.

In all her long existence, Maxis was the only one who'd ever made such sacrifices for her. The only one who'd ever put her needs above his own.

And he'd given her the two greatest blessings of her life. Hadyn was so like his father, not just in form and mannerisms. He held the same loyalty and honor. That need to protect whatever he loved above all else, as if they were sacred objects.

Unlike Maxis and his brothers, both of their children were Arcadian. Human born, and trained to be dragonslayers like her and her people. Nala and the others had taken a morbid thrill over the fact that both of them were some of the best hunters among their tribe.

When Edena had made her first kill, they had celebrated with an overzealous glee that still sickened a part of Seraphina's soul.

Now that she thought about it, Max hadn't even asked her about their children's base forms. He hadn't cared. They were his progeny and that was all that mattered to him. Not whether or not they were Arcadian or Katagaria.

Regardless of their birth forms, they were his, and therefore, worth his life. Even though they were strangers and he'd never met them.

And her people dared to call *him* the animal. In his own way, he knew more about love and decency than any man she'd ever met.

In that moment, she made a decision she knew would make him furious. But he'd already suffered enough for her stupidity. She wasn't about to watch him be slaughtered for no reason. Not when she knew she could help it, and him.

"Blaise? If you care for your brother, stop him from leaving. He's off to face a demon who plans to slaughter him and bring back the reign of the Sumerian demons."

Max cursed under his breath as Blaise moved to block the door.

"Did you perchance forget to mention a minor-major detail, brother?"

Maxis sighed heavily. "I didn't forget. I intentionally left it out."

Blaise sputtered. "Hell of a detail to omit. Care to elaborate now?"

"Not really. If you'll excuse me . . ."

Blaise completely blocked the door. "Don't make me call out Kerrigan. I might not be able to kick your ass, but he has a good chance of it."

"Not amused. And I don't have time to waste. Now move aside or else I'll move you, and you won't like the bruises caused by it."

"Why? You really want to die that badly?"

Max laughed, low and evil. "I'm not a mandrake, Blaise. Have you any idea how long it's been since I've killed in my true form? How much I've missed it? For too long I've been forced to live in a cage. They want a battle? Bring it. This is what *I* was spawned for. If it's a true-born dragon they want, then I say they should actually face one, and not one of the pussy half-bloods they've been battling. Let them taste my fiery wrath as I send them all straight to their respective hells."

Seraphina shivered at those growled words. He was right. She'd only seen his real form once and it'd terrified her to such an extreme that he'd promised to never transform around her again. While she'd killed dozens of Katagaria and other breeds of dragons, they were nothing like him. Drakomai were the oldest and deadliest of their species. They were so powerful that even when Nala had tried her best to force him to transform, he'd been able to hold his human body. No matter the pain they'd heaped upon him. The most they'd gotten from him involuntarily was his wings had jutted out of his back.

Nothing more.

She couldn't imagine going up against him in battle. It'd have to be terrifying.

But Blaise didn't shirk as he continued to block his way. It was comical, really. "Fine, then. I'll bleed all over you and make Quinn pissed when he has to repaint the room."

Max let out a frustrated breath. "I swear to the gods . . ." He picked Blaise up and physically set him down on the other side so that he could pass. As he started out the door, Blaise let out a shrill, haunting cry.

With a fierce snarl, Max turned back on him and covered Blaise's mouth with his hand. "Stop it!"

Blaise bit him.

Cursing his brother and insulting their mutual mother, Maxis snatched his hand away. "I can't believe you did that!"

She had no idea what that was about until the door was thrown open to show another male dragon. Slightly taller than Maxis, he had long brown hair liberally sprinkled with auburn highlights. Hair that was disheveled by sleep. Even though he was fully grown and muscular, he frowned at them like a small, irritable child who was angry at being awakened.

Realizing there was no imminent threat, he rubbed at his eyes . . . a gesture that reminded her much of Hadyn in the morning.

What the hell are you two hatchlings doing? I thought you were under attack. The thickly masculine words whispered through her mind as if he projected them there. He scratched at the whiskers on his cheek.

Blaise shoved at Maxis. "He's planning to leave us behind and go fight demons on his own for his dragonswan. Go on and tell him how stupid he is. I tried and he's too stupid to listen."

The dragonswain arched a brow at that. His sharp, steely gaze went to her and narrowed with a bloodlust that scared her. Shaking his head, he let out a frustrated sigh as he returned a furious glower to Maxis. *So can I kill her now?*

Eyes wide, Seraphina stepped back. "Excuse me?"

"No!" Maxis snapped. "And stop asking me that."

Completely ignoring her, the newcomer looked up at the ceiling. *It's so not fair. I lost my Edilyn and yet* this *bitch lives and returns? Why, gods? Why?*

His jaw ticcing, he looked to Blaise. *Is there not some transmutation of souls we can do? Place my mate's soul in her body?*

"Maybe."

Max growled at them. "Stop it! Both of you! You're not going to swap out her soul."

Curling his lip, the dragonswain who kept speaking only through their thoughts gestured toward Seraphina. *I don't understand why you continue to protect her. She's never brought anything save utter hell and misery to your door. You told me yourself that she could barely look at you when you lived together. So why are you so eager now to die at her command? Let her rot in whatever mess she's woven. It serves her right and is all she deserves.*

Seraphina winced at a truth she hadn't even realized Maxis

had noticed. To her ever shame, Illarion was right, she'd had a hard time looking at her mate when they shared a home.

"Enough, Illarion! She's the mother of my young and I will not have you say another word against her."

Illarion's jaw went slack. *You spawned with her? Are you infinitely stupid?* His gaze went from Maxis to lock on hers with a frigidity that sent shivers down her spine. *Instead of saving their race, Max, you should have cut that ungrateful whore's throat and devoured her unborn young when you had the chance. Save us all the misery and heartache they've caused us since then. Not to mention the indigestion and ulcers.*

He raked another cold sneer over Seraphina. *Be grateful you're his mate. That alone stays my hand from ripping out your heart and feasting on it . . .* Arcadian. The way he spat the word in her mind made it sound like the worst sort of insult.

"If not for them, Illarion, you'd have never met your Edilyn."

Illarion winced and looked away. *You're not helping your cause, brother. You're only reminding me why I hate them all and what they've viciously taken from me. . . . Now, what's this infernal madness you're about?*

Max glared at him. "You're the only being alive who can talk to me like that and not be gutted on the floor."

"Um, yeah," Blaise said in an irritated tone. "Why does he get that favoritism? You'd lay me out cold for it."

Illarion cut another malicious glare at Seraphina before he answered Blaise's question. *Before you were born, Blaise, I was the one who found Max after her tribe all but gelded and skinned him alive. They had him muzzled with a metriazo collar that restricted his ability to use his magick in any way. He couldn't even transform to heal himself. Had I not found him when I did, he would have died. I doubt he'd have made it through another three hours in the condition he was in.*

Blaise sucked his breath in sharply at what that meant as Seraphina closed her eyes in sympathetic pain and horror. What Illarion didn't know was that she hated her own self for the part she'd played in that, far more than he ever could. It was a moment that had haunted her day and night. And in particular, every time she'd looked into the faces of her children and had to explain to them why their father wasn't with them.

Why it was all her fault and why they were to never blame him for it. They knew she didn't blame him. How could she?

His lip curled, Illarion circled her. *Had an enemy found him, he'd have been gutted and tortured even more. I don't say worse, because no one could have done him worse harm than you and your tribe did.*

"Enough," she breathed, unable to stand it.

But he took no mercy on her. *They'd even clipped his wings to ground him.*

"Stop!" Max snarled.

Now even Blaise glared at her. What could she say? They weren't supposed to do that? That she'd fought her sisters to stop them from torturing her mate, and had only ceased fighting against them for fear of miscarrying her children? She'd been as horrified by their actions against Maxis as his brothers were.

But she'd been powerless to stop it. Truthfully? She'd never gotten over her own sense of hopelessness that day. That feeling of just how little control she had. It'd been the hardest lesson of her life.

Maxis broke between his brothers to approach her. To her shock, he gently lifted her chin until she met his haunted gaze. "My wings grew back together."

After two hundred years. Leaving you at the mercy of enemies you couldn't escape until you could fly again.

He glanced over his shoulder toward Illarion. "It taught me to be a stronger fighter. Now leave it. This isn't about me or the past. It's about my dragonets and their survival today."

Illarion moved to stand at Maxis's back. He placed his hand on his brother's shoulder. *You are the only parent I've ever known. And you're my best friend. I will not let you fight alone.*

Blaise nodded. "Three dragons are better than one."

Scoffing, Max dropped his hand from Seraphina's face. "Two dragons and a mandrake."

"What exactly is a mandrake?" she asked, not quite sure of the exact difference between them.

"They're the children of dragons seduced by Adoni who wanted to tame them. Born from the womb of an Adoni mother, they were hybrids of the two races at first . . . until they became a separate species by themselves."

Blaise nodded. "My father was the leader of the mandrakes under King Uther Pendragon. When I was born looking like this—" He held his hands out to show off his face. "—my demonic mother decided she had no use for her *special* mandrake son. She handed me over to my father, who then took me out to the woods and left me to die."

"I'm sorry."

He shrugged. "Don't be. Got over it. And given my mother's wonderful personality, and my father's oh-so-kind temperament, prefer it to having been kept by either of them. Normally, I just tell folks I know nothing of my parents and leave it at that. It's easier than dealing with their pity for something that really doesn't affect me."

Like Maxis. It'd never bothered him, either, that his mother had abandoned her nest and left him to either die, or survive on his own. Something Seraphina hadn't known about him until he'd seen one of the women in her tribe nursing her infant.

He'd stopped in his tracks to stare at them with a curious scowl. "What is she doing to that poor child?"

Seraphina had laughed at his shocked question. "Nursing it."

Perplexed, he'd deepened his frown even more as he looked back at Seraphina. "Why? Is it ill?"

Seraphina had paused to stare up at him as she realized he was in earnest. "It's what a mother does with her young to feed them. Were you not so nursed?"

"No. Never. I was only fed by demons whenever I was ill and I only met my mother once, when I returned to my nest to bury my skin, and she was laying more eggs there. At first, I thought her an interloper. As I went to drive her away, she clipped my wings as punishment, and told me who she was."

It'd been her turn to be completely stunned by the disclosure. She couldn't fathom what he described. "Why did she abandon you?"

He'd been as baffled by her as she was by him. "Why would she stay?"

Aghast, she'd laughed nervously at his inability to comprehend basic human decency and the role a parent played in their children's development. "To feed you. Clothe you. *Protect* you."

"I was fully drakomas then. I required no clothing. As for food, I found my own, and was more than able to scurry and hide from or fight whatever pursued me." There'd been no animus or condemnation for his parents in his tone. Simple acceptance. To him that was what a mother did.

She birthed her children and left them behind to fend for themselves. Whether they lived or died was solely up to them.

Seraphina had struggled to comprehend it. But as an animal, he couldn't understand why she was so baffled.

As they'd headed for her tent, he'd glanced back at the nursing mother one last time. "Should we have children, would you nurse my dragonet in such a manner?"

What an odd question. "Of course."

A slow smile had spread across his handsome face.

She cocked her head at the curiousness of it. "What?"

"I'm glad to have an Arcadian mother for my dragonets. Perhaps the gods have finally forgiven me."

"For what?"

"For surviving what should have killed me."

She'd never really understood what he meant and he'd refused to explain it further.

Now, Seraphina stared at the three dragon brothers who'd

never known a mother's tender loving touch. Never known what a real family was. Not that she had that much experience herself. Her own family had been brutally slaughtered by a dragon raid when she'd turned fourteen. Her mother's last act had been to wrap her dragon cloak around Seraphina and shove her into a small knoll where the dragons couldn't reach her. Made from the scales of the dragons her mother had slain, it had protected her young body from their dragonfire as they razed her village.

But that act had left her mother exposed to their fury and attack.

And she'd died in agony, trying her best to save her daughters and tribe.

It was why Seraphina hated the Katagaria so much and had vowed to see them in their graves.

When she'd learned that she was mated to one . . .

"Kill me." Maxis had handed her his own dragon-headed dagger and lain back in bed, arms spread, his throat offered in sacrifice. "If you can't bear this union, then free us both from it. I'd rather be dead than damned to no comfort whatsoever."

Growling in fury, she'd straddled him, fully intending to take his offer. But as she looked into those calm, receptive, *human* eyes that waited for her killing blow, she'd been unable to deliver it. While she, like her mother before her, had slain countless dragons in battle, she'd never murdered a man.

Not in cold blood.

As if reading her thoughts, he'd fearlessly covered her hand with his and pressed the blade against his throat. So close, he'd drawn his own blood.

"Finish it, dragonslayer. Free yourself from the Fates' curse."

Her gaze had gone from his eyes to the scars on his body from his own battles against her people. Every thought in her mind had screamed at her to take his life, to end him right then and there.

He's an animal. An enemy . . .

His muscles had tensed as he pressed the blade even deeper into his neck.

With her battle cry, she'd pulled the dagger away from his throat and thrown it aside. Then she'd buried her hands in his hair and kissed him, rolling in bed until he was on top of her.

His body wedged between her legs, he'd held himself completely still as he stared down at her, waiting for her to change her mind.

She'd wanted to curse him. Hate him. But she'd lost her heart to those tormented, pain-filled eyes. To the sweetness of his lips and hair the color of honey and laced with small braids and feathers. He didn't touch her like an animal. He touched her like a tender man who saw only her and no one else.

Knowing she was consigning them both to an uncertain future, she'd drawn a ragged breath. "Finish the mating, dragon. May the gods have mercy on us both."

But they never had.

Rather, they'd taken perverse pleasure in driving a wedge between them every day until Maxis had finally had enough of her and her people, and walked away with his heart as shattered by betrayal as hers.

It'd tied her mother's death for the worst moment of her life.

Until she'd discovered his escape from her tribe, she'd fool-ishly thought that his death or absence would be a relief. That it would restore her life to what it'd been before she found him, and make everything right again.

It hadn't. Instead, it'd almost destroyed her.

Too late, she'd realized what she'd held in her hands and not seen. What her dragon lord had actually meant to her. Every-thing wonderful he'd brought to her life.

A dragon hunting party had taken her family and childhood innocence in the span of one brutal night. But a single, fierce dragon lord had given her a soul and a heart. He'd taught her to smile and love again.

To trust.

Most of all, he'd taught her to laugh and to live in ways she hadn't known existed.

Then, in one single act to save himself, he'd banished her back to darkness, leaving her there bereft and heartbroken.

And she couldn't even blame him for it. He'd endured more than any creature should have to.

Tears gathered in her eyes as she stared up at him again and those memories haunted her anew. He was as beautiful now as he'd been then. "Gods, I thought this would be easier to do."

"What?"

"Consign you to death. Again." Seraphina bit her lip as she glanced between them. "I don't know what to do, Maxis. Even though they can't use our children for the spell they have, Nala will gut them if I fail to deliver the Dragonbane's heart to her."

Why him? Illarion asked.

She shrugged. "The spell they have requires the heart of the father of our race. The firstborn Apollite-dragon who drew first blood."

The Dragonbane.

Max met Illarion's gaze and knew the secret the two of them had shared for five thousand years. They weren't just bound by their mother's blood. They'd been bound by one prince's and pantheon's savage cruelty.

Blaise cleared his throat. "You know . . . having been raised around the queen bitch of the fey folk and watching the nasty shit she's pulled on everyone. The backstabbing. The lies. Half-truths, et cetera, I just have to ask one simple question. . . . Has anyone bothered to find out what this spell will actually do once it's cast?"

Max laughed bitterly. "I have a really good idea since they have Hadyn's Emerald Tablet."

Blaise's eyes bugged at the mention of that. "Combine that with what you guard—"

And your heart, Illarion finished.

"Bishhhh!" Blaise made the sound of an explosion as he flung his hands out.

Seraphina scowled. "I don't quite understand what you're saying."

Max locked gazes with her. "They're not just planning on destroying this Stryker. They're planning on releasing the Destroyer, reuniting the gods of Chaos, and reestablishing the old order."

Blaise nodded. "If they succeed in this, honey, it ain't just your kids they'll kill. It's every creature who has an ounce of light energy in them."

Illarion let out a silent sigh. *Which means all of us and everyone we love, and a few we're not that fond of, either.*

5

"You fed the children to your demons while we were gone? Have you lost your mind?" Completely slack-jawed, Nala stood in the center of the dimly lit room, staring at Kessar. While the red-eyed demon towered over her, she refused to be intimidated by him. Especially right now when she was so furious.

He had fed the children to his demons. She just kept repeating that over and over in her mind, because she couldn't believe he'd do something so dumb the five minutes she'd left him alone.

This matter was far more serious than he could guess. One didn't just lightly go for Seraphina's throat.

One only did so with a huge army.

And he was shy a few thousand demons.

He scoffed at her anger. "You would do well to choose another tone, lest I add you to our menu. Remember, but for my good will, you'd still be collecting bird shit out in an open field where your gods left you to rot."

"And you'll find yourself in the middle of a massive shit storm when Seraphina learns of this! She'll never lead you to her mate now. You can forget ever finding him."

"She won't have to. Once we control her spawn, they'll be able to sniff out their sperm donor for us. It's a much easier and quicker solution than yours." A slow, evil smirk twisted his lips. "Besides, she hasn't returned. I'm thinking she's already betrayed us."

Nala struggled not to roll her eyes at the bastard, but given what he'd done to the last member of her tribe who'd made that mistake, she didn't want to test the demon's patience. While she might be basilinna and a fierce warrior in her own right, she was no match for the ancient demon and his terrifying skills. And that only pissed her off more.

She and her tribe had once made the gods themselves flee in terror. But the gallu were another entity entirely. And they'd been birthed for no other purpose than to end pantheons and shatter the gods.

Which made them extremely lethal, even to the Scythian Amazons. The only member of her tribe who could stand against them was Seraphina. No one was quite sure why. While Seraphina had always been extremely skilled, something had happened after she'd mated to her dragon that had kicked her abilities up to an entirely new level.

Since then . . .

It was why Zeus had frozen them in stone. That had been the only way to stop them from defeating the Greek gods they'd fought against.

"My lord?"

They both turned to see Kessar's second-in-command, Namtar, approaching with a nervousness that didn't bode well.

Especially not for Namtar. Grateful to get Kessar's ire off her, Nala let out a relieved breath at the demon's timing.

Bowing to Kessar, he gulped audibly as a bead of sweat rolled down his dark caramel skin. It was obvious he'd rather be anywhere else in the world than right here, right now.

He cleared his throat and finally spoke to Kessar. "We have a slight problem, my lord."

The expression on Kessar's face was one of barely restrained murder. "How so?"

"The children . . ."

"Turned gallu."

Namtar shook his head slowly. "No, my lord. They appear to be immune to gallu bites."

Nala wasn't sure which of them was the most stunned by that disclosure. "Pardon?" she gasped before she could think better of it.

Namtar cut his handsome gaze in her direction. "They are not completely Greek. Nor can they be completely *vrykolakas-kynigos*. They appear to be something else. We're not sure what."

Now there was a word she hadn't heard in a long time. It was the original term for her species that the Greeks had used.

Ignoring her question, Kessar stepped forward. The red in his eyes intensified as he raked a sneer over her. "What information have you withheld from us about your champion?"

She swallowed hard. "None . . . I swear!"

Kessar refused to believe her denial. It was too convenient. How could she not know? These were members of her tribe, born into it. Had lived with her for years after their father ran off. Their mother was her primary champion.

Surely Nala knew who and what she'd harbored amongst her people?

Pissed, and cursing under his breath about how he should have left her and her Amazon tribe to rot, Kessar headed from his small throne room to the cell where he'd tossed Seraphina's children. Since the gallu were being hunted by the Daimons who were preying on them and using their blood and souls so that the Daimons could walk in daylight, they'd been driven underground and into virtual extinction.

For the last few years, Kessar and his handful of loyal demons had played a deadly game of hide-and-seek with their former allies. And all because of a "small" falling-out he and Stryker had had over who to kill when and how. And the fact that Stryker had taken issue over Kessar going after his wife, daughter . . . and, well, *him.*

Though why it would bother the Daimon, Kessar couldn't fathom. That was what happened in war. Goals changed. Borders shifted. Battles were won and lost, and new ground gained, while some was lost.

It happened and should be expected. As a commander, Stryker should know that as well as anyone.

In the end, friends and allies didn't matter. Only your cause did. Your allegiance.

But sadly, their alliance against the Olympians had dissolved after Stryker had awakened the Greek god War, and the ancient trouble-making entity had turned them against each other. They were no longer unified or after the same things. With one particularly bad night, they'd turned on each other and had splintered.

That was the problem with friends.

When the time came, and it always did, for the friendship to dissolve, those friends turned to enemies. And they knew the best place to strike to cripple you.

Yet now the tables were turning. When Stryker had allowed the Dark-Hunters to place the Sumerian amulet around Apollo's neck and temporarily drain the god's powers, he'd unknowingly opened a door for Kessar to slip in.

And brought to Kessar a whole new group of allies to play with and feast upon.

Just like Stryker, Kessar knew exactly how and where to make the coup de grâce against the Daimons who'd turned on his gallu brethren. And he wouldn't hesitate to take it. An eye for an eye. Throat for a throat.

Testicle for testicle.

It wasn't in the nature of his species to let any slight go. The gallu had been bred as the final "fuck you" of their ancient gods to destroy the world should the world destroy them. Knowing that, Stryker should never have turned on them and declared them a food source for his people.

That was the ground the Daimon was going to be buried upon.

At least that was Kessar's thought as he opened the door to the cell where the young Were-Hunters had been chained. He'd expected to find both of them where he'd left them.

Instead, the sight of the smoking remains of three headless gallu greeted him. Stunned by the sight, he cocked one regal brow. The chains that had held the young dragons had been ripped from the walls and the metriazo collars that he himself had placed around their necks to block their magick and keep them tame were laying in pieces on the ground at his feet.

"What the hell?" he asked slowly.

There was no sign of either young adult dragon. Gaping to the point he exposed his fangs, he turned toward the Amazon queen.

Eyes wide, she stared at the damage they'd wrought. "What happened?"

Namtar shook his head. "I honestly don't know. By the time Neti and I got the door open, this was what we found. How could they do this?"

Kessar toed the remains of the gallu closest to him. There were very few creatures capable of this. And only one he'd ever fought against who could do such. A chill went down his spine at the prospect of facing *that* hairy bastard again. "What is the name of their father?"

Nala scowled. "I'm trying to remember. We never really used it. Um . . ."

You've got to be shitting me? She really couldn't recall something so banal?

Or something so vital?

He met her vacuous gaze. "Was it perchance Maxis Drago?"

"Yes!" But the joy quickly faded from her gaze as she realized it wasn't a good thing that he knew the dragon's name. "How did you know?"

How did he know . . .

Sick to his stomach, he exchanged a glare with Namtar. "Son of the lilitu."

It figured.

Still, she had no clue of the monster she'd unknowingly harbored. "What's that?"

He laughed at her stupidity. But then, being female, she wouldn't have ever drawn the attention of a lilit demon. They preyed exclusively on males, and in particular, male demons and gods. "In short, our mothers. The gallu were originally hatched in the eggs of the lilitu."

"Are you telling me that he's your brother?"

How he wished it was that simple. "No. We were bred differently by our gods. Designed for a specific purpose. He was truly born from the forbidden coupling of a lilit mother and an arel father, and raised to be a tool for the ancient gods." Kessar pierced her with a harsh glare, before he rammed home exactly what kind of creature they were dealing with. "And it's said he turned on his own mother in a fit of anger, and tore out her throat with his own teeth."

"You're serious?"

He nodded as he lifted his shirt to expose the wound on his side that had never healed. A vicious bite scar that ran from nipple to hip, and forever oozed with dragon venom. "He is not just *your* Dragonbane. He is my personal plague and the one creature in this universe I would give anything to have in battle one last time."

"Anything?"

"Anything . . . More than that, he has in his possession something he protects that's a lot more powerful than the Emerald Tablet." He lowered his shirt. "Forget restoring the old world we once knew. With what he has, we could reign as gods ourselves. We would have the power to not only take life, but to create it. To make and destroy entire worlds, and pantheons."

Completely shocked, she gaped at him. "Are you telling me that dumb, idiot dragon who lived in my village—"

"Is one of the most powerful and ancient creatures who has ever roamed this planet." Kessar laughed bitterly. "He was never a dumb animal, you stupid bitch. But for the curse placed on his mother, he would have been born a Naşāru."

A being of purest light, they were the protectors of order and the defenders of the primal gods. Resolute warriors of the highest honor and noblest hearts. Their place was to remain away from the world and those who lived in it so that they wouldn't be corrupted by evil.

But once exposed to the world, they became the deadliest of all its creatures.

And none more so than Maxis.

"What curse?" Nala asked.

Kessar folded his arms over his chest. "After Lilit made the mistake of seducing a god and becoming pregnant with his child, his goddess wife cursed her and all her kind to never birth a live child, or to carry a fetus in their wombs. Rather they were all to lay eggs and only have serpent children. And so the first race of dragons were born from the cursed lilitu. Because of what those children were, their mothers hid them away and left them to die in caverns and caves. Over time, the gods learned that these children were excellent survivors and that their solitary natures made them the perfect vassals to guard their most sacred objects."

"And what is this object he protects?"

"The Sa'l Sangue Realle."

She frowned. "Never heard of it."

Kessar scoffed at her ignorance. "It's a bowl his mother stole from his father that can grant immortality to any who drink from it. And take immortality from those who have it. Any weapon that is dipped into a liquid held by it can kill anything it pierces. More than that, it grants total omnipotence and omniscience."

"And you're sure *he* has it?"

Kessar backhanded her. "I know the creature I seek." He gestured to the bodies on the floor. "And I know how rare a species it is that can render three gallu dead with this kind of ease, especially in adolescence." He grabbed her by the throat and yanked her closer. "Find their bitchtress mother. We have to leash them and their father, and find that bowl. If you fail, I'll take great pleasure in spending the rest of eternity making you my own personal bitch."

Brace yourself, Deenie. I can't go any farther."

Edena held tight to her brother's neck as Hadyn lost altitude and headed for the burned-out ground far below them while they flew out of the reach of the demons they'd escaped. Wounded herself, she wasn't able to take dragon form at all. And as they crashed and he hit the ground hard, she felt for him. But true to his nature, he coiled himself around her to protect her as best he could.

When they finally stopped falling and rolling, he was flat on his back, his wings spread wide with her tucked in tightly between his massive claws and nestled against his chest. She heard his heart pounding beneath her bruised cheek. They were in some kind of valley underneath a vast, dark sky that was filled with bright stars. A sky she didn't recognize at all.

"Hadyn?"

He groaned.

"You alive, little brother?"

"No," he groused with a light, pain-filled laugh. He loosened his hold so that she could slide out from between his massive talons and check on his wounds. Panting and weak, he tilted his massive spiked head to the side and stared at her with those eerie gold serpentine eyes. "Did they bite you?"

She shook her head. "Are you turning gallu?"

"I don't think so." He hung his huge tongue out the side of his mouth like a dog that was playing dead. "But at this point, I wouldn't mind so long as it stopped hurting. Ugh! Braaaiiinsss. Me neeed . . ." He paused to stare at her. "Ah, crap. I'm here with *you*. If I need brains for sustenance, I'm going to starve."

Rolling her eyes, she shoved at his claw. He had a twisted sense of humor, but she appreciated him trying to cheer her in the midst of their dire predicament. He was always good at that. Always precious to try and make her see the better side of things when it definitely wasn't her nature to do so.

It was why she loved her brother so much. Why she would kill or die for him.

Thank the gods Hadyn was all right and still Hadyn, not some horrid gallu slave.

Oddly enough, when the gallu had gone to feed on him, instead of becoming one of them, the feeding had thrown him into his real body in spite of the collar he'd worn. Something he'd needed badly since being trapped as a human for so long had been slowly killing him.

Little had they known, her brother was a Katagari Drakos—like their father—who needed to be in his dragon form more than his human one. A secret the two of them had kept from everyone, even their own mother, for fear of what their tribe might do to Hadyn should they ever learn the truth. Both of them had grown up with the horror stories of how their father had been driven from their tribe over his animal birth.

She would kill before she allowed them to drive her brother away. Or harm him in any way.

And as they lay there, she realized how ragged and raspy his breathing was becoming. Instead of clearing, it was worsening.

Edena cupped his dragon cheek. "Slow your breathing before you hyperventilate."

"I'm trying."

"Hade? Look at me." She stroked the scales of his snout to soothe him. "Focus and breathe. In . . . out . . . in . . . out." She repeated the steady and slow rhythm until his ragged breathing returned to normal.

Since the hour of their birth, he'd always had trouble with his lungs. No one was quite sure why. And the condition had only worsened when he became a dragon at puberty. It left his voice very deep and raspy. Barely more than a whisper that required others to listen very carefully in order to hear him whenever he spoke.

Nala had wanted their mother to abandon him to the elements and not waste valuable resources to raise such a weakling. But their mother had refused and fought a hazard to keep him with them. He was her son and she refused to let anyone harm him.

Over the years, Seraphina had taken the heads of any who went after or insulted Hadyn in any manner.

At least, whenever she heard it.

Only Edena knew the real heartaches her brother endured on a daily basis. Since there was nothing their mother could do, he kept most of it from her, and begged Edena to do the same. He was far stronger than anyone knew.

Even stronger than she was. Without him, she doubted she would have made it through the misery of their lives.

Coughing, he rolled to his side so that he could breathe more easily.

She patted his back, taking care to avoid the cuts the demons had left behind. "Where do you think we are?"

"I don't know."

It was so dark here. And cold. But at least they were no longer frozen in stone. They finally had movement again.

"Should I try to call Matera?"

He wheezed and shook his head. "It could alert the others where we are." He wrapped his tail around her and sent a wave of warmth through it for her.

Pressing her cheek against his scales, she smiled. "Thank you."

He tucked his wings in around her to make a leathery blanket. "Are you warm now?"

"Yes. How did you know I was cold?"

"You're always cold. There's not enough fat on you to keep you warm."

She laughed. "I'm big enough to whip you."

He snorted a rude sound of denial. "Only because I let you win."

Suddenly, there was a loud, fierce sound over their heads.

Something that rumbled like vicious thunder. Bright lights danced across the landscape.

"What is that?"

Hadyn immediately returned to being human, even though it was extremely difficult for him to do so. "I don't know. But I doubt it's good."

She took his hand in hers as they stepped back into the shadows and watched the strange things that flew in the sky over their heads. Worse? They could hear voices as others searched for them.

What's a military installation? she projected silently to her brother.

I don't know. But I don't think we're supposed to be here, and I'm pretty sure that if they catch us, they're going to put us in another cage.

And that she couldn't argue against either.

Keeping to the shadows, they ran along a wall of some sort, away from the sounds and machines they didn't understand. Looking at the vegetation, she guessed that they were in a desert. But she had no idea where.

Or what time period.

As they reached the end of the wall, she pulled up sharply. She stopped so suddenly that Hadyn slammed into her before he saw what had caused her new panic.

There in the darkness was another group of demons waiting to recapture them.

6

"Here. You look like you could use this. It's hot cider with rum. It helps with pre-battle nerves."

Seraphina stepped away from the group that was assembling to save her children to thank Aimee. She took the peculiar cup that smelled quite delicious. And as her gaze fell to Aimee's distended stomach, she realized a fact that had escaped her earlier attention.

The bearswan was Arcadian. She had to be. Aimee wouldn't be able to shapeshift while pregnant. That was one of the worst drawbacks of being a female Were-Hunter—you were locked into your base form for the duration of any pregnancy. Should anything force them to shapeshift while they carried another life, both mother and child or children would die.

Gods, as bad as her own fears had been while she carried her children, she couldn't imagine the uncertain horror Aimee must deal with. At least she and Maxis were the same species. How could an Arcadian bear stand being with a Katagari wolf?

How had they even courted? Or conceived? Common thought was such couples were sterile. But then, their very existence defied all natural order. Given what Lycaon and the gods had done to them, there was no telling, really, what a Were-Hunter could or couldn't do.

"You're mated to a Katagari?" The question was out before she could stop it.

Aimee's features turned to stone and all friendliness evaporated from her eyes. "Careful where you go with your next words. My mother was Katagari. My father Arcadian. And they died as bonded mates."

That stunned her. Bonded was the highest declaration of love for their species. It meant the mated couple had made the mutual and conscious decision that rather than let death separate them, they chose to combine their life forces into a single cord. Whenever one mate died, the other would follow them into eternity.

Very rarely did Arcadians make such an unbreakable pact. It just wasn't practical. And even though Maxis had asked it of her and she'd refused him out of fear, she'd always assumed it would be even more rare for the Katagaria to make so strong a commitment. Most Arcadians believed them incapable of comprehending it. To her eternal shame, she'd refused to bond with Maxis, hoping that one day death might free one of them to find a mate of their breed.

But that was before she'd had his children. They and his absence had taught her an appreciation for her mate that she wished she'd had before he left.

"Did their differences ever bother you?"

Aimee's features softened as she placed her hand over her stomach and lovingly caressed the unborn children she carried. "What bothered me was having to hide and lie about my true form because of the prejudices *others* hold. Having to hide and run with my parents and brothers before we were granted the license for a limani. The fact that my parents had to live in secrecy from even their own families, or risk harm to themselves or us."

Seraphina could only imagine. The gods knew her tribe had never been kind to Maxis. The only thing that had saved her children was the fact that they were Arcadian born and her skills with a sword had forced the ridicule to stop. No one wanted to go against her battle skills or face her maternal devotion.

Even so, Hadyn had borne the brunt of it. It'd forced him to grow up much faster and harder than he should have. And there was a deep-seated bitterness in his eyes that tore at her heart every time she caught his unguarded expressions. He'd never been fairly treated among her people and she knew it.

Just like his father.

For that alone, Seraphina could almost hate her tribe.

Yet Aimee's words gave her comfort that maybe Hadyn would one day find a woman who could love him as he deserved to be cherished. "Thank you, Aimee."

She inclined her head. "Any time."

"May I ask another question?"

"Sure."

"Did . . ." Seraphina paused as she tried to think of a gentler way to phrase her question. "Does it ever bother you that Fang is a wolf?"

"Because I'm a bear or an Arcadian?"

"Either."

Aimee shook her head. "No. It never mattered to me that he was Lykos Katagaria. Though I didn't want to admit it, I lost myself to that face the first day I saw him. But it scared me how others—and in particular, my mother—would react to our union. And it terrifies me what they might do to our young once they're here. My mate comes with some rather scary enemies. And not just in our community." She cast her gaze to her massively large brothers. "But the good news is, I come from a scary, over-*bear*ing family."

She laughed at the bad pun. Then turned serious as she remembered why she was so harsh against the Katagaria. Those memories still woke her up at night with terrors that never faded. "But you never had the Katagaria tear apart your family, either."

The anger returned to Aimee's eyes. "No. I watched my older brothers and parents be viciously slaughtered because of lying Arcadian bastards and their needless hatred and intolerance for their Katagaria brethren . . . and my brothers they slew *were* Arcadian. But they didn't want to believe it. . . . Honestly? I'd rather lie down with the animals at night. From my experience, they're a lot less likely to go for my throat than their human counterparts."

Seraphina swept her gaze around the small group gathered on the third floor of Sanctuary as they prepped a rescue for her children.

Different species.

Katagaria *and* Arcadian.

All working together to save two teens they'd never met and knew nothing about. Each prepared to bleed and die for them.

She couldn't fathom it, and she knew in her heart that her tribe would never do something like this to save strangers, especially Katagaria children.

Aimee had a vicious point.

Not wanting to think about it, she was just about to take a drink when three more wolves came up the stairs to join their raiding party, leading an attractive human female . . . each of them carried a small child in their arms. Three boys and one girl, ranging in ages from about a year old to around six or so. But then given the fact they were Were-Hunters, the children could be older than that. Unlike their Apollite cousins and humans, Were-Hunters aged much slower, and what might appear to be a six-year-old Arcadian Were could easily be as old as ten or even eleven or twelve.

Sound asleep, the babies were nestled in the arms of the adults.

Fang came over immediately to take the girl from the sole human. "What are you guys doing here?"

The human kissed his cheek. "Like big brother would let you face this alone. Or leave me by myself at the house with an imminent threat of any kind, even though I've got two packs of wolves denned in every house in and around my block? Get real. This is a blood alert, so here we are until it's cleared and everything's safe and quiet."

Fang laughed. "Well, I'm glad to see you. Maybe you can talk Aimee into going to bed. She's not listening to me and she's been up for almost twenty hours straight."

Tsking, the human walked over and hugged Aimee. "What have I told you about resting those puppies?"

"I know. I know. I was going to bed when all this happened. It's hard to sleep when my family is up here planning to go break badass on a horde of Sumerian demons who were created to eat gods for fun."

The female wolf who held a small infant boy had the same chiding expression on her face. "You need to rest, Aims. C'mon. Let's put these pups to bed and Bride can ride herd on you for a few hours." She handed the infant in her arms to Aimee, then took the girl from Fang. "I'll be back in a few to gear up for battle."

Fang kissed her cheek. "Thank you, Lia."

Seraphina froze as the small group drew near her. The voluptuous, auburn-haired human offered her a kind smile. "I'm Bride Kattalakis. Fang's sister-in-law and mate to his brother Vane, the dark-haired cutie next to him." She brushed her hand over the head of the sleeping eldest boy. "This is our son, Trace, and the girl is our daughter, Trinity."

Seraphina inclined her head to her. "Nice meeting you."

"You, too."

The female wolf had a strange hair color that was white-blond at the roots and slowly darkened to black at the ends. Her brown eyes were every bit as friendly. "I'm their brother Fury's mate, Angelia. Call me, Lia, though, everyone does. . . . The two younger boys are ours. Asher is the older, blond one, and the dark-haired baby is Ryan."

She must have had a peculiar expression on her face because the next second, Lia laughed. "Yes, I know. Fury and Fang are Katagaria. Vane and I are both Arcadian Sentinels. And all the children are Arcadian . . . so far. But since both Vane and Fury changed their base forms during puberty, we're waiting to see if the kids remain Arcadian or switch in a few years."

Her eyes widened. "They can do that?"

Aimee laughed. "Yes. *We* can when we have mixed parentage. I started out as a cub and switched myself."

Now that was something Seraphina had *never* known about or considered. Could that have happened to one of her children? Edena had been acting very peculiar and secretive. Seraphina had foolishly thought it might stem from a crush on a male she didn't care for. But that might explain some of her daughter's more irrational behavior . . .

Could Edena have switched from Arcadian to Katagari and been too afraid to tell her about it?

She wasn't sure what upset her more. The fact it could have happened or that her daughter wouldn't trust her with the truth. That Edena would be afraid of her own mother judging her for something the child couldn't help.

As the women drifted away, Fury, who had white-blond hair similar to Blaise, came forward. He shifted Trace in his arms. "Don't worry. You'll learn our names quick enough. And I'm easiest to remember as I'm the one most likely to say or do something really stupid or offensive. But don't be offended. I'm socially awkward and mentally stunted." He wrinkled his nose in a very wolflike gesture. "Once they learned I wasn't Arcadian anymore, I was harshly ejected from my Arcadian pack before I got fully mannered up. Lia and Bride keep trying to school me on how humans behave, but I'm learning it's really hard to teach an old wolf new social skills. So don't let me hurt your feelings. I don't mean nothing by it."

She smiled at him. "Same here. I don't really understand this time period or . . . how all of you do things."

He ran his gaze over her wardrobe. "Fourth century BC? Steppe tribe?"

"Amazon. Not sure what you mean by fourth century BC."

He stroked the sleeping baby's back in a very human, fatherly fashion. "What emperor or warlord got on your nerves the most?"

"Philip of Macedon, and his son Alexander."

He let out a low whistle. "Yeah, you're ancient. You pro-Rome, or hate their guts?"

"Not my favorite group."

"Fair warning, then. There are two of them in this city, Roman and Valerius. They're on our side. Try not to kill them. Especially Val. Once you get past his assholishness, he's actually a decent enough guy. And his wife's one of Bride's best friends. She'd be real put out if you killed him, which would upset Vane and, well . . . you know, shit rolls downhill."

Seraphina laughed. Yes, yes, it did. "Thanks for the warning."

He inclined his head. "Let me go tuck my nephew in with my sons and I'll be right back."

Isolated again, she returned to listen to the small group continue to discuss the best way to attempt a rescue for her children and not get eaten by gallu in the process.

For the first time, Seraphina understood how Maxis must have felt when he'd found himself thrust into her tribe after their mating. How completely alienated he'd been, and how foreign the surroundings and customs and faces. Because she'd been born among the Amazons, she'd always known their traditions. Known their language and felt a part of them. How they fought and went to war.

Yes, she'd been orphaned after the attack on her village, but she hadn't been the only survivor that night. Her aunt's Amazon tribe had welcomed them in with open arms and great compassion. Each of them had been given adoptive families and treated as natural-born daughters.

From the moment of Maxis's arrival in her village, they'd received him as an outsider and had never allowed him to forget the fact that he wasn't one of them, and would never be fully accepted among her race.

When Maxis had first seen the number of Drakaina tents, he'd slowed his horse and worn a look of feral reservation in his eyes.

"Don't tell me you're afraid."

"Not afraid. Only disquieted." His gaze had gone to the collection of cloaks and shields her tribeswomen displayed outside their tents that were made of the tanned scales and skeletons of past dragon kills they proudly flaunted as war trophies. "What is the penalty for killing an Amazon in combat?"

"None, so long as it's fair and open. Murder, however, is punished swiftly and severely. I wouldn't advise doing that. No matter how tempted someone might make you."

And when they'd neared Nala's grand tent where a row of dragon skulls were mounted on dragon-spine posts, he'd arched a brow at her. "I think I know that guy."

She'd laughed, until she realized he wasn't joking. "Seriously?"

"Aye, but it's all right. I owed him money." He'd winked at her.

His sense of humor and extreme intelligence had always caught her off guard. It was what had always charmed her about her mate.

Maxis was never what she expected.

"Are you all right?"

She swallowed hard at Samia's question that dragged her away from her memories and back to the present. "Thinking about the past."

Sam nodded with a sympathetic smile. "I heard you were recently awakened from a curse where you were all turned to stone? What'd you do?"

"Fought for the wrong set of gods, and were too successful at it."

Sam sucked her breath in sharply. "That would do it. So who did you piss off?"

"Zeus."

"Ouch."

Seraphina didn't comment on that as her gaze dropped to the low cut of Samia's shirt where a part of a double-bow brand mark peeked out.

The symbol of a Dark-Hunter—they were immortal warriors who'd sold their souls to the goddess Artemis to fight in her army and protect mankind from the Daimons who preyed on human souls to elongate their lives. Since they hunted the cousin race that had birthed the Were-Hunters, they were normally avoided or considered enemies to her people.

How odd that Samia would end up mated to a Were-Hunter. . . . That had to be the strangest union of all.

"Are you still in service to Artemis?"

Sam shook her head. "I got my soul back." She jerked her chin toward Dev, who was shoving at his twin brother. "It's an adorable werebear who owns me now."

"And you're happy?"

A wicked smile spread across her face. "He's a very special kind of happiness."

"Meaning?"

"He loves to tease and nettle me to the brink of murder,

but I wouldn't have it any other way. He is everything in this world to me." She wandered back to Dev to give him a hug from behind.

A part of Seraphina envied Sam that easy camaraderie with her mate. She'd never really had that with Maxis. Some of it was the fact that he was so much taller and more massive than her, even in human form.

But mostly it stemmed from the fact that she was acutely aware of the their "other" differences. The fact that he stood out radically from other males.

Even in this group.

Both he and Illarion, and Blaise. While they weren't the largest in their human incarnations, there was something more feral and innately powerful. Something about them that warned they were much more than they seemed. They exuded a quiet, lethal predatorial confidence that other species lacked.

An air that said they were the pinnacle of the food chain and that anyone else could be added to their menu at any time.

At their sole discretion. And there was nothing anyone could do to stop them.

He also moved with an exquisite grace. A fluidity of muscle and sinew that was both beautiful and unnerving—like watching a sleek jungle cat stalking its prey on the savannah.

Maxis was the perfect killing machine.

It was what he'd been conceived for. All he'd been created to do. Since the dawn of time, his species had existed for no other purpose than to kill and breed. To guard and protect.

To survive in solitary seclusion, under the harshest of environmental conditions, hot or cold, feast or famine. While other creatures needed social interaction to save their sanity, dragons didn't.

Females were biologically driven to find males twice a year to spawn and carry on their species. Unless a male caught the scent of such a fertile female, they were content to remain celibate, and reclusive.

Alone for centuries.

Being merged with humans had changed that. Arcadians, because they possessed human hearts, formed communities and tribes or patrias of dragon clans, as did many of the animal-hearted Katagaria.

But Maxis had remained solitary even after his transition.

Until they'd been designated as mates. With her alone, Maxis had been unbelievably attentive and affectionate. Insatiable. And true to his dragon's blood, he'd made her his own sacred object that he'd held and guarded, and dared anyone to threaten or harm. She'd been the one thing he'd kept diligent watch over.

He seldom even slept whenever she was with him. No one could come near her that he didn't watch them with careful suspicion, ever ready to attack if they said or did anything to hurt her.

And the entire time he'd lived with her, he'd sought out her company, and made her feel as if she were the most beautiful and precious woman in all the world.

Given that absolute hunger he'd possessed for her, she had no idea how he'd managed to leave and return to his monastic ways. Even now, he kept glancing at her with that familiar, scorching heat in his eyes that said he wanted to find a secluded nook for them . . . kept holding his mouth as if he were tasting her already. It left her breathless and starving, and for that, she could almost hate him.

She had seriously underestimated how much impact his presence would have on her. How traitorous her body would be once it was this close to his. Dear gods, it was unbearable to be under that golden scrutiny again and not have some way to taste those lips. To run her hands over his long, languid body and enjoy the wealth of tawny skin . . .

Did all mated couples feel like this? Did they have the same overwhelming need whenever they were together?

But then Seraphina knew from experience that the other Arcadian Draki didn't respond this way to their mates. In fact, the females of her tribe, even those already mated, had been drawn to Maxis in a way that had viciously pissed her off. Any time they thought they could get away with it, they'd cornered him and called it "curiosity" over the fact that he was Katagari and they'd never been that close to a Katagari Drakos before outside of battle, especially one in human form. They'd claimed they only wanted to see if there was any difference between his kind and male Arcadians.

It was that very thing that had led to their first real fight when she'd returned to her village from a hunt to find him gone. Her tent empty.

No sign that he'd been there at all. Something that was a viciously rude public slap in the face, as it was expected for mates to receive their warriors on their return. He should have been there with the rest of the males and children and elder villagers to celebrate as the returning war party rode in a parade to Nala's tent. Since Seraphina was the queen's champion, he was supposed to be waiting outside Nala's tent to greet both her and Nala.

As her mate, his absence was well noted, especially since they'd left a space of honor for him to stand.

Instead of cheers, smirks, and snide innuendoes had greeted her.

A quick interrogation of her neighbors and she'd learned Maxis had left her village just after her raiding party had ridden out. No one had seen him since.

Angry and concerned, Seraphina had headed into the woods, with her tribe's wild speculations about his activities ringing in her ears. Everything from he'd gone hunting humans, to he was practicing the black arts and conjuring foreign gods.

Because they were mates, she had no problem picking up his scent to track, even though it was days old. It was the same ability that had enabled her to locate him here in Sanctuary.

Unless Maxis blocked his scent and used his powers against her, Seraphina could find him with ease.

That was also the first and last time she'd seen him as a dragon.

Without thinking, she'd tracked him into a dark cave where he'd taken refuge to await her return. Because it was a full dragon's den where he'd placed his own belongings without her knowledge, she hadn't realized it was his.

Until that moment, she hadn't given any thought to the fact that Maxis had come to their marriage with nothing more than the dragonslayer's sword he'd taken from his brother's killer, the clothes on his back, and the horse she'd given him as a wedding present.

As she'd stumbled upon the sleeping dragon, she'd unsheathed her sword, intending to kill the beast. His ears had twitched as he detected the subtle sound of metal scraping.

With the fierce rumble that said he was preparing to let loose fire, he'd opened his eyes and turned toward her with a vicious, feral growl. His deep blue scales had turned bright red—a battle color . . . then green as he focused his gaze on her and relaxed. He'd folded his wings down to lay against his back, and slid his tail beside his rear left foot—a dragon's position of peace and acceptance.

"Sera?"

The shock and horror, as she realized this was what the gods had mated her to, had claimed her so fully that she really didn't remember the next few minutes. Only that when she returned to her senses, Maxis was human and holding her against his chest as she sobbed violently. Something that wasn't in her nature.

"I'm so sorry." He'd kissed the tears on her cheeks as he sought to soothe her. "I didn't mean to frighten you."

Once the shock had worn off and her mind worked again, she glared at him.

He's a dragon. A full-blooded, horrific dragon.

A dragon.

Yes, she knew how stupid that sounded. She'd known what he was.

But knowing and seeing . . .

It was *so* different.

He was one of those awful, murderous things that had brutally slain her entire family. Her mother and sisters. Without regard or mercy. One of the animals that held no care or concern for her people. Who preyed on them as if they were cattle.

As if they were *nothing*.

And as she'd glanced around the dark cavern and saw his trunks of treasure and lair—the things he valued—she'd realized that this was what he considered his home.

Not her tent. Not her tribe.

Not *her*.

This was his home. His den.

He's an animal. The pile of straw on the floor attested to that. Straw like what her horse slept upon. No bed or pillow. Or blanket.

He even had a trough of water.

Disgusted, she'd shoved him away and risen to her feet as the brutal reality slapped her hard.

His expression shocked, he stood. "What's wrong?"

She didn't know where to begin. The question wasn't what was wrong. It was what was right. "You were supposed to be in the village to welcome me home. Why weren't you there?"

He'd laughed derisively. "Really didn't want to see the lot of you returning home with the bloody hides and scales of my brethren dripping from the backs of your horses as you dragged them through the village. Damn sure didn't want to celebrate your sneaky victories and bloodshed."

Sneaky? That had only made her fury grow. How dare he dismiss the danger in what they did! "I'm your mate!"

Heat had darkened his deceptively human cheeks. "And I'm yours! You just took one look at me in my real body, and screamed for an hour, and then went into shock at the sight of me. How would you have felt had I done that to you the first time I saw *you* naked?"

"It's not the same!"

"Isn't it? Or better yet, what if you'd come here to find human skulls and bones littering the floor and decorating the walls? Huh? How would you react to human fat burning as oil for my torches? Yet you left me alone in *your* village that's held together with the remains of dracokyn. And that includes the tent where you sleep. Do you really think it's escaped my notice that the posts of it are made from the bones and tusks of drakomai? Or that the candles that burn throughout the village are made from dragon fat? You think I don't know that smell?"

Unwilling to cede the point since he was right, she didn't bother to contradict him. Instead, she moved on to something he couldn't argue with. "Your place is at my side!"

"Aye, *at* your side. Not beneath your feet to be trod upon. I am not an Amazon male who caters to your every whim and begs for a kind word from you. You do not own me. I am not your property! And I will not allow you to treat me as such!"

"And I will not allow you to embarrass me in front of my basilinna or my tribe. I've worked too hard to reach my position—"

"As a murderess?"

"Dragonslayer."

"Nay." He shook his head. "Sneaking into a lair while a dragon sleeps and cutting his throat isn't noble. It's murder. You don't hunt. You tiptoe to slaughter."

"And what do dragons do? You attack sleeping villages! Is that not murder?"

"No, we don't. *We* don't attack, ever. Katagaria are not drakomai. Do not insult me by mistaking my brethren for one of them. They are a different breed entirely. Made by an Arcadian king and a psychotic god who wanted to please him. Merged with Apollites by dark magick. 'Tis the bloodline of *your* kind that taints those poor bastards. Drakomai are not raised to attack unprovoked. We don't hunt for any reason except to eat, and we don't prey on man. That is not in our natures. So long as you stay out of our territory and dens, we leave you in peace."

"You lie!"

He shook his head. "We are solitary beasts who only war when confronted."

She'd gestured at the trunks of treasure that surrounded them. Gold and jewels that glimmered in the dim light. "And what of that? Are those not your war trophies?"

Sincere shock had marked his handsome features. "Hardly. I have no need of treasure or money. Those are things given over to me for my protection. I hold them in trust for their rightful owners."

"You expect me to believe that?"

"Believe it or not, that's up to you. It's the truth. Everything *I* own, I placed in your tent."

"And why weren't you in my tent on my return?"

He'd stared at her in sullen defiance.

"Answer me!"

His eyes had snapped the same fire he could have easily breathed all over her. "You don't take that tone with me. I don't speak to you in such a manner and I demand from you the same respect I show my mate."

Fury had simmered deep in her and she'd wanted to beat him for that. In Amazon culture, the men bowed down to their women and were, in truth, subservient to them. But she knew he didn't come from that kind of environment. And she did her best to understand and respect it.

Yet it was difficult when it went against everything she knew.

"Fine, then. Please, explain to me why you humiliated me today."

He'd snorted in shocked disbelief and repeated her words back at her. "Please explain how I humiliated *you*?"

"By not being there when I returned. You showed a total lack of regard for me and my standing in the tribe. And they all laughed at me because of it."

His jaw had gone slack. "I didn't know that." His brow furrowed by earnest regret, he'd closed the distance between them and cupped her cheek in his warm palm. "If this is true, then I'm so sorry, Sera. I had no idea that was your custom. No one told me. I swear, I never meant to hurt you."

It was so hard to be mad at him when he looked at her like that. When he touched her with such loving sincerity. She felt her anger wilting. But worse than the anger was the underlying hurt, and their mockery that stung much deeper than she wanted to own up to. "Why weren't you there?"

Then she saw it. The bitter agony in his eyes. His own hurt and embarrassment. "In the future, if you will call out to me on your approach, I shall make sure to be in attendance on your arrival."

"But you won't stay in the village while I'm gone?"

He'd shaken his head.

"Why?"

His gaze had burned into hers. "You know why, Sera. My speaking it aloud will only anger you, and solve nothing. And we both know the only thing you can do is leave . . . which you won't do." He'd placed a tender kiss to her lips. "I don't wish to fight with you any longer. Come, let me make amends for my unintended slight. I promise, by the night's end, I'll earn my way back into your good graces."

And that he had. He always did. No matter how much she wanted to stay angry at him, he had ways of making her smile. Of melting her ire until she was laughing and happy again.

That was his greatest magick of all. His ability to wash away her pain and drive out her demons with nothing more than a teasing smile, warm hug, and tender kiss.

Worse, he'd been right that day. The members of her tribe had always been too free with their hands on his body. Even though they knew he was mated and off-limits—that he couldn't do anything had he wanted to—they'd constantly tried to corner him so that they could compare him to a "regular" man. Get a "hands-on" comparison.

To Maxis's credit, he'd done everything he could to avoid them and their cheap caresses. Everything he could to fit in and please her. To make their union work.

If only I'd met him halfway.

Seraphina winced as the guilt of it settled hard on her shoulders. She'd asked things of him that were so far beyond tolerance, she still couldn't bear to think on them. Things he'd suffered.

To please her.

She hadn't deserved him and she knew it. Unfortunately, that realization had come too late. She'd listened to the wrong people and allowed their venom to color her heart. Had allowed their beliefs and opinions to interfere with her relationship with Maxis. Instead of trusting herself and her husband, she'd trusted them.

And learned the hard way that too many people spoke jealousy under the guise of "truth" and "good intentions." When honestly, their only purpose was to make others as miserable in their lives as they were in theirs.

And instead of having a devoted husband at her side when her children had been born, as Aimee would have with Fang, she'd been completely alone.

The loss of what should have been was what made her saddest of all. Her pride and blind stupidity had robbed them all of the family life they should have had.

But there was no way back. And she had no one to blame for it except herself.

"So how do we find where they're holed up?" Dev asked Fang, distracting her from her thoughts.

"I called Thorn, and because they're gallu, he's clueless. Since they don't fall under his jurisdiction, he doesn't deal with them and knows nothing bout them. I tried to call Sin and got no answer, so I left word with Kish to tell him what was going on. He said he'd have him call me ASAP."

Dev glanced over to his younger brother Kyle, who'd joined them a short time ago. "What about Kerryna? Doesn't she know them? They are technically her family, right?"

Kyle made a rude bear sound. "Um. Yeah. They're hunting her so they can enslave and use her to awaken her evil sisters. Needless to say, she tends to keep as far away from the gallu as she can. Kind of like you and Rémi. As much as she loves us, she's not volunteering to help with this fight. And if we ask for that favor, her hubby will tear our heads off and make us bearskin rugs. Charonte are *ridiculously* protective that way, especially when it comes to the mother of their young. Xed basically chased me out of the club for even trying to talk to her about the gallu."

Dev snorted. "But she can give us intel, right?"

Kyle gave him a droll stare. "Let me reiterate. He chased me out of the club . . . with barbecue sauce. While smacking his lips and calling my name."

"And?"

Fang answered for him. "Give the kid a break. They basically locked her up from the moment of birth, so she hasn't really interacted with them . . . and while she's born of the gallu, she's not really one of them. From what she's said in the past, they're a separate beast."

Seraphina felt sick at where this was going. And how slowly. They didn't have much longer before Nala would return here and demand she leave.

Or worse, discover that she'd lied and Maxis was here, after all. In retrospect, maybe she shouldn't have come. She could have screwed this up on her own.

Really, she didn't need any help at all.

Off to the side, Maxis passed a look to Illarion that said the two of them were speaking in their heads. Then he locked gazes with her. "I might be able to find them. But it will require my mate to trust me and do something that's repugnant to her."

Her eyes widened at that. "What?"

Illarion took his arm and vigorously shook his head no.

Maxis ignored him. "It'll be fine."

Illarion rolled his eyes. He mouthed a silent curse at his brother.

Blaise burst out laughing, then stopped as he realized the rest of them weren't in on their private conversation. Clearing his throat, he slinked off to a corner to examine a spot on the wall, even though he was blind.

Seraphina scowled. "What's going on?"

Max hesitated as he swept his gaze around everyone gathered there. This motley hodgepodge was his family and he didn't want to risk losing any of them. "I can track the children."

"There's no way," Sera said affirmatively. "They have them shielded. If it was possible, I would have done it already."

"I can find them." His tone held absolute resolve.

Her doubting expression was as comical as it was beautiful. But then she'd always underestimated his abilities. Most creatures, to their detriment, did. "How?"

"If you'll trust me. Completely. I can do it."

Fang cocked his head as if he now understood what was going on. "You're part Oneroi?"

Max snorted at the assumption that he was one of the gods who raided human dreams so that they could siphon off emotions. "Don't insult me. I'm not Greek. I was captured and dragged to Arcadia. It was never my homeland."

Fang's jaw dropped. "Seriously?"

Illarion nodded. *While I'm a son of Ares, we're related only through our mother. Max is a lot older. His powers much stronger and more akin to those of the gods than a typical Were-Hunter.*

Even Dev was awed. "So what are you, then?"

"Xarunese."

"Bless you," Dev said drily. "You need a Kleenex? Benadryl?"

Max sighed heavily at the bear's fucked-up sense of humor. "Land of Xarun. Much like Atlantis, the gods took issue with it. What little remains sits at the bottom of the Black Sea. I'm one of the very few who survived the sinking."

"Ouch."

Max inclined his head to Kyle for his verbalizing the pain of *that* particular nightmare.

"So wait a minute." Dev cocked his head as if he just realized what Max was telling them. "You're not Greek or Apollite . . . how exactly are you Katagaria?"

Carson Whitethunder, the hawk who was also their resident vet and doctor, passed a smirk to Dev. He and Aimee were the only two creatures here who had ever seen the mark that was branded on Max's thigh. And only because they had treated his injuries. Aimee when Max had first arrived one heartbeat from death, and Carson decades later after a couple of their grittier confrontations with enemies who'd tried over the years to destroy the Peltier family. "Haven't you ever wondered why, in over a hundred years of living here, Max has never stepped a single foot outside of this building?"

Dev snorted. "We're all freaks here. I don't judge."

Max glanced to Seraphina as he remembered the less than pleasant way she'd handled the news when she'd first learned what that mark was. Why he bore it.

He'd never intended for anyone here to learn about it. But it was time to come clean.

"Remember that you're all bound by the Omegrion laws. None of you can attack me on Sanctuary grounds."

"Sheez, boy," Dev groused. "What are you? The Dragonbane, or something?"

Max inclined his head to him, and as soon as he did, it sucked every bit of oxygen from the room. Half the shapeshifters around him took a step back, as if terrified being near him would taint them.

All humor and friendliness evaporated from Dev's eyes as he gaped. "Are you shitting me? *You're* the sole reason for the war between the Katagaria and the Arcadians?"

Illarion stepped between them. *It's not that simple, Dev. Calm down.*

Dev curled his lip. "Not that simple, my ass. You murdered Lycaon's heir in cold blood and started this bloodbath between our people, and you're telling me it's not that simple?"

Max felt that same sick knot in his stomach he got any time someone saw his mark and recognized it.

He was the most hated among his people.

No, not *his* people.

They were Greeks and Apollites.

He wasn't. He'd never really been one of them. Forever a hated outsider. An interloper who'd been mistaken for them since the day Dagon had captured him and mixed him in with their ancestors.

Unable to bear their rejection, he met Sera's gaze and waited for her to condemn him as well.

Seraphina choked on tears as she saw the familiar agony in that golden gaze. The reservation and acceptance of the fact that he didn't belong to anyone.

For the first time ever, she saw *him*.

Worse, she saw herself in the way the others reacted as they shouted and accused him of crimes and misdeeds. Judged him without a hearing or without understanding. Like her, they had accepted him only a few minutes ago and now they were attacking him, without listening. They were so busy condemning him over the stories they'd all been told that none of them even asked him what had happened.

They acted as if *they* knew.

But none of them had been there. With the exception of Maxis, none of them had been born.

Yet they were the experts, with *all* the answers.

"Enough!" Fang shouted, holding his hands up to get the others to settle down. "We'll deal with the Dragonbane issue after this is over. Right now, we need to focus on getting the kids away from the gallu before they convert them. Regardless of anything else, they're innocent in this."

His eyes haunted, Max held his hand out toward Seraphina. By the expression on his face, she could tell that he expected her to react the same way she had the first time she'd learned he was the Dragonbane.

To refuse him completely and shirk away as if he were poison.

This time, she did what she should have done then—she took his hand and smiled up at him. "I trust you, Lord Dragon. Lead me to your lair."

But as he closed his hand around hers, a chill of foreboding rushed over her spine. With this one action, she was either saving all their lives . . .

Or consigning them to death. And not just them. Her children were counting on her to not screw this up. Yet what choice did she have?

There was no one else to turn to.

Yes, Maxis was the most hated enemy of her people. But he was the father of her children. And he was the only chance she had to save them.

Please gods, let this be the right choice.

7

Seraphina let out a slow, nervous breath as she cast her gaze around the huge attic where Maxis had made his home. It held "modern" things she couldn't even begin to comprehend, but aside from a few of those, it reminded her so much of his sparse cave that it raised chills of déjà vu on her body.

Those were definitely the same trunks from his cave that lined the right brick wall. This was his home in a way her village had never been.

And that made her saddest of all. He'd found a comfort here with strangers that he should have known with her. His mate.

Maxis used his powers to light four huge iron candle stands. The light flickered and merged with the rays of the dawning sun to cast their shadows against the wall.

Illarion and Blaise followed them into the room and closed the door. By the way Maxis continued to grimace and act toward his brother, she assumed they were having a private conversation in their heads.

Sighing, she met Blaise's blank stare. "He doesn't think much of me, does he?"

"I'm trying to remain impartial, but if one-quarter of what Illy is saying is true . . . do your people really make jewelry from the tusks, scales, and bones of dragons?"

She felt heat creep over her face. "We don't hunt mandrakes."

"From what I'm hearing, you don't know. Your people don't exactly bother to find out if they're hunting Katagaria or not. You basically kill indiscriminately and go after any large serpent that isn't Arcadian."

"Stop, Blaise," Maxis said in a gentle tone. "She's not to blame in this."

No. We are, you and I. I curse the day I ever let you talk me into saving their kind. Illarion raked her with a chilling stare. *We should have let the gods have them all.*

"Enough, Illarion. And I didn't talk you into shit, as I recall. You were in it more than I was. Besides, what's done is done. Now either choose to be part of this solution, or leave. I'm not about to tolerate your incessant bitching. I have to focus."

Illarion threw his hands up. *Fine. Let's see how she handles this. After all, she never bothered to ask you anything about what you really are. Where you came from. How you were dragged into her world to become part of it. The three years you lived with her, she never once cared enough to learn.*

Maxis growled at his brother. "Stay out of my head and thoughts. . . . I swear, I should have eaten your egg instead of nesting it."

Seraphina arched her brow at that. "You nested him?"

"Sadly, yes, and I did a piss-poor job of it, too. As you can see."

Illarion rolled his eyes.

Blaise laughed. "Max attempted to nest all of his siblings. At least those of us he could find. Once a year while she lived, he'd journey to where our mother placed her eggs and collect them so that they wouldn't have to hatch alone, and flounder for survival."

The irritated look on Maxis's face told her he didn't want his brother sharing that tidbit with her. But she was glad that Blaise had spoken.

And Illarion was right. There was a lot she'd never bothered to learn about her husband.

"Did you nest Hadyn?"

Maxis nodded. "He was the first I found, just days old. Wandering and lost, like a little bug."

No wonder they'd been so close.

Max taught us the Bane-Cry to clear our lungs and so that no matter how far apart we were, we could always call out to each other for help, should we need it. And while the rest of our siblings might not respond, Max would always come to us if he was physically able to do so.

That thought brought tears to her eyes. And it was that capacity for love that she missed most about her mate. No, he wasn't the animal her tribe had accused him of being. *How could I have ever let you go?*

"Neither here nor there," Max said, passing an annoyed grimace at each brother in turn. He led her toward a large area of the attic that was curtained off.

It wasn't until he pulled the heavy, dark blue brocade curtains back that she realized this was where he "nested" nowadays.

It actually made sense. Since he slept in dragon form, he'd be far too large for any kind of bed. And again, it reminded her of how different they were. Of the fact that in spite of his male beauty and form, he was still an animal at heart.

As if he heard that thought, Illarion sneered at her. *This is a bad idea.*

Sighing heavily, Maxis passed an aggravated stare at his brother before he took her hand and pulled her inside the curtained-off area. His gaze scorched her with that peculiar mixture of jaded worldliness and precious innocence that was uniquely his. "I know that you've never seen me as anything more than an animal and I'm well aware of what you think of my species. Just remember this is for your children and hold that thought tight."

She opened her mouth to deny it, but he placed a gentle finger over her lips. "Don't lie. We both know the grisly truth. I am an animal. Hatched and spawned." He stepped back. "Blaise? Can you hold her for a minute? I'm not sure how she'll react to this."

It was on the tip of her tongue to tell him not to treat her like a child when he shifted so fast that she almost screamed in terror of it.

She'd forgotten just how large his dragon's body was. How massive and terrifying.

Even as spacious as the attic was, Maxis had to crouch low and could barely move about. He completely filled the area. For that matter, he couldn't turn around. Rather, he had to back himself against the wall where she assumed he slept. Heavens, he was humongous.

"You okay?" Blaise rubbed her arm for comfort.

Swallowing hard, she nodded. "It's just been a long time since I was this close to a living dragon. And never one that wasn't trying to kill me." Because they prided themselves on being human, her tribe rarely took dragon form. It was considered a loss of control . . . similar to throwing a temper tantrum.

Maxis's iridescent scales glimmered like jewels in the dim light. And as he moved, she saw on his wings the vicious scarring Nala and her tribe had left behind. Guilt stabbed her hard for the part she'd played in that.

"I'm so sorry, Maxis," she breathed.

Max froze at the sound of her earnest words. This was a far different reaction than she'd had the last time she'd found him in dragon form.

There was no screaming in terror. No running or attacking.

Instead, she approached him slowly and placed a gentle hand

on his scarred wing that had never properly healed from his harrowing. While he could fly with it, it wasn't particularly comfortable to do so.

And no one had ever touched him like she did now when he'd been in his real body.

Like he mattered to them.

Not even Aimee . . .

Lifting his head, he waited to see that familiar contempt in her gaze for his dragon form. Yet it wasn't there. For the first time ever, Sera ran a curious hand over his scales. And though it made no sense, it comforted him.

"You're so warm."

We're not like other reptiles. He sent his thoughts to her. *My personal belief is that it comes from our ability to make fire. For some reason, it seems to elevate our body temperatures, especially when we're dragons.*

She smiled sadly at him. "No. You're definitely not like anyone else." Biting her lip, she touched the scar on his hind leg that marked him as the firstborn of their race. The dreaded Dragonbane. "What do you need me to do?"

Trust me. You need to lie with me and let me guide you from this realm to wherever they've taken our dragonets. But if you fight me in this, you'll do irreparable harm.

"You trust me?"

Max hesitated. Honestly? He was terrified of what she might do to him. But he had no choice. It was the only way to locate their children. Since he'd never met them, he couldn't even begin to track them without her. Any creature could use their scent to lead him astray. Only their mother would be able to hone in on the real truth of them. Nothing would fool her maternal senses.

Yes.

And still he saw the fear she hid behind her eyes as she knelt by his side.

He rolled slightly so that she could settle comfortably in the shelter of his arms. Yet she was so tiny now. No wonder she feared him. One talon was almost the size of her entire body. A fact she didn't miss, either.

Her hand trembling, she reached out to touch his claw.

It's sharp, he warned. *Mind the edge.*

She drew back to rest behind his dewclaw. "How did you ever get captured by Dagon?"

Max came to help me, when Dagon had me trapped. Fury darkened Illarion's eyes. *My powers were bound so that I couldn't fight or protect myself.*

It wasn't your fault I flew in blindly, Illy.

Because I called in a panic and you were too worried to be cautious.

Max sighed. *It doesn't matter. I don't really need a reason to be stupid. Can find plenty of reasons to partake of that particular vice on my own.*

Illarion snorted as he and Blaise moved forward to help settle Sera against him.

Blaise stepped back. "I'll keep guard at the door to make sure no one disturbs you."

"Thank you." Sera was rigid in his arms.

Illarion moved to the curtains. *I'll wait to join you.*

"What do you mean, join us?"

He smiled, but didn't answer before he closed the curtains and left them alone.

She turned her face toward Max. "What did he mean?"

Nothing. Close your eyes and think of our little ones. Imagine being with them and let your thoughts stay with them. Whatever happens, don't let anything or anyone distract you.

Seraphina wasn't sure what to expect. Honestly, she was terrified. But there was something innately soothing in the way Maxis breathed. His radiating warmth seeped into her body, lulling her. It reminded her of the nights when he'd held her in his arms, waiting for her to fall asleep so that he could sneak away and seek his rest in his cave. Because his native form was that of a dragon, it took concentration and energy to hold a human form, especially during the daylight hours.

Very few Katagaria could hold human form while wounded or when fighting. Only the strongest of the strong managed. But no matter how powerful the beast, when they slept, they invariably returned to their native species. It was as involuntary as shapeshifting when struck by an electrical shock. Anything that disturbed the electrical currents around the cells would shift them.

So Maxis had always taken care to leave her tent and village any time he needed to rest. He'd never trusted them to not harm him.

"Why are your scales so soft?" she breathed as she struggled to stay awake against the sudden exhaustion caused by the warm, soothing comfort of his body.

"All drakomai have supple scales."

"They're like feathers."

"Are they?"

She nodded, sinking herself even deeper into them. It was the most pleasant and comforting sensation. Like a luxurious bed. Better still was the scent of sandalwood and vanilla that was uniquely his. She'd forgotten that delectable scent of his skin that had once caused her to covet any item of clothing he wore.

Why had she ever feared this?

Before she could stop herself, she turned her face into the scales and inhaled the masculine scent of them.

Maxis cursed as he felt her caress all the way through his body. For a full minute, he saw stars from the intensity of lust that struck him like a physical blow.

Damn it! He'd forgotten how intense these feelings for her were. How much he craved being with her. While his body could be mildly stirred by others, it was nothing compared to what it felt now that his mate was with him again.

Worse . . .

"You're entering your fertile cycle, aren't you?"

She answered by burrowing deeper against him. By balling her fists into his scales.

Max sucked his breath in sharply as every hormone in his body was fired by her touch. "Sera?" he tried again. "Can you hear me?"

"Yes?" That breathless tone raised chills all over his body and was its own form of a caress.

Its own form of torture.

Biting his lip, he knew this wasn't the time or place. But it wasn't easy to distract himself from the warmth of her pressing against him. From the curve of her lush, full breasts that practically spilled out of her top, and the invitation of those lips that he wanted to taste until he made them cry out in pleasure.

He was just about to give in when he felt a strange break in the ether around them.

It wasn't Illarion.

Fully alert, he lifted his head to search with all his senses. The ancient, arcane evil was one he hadn't felt in a long, long time.

And it wasn't alone.

"Maxis?"

His heart pounding from the sudden adrenaline surge, he manifested the two of them in the darkness and tucked Sera behind him to protect her. He searched the nebulous area around them that reminded him too much of Irkalla.

And now that he thought about it . . .

Why would they be *here*? Was he mistaken?

Every single nerve ending in his body crawled with warning.

Well, this can't be good. Terrified of what Kessar intended, Max shifted back into his human form and faced Seraphina. Gods, he'd forgotten just how beautiful she was. How much she'd once meant to him.

How much she still did, in spite of his common sense and best denials. But no time now for dawdling. It was time to do what he'd brought her here to do.

Cupping her beautiful, round cheeks in his hands, he smiled down at her. "Do you trust me?"

He saw the uncertainty in those hazel eyes as she searched his gaze warily. "Yes. Why?"

Max didn't speak. He couldn't. What he was about to do, she might not ever forgive. Yet it was something that had to be done. Let her hate him if she must.

At least this time, her hatred would be justified.

Seraphina knew something was wrong by the light in those golden eyes, but she didn't know what it was. Instead of speaking, Maxis tightened his arms around her and pulled her flush to his hard, muscled chest. Leaning down, he nuzzled his face against her neck. His warm breath scorched her skin and raised chills all over her body. Worse, it made her breathless with a heated longing that wanted him inside her so badly it was almost impossible to resist.

Just as she was about to ask what he was doing, she felt the sharp sting of fangs sinking into her jugular. She cried out and started to fight, but it was useless. He had her completely subdued.

Completely at his mercy.

Weak and confused, she didn't understand why he was doing this to her. Was he trying to hurt or kill her? To punish her for what she'd done to him? Did he intend this to be his revenge? Kill her and their children?

Her head reeling, one moment she was in his arms in the darkness. The next, she was back in his bedroom, lying on the floor behind the closed curtain. Alone.

"Maxis?"

What? Why was she here?

What was he thinking?

The curtains parted instantly to show Illarion, looking every bit as befuddled as she felt. *What happened?*

"I don't know." Feeling sick and weak, she wiped at her neck to find the smallest trace of blood there. "He drank from me?" She hadn't even known that dragons could or would do that.

The color drained from Illarion's features. *What?*

She showed him her bloodstained hand. "He bit me . . . *bit me,*" she emphasized, gesturing toward her neck, "and then I woke up here. Why?"

Blaise came rushing up behind Illarion. "What's going on?"

Illarion let out a deep, guttural growl. *Max just took her blood so that he could track their dragonets on his own, then sent her back here without him.*

Cursing, Blaise ground his teeth. "Why would he do that? We had a plan! A fairly, almost decent one . . . That could have almost worked. Maybe, in the right light and with good timing. Why would he alter it?"

Because this was his *plan, all along. To face them without putting any of us in danger. The stupid bastard plans to battle them alone. 'Cause he's an effing idiot! I knew better than to trust him. I knew it!* He shook his head. *Why did I ever trust him?*

Horrified, Seraphina pushed herself to her feet. "We can't let him do that! One bite. One scratch and he'll become a gallu!"

Illarion laughed bitterly at her concern. *That's not our worst fear.*

"How in the name of the gods is that not our worst fear? Barring his death, that is."

Illarion sobered as he faced her with a dry, cutting glare. *You really, truly don't know* anything *about my brother, do you?*

8

Max felt the forbidden darkness that stalked him. It was the same one he'd battled the day Hadyn had died. The same evil that had been after all of his kinikoi since the hour they had taken up their sacred posts. Because of who and what they were, danger was a natural part of their existence. They'd always known of it and accepted it as an ever-present threat waiting to explode and kill them and anyone in their vicinity.

It was why they kept to themselves and did

their best to let no one close to them. Because anyone they cared about could be used against them, at any time.

Given that, he should have known better than to ever try to have a family with Seraphina. But she'd been so irresistible that night when he'd been in mourning. He'd needed physical comfort to ease his grieving heart and she'd needed a male to ease her cravings.

Now . . .

In dragon form, he banked a hard right, skimming away from the foreign sounds he'd never heard before. In his mind, he carried Sera's memories of their children. And the total love, devotion, and adoration she bore his dragonets warmed him deeply. If he closed his eyes, he could almost pretend that she loved him, too.

And what he hated most was how much he wished he had that part of her. But at least she loved a part of him.

The *best* part.

Quick-tempered and lighthearted, Edena was the very image of how her mother had looked in the bloom of her youth. Long, flaming red hair with bangs that were forever obscuring her eyes and causing her mother to chastise her for hiding their vibrant gold color from the world.

His son was strong and tall, defiant, and far too quick with his snarky comebacks for his mother's patience and sanity. Hadyn's hair was a deeper shade of auburn, and his skin the dark olive of Max's. Where Edena had her mother's porcelain skin with a bit of freckling across her nose, Hadyn had none whatsoever. Both had Max's high cheekbones and the sharp catlike shape of their mother's eyes. But it was Edena's deep dimples that weakened his heart most. Like her mother, she had a smile that could light up the darkest night and weaken the sternest resolve.

May the gods have mercy on any man she ever turned that smile against.

And he was so grateful that they'd been born human. That they'd both been spared their mother's hatred for his kind. That neither child had ever seen in Sera's eyes the contemptuous condemnation he'd glimpsed directed toward him at times, whenever he did something too dragonesque around her.

But those days of hiding his true nature were behind him. If they wanted to tilt the dragon . . .

The dragon was here and he was ready for war.

Bring it, bitches.

Angling his wings down, he swooped low, following their scents until he was sure his children were near the crumbling remains of an old temple. Then he partially changed over to his human form, leaving only his wings so that he could keep a lower, yet equally lethal, profile as he scouted the entire area. A chill raised the hair on the back of his neck as he listened to the winds rustling the ground around him.

He still felt the presence of haunting evil. It caressed everything around him. But more than that, he caught the scent of something even more peculiar. . . .

Arcadian.

What the hell?

His nose twitched at the familiar odor. It was similar to Illarion and yet entirely different. Not his child, but a relative.

Dissolving his wings, Max crept along the shadows, listening intently for any sign of his enemies.

This was a den of dragons. But not just any den . . . Scowling, he peered through the window at the people inside. They were both wolf and drakos. Two groups that didn't normally associate together.

Even more peculiar, they were speaking an older dialect of medieval English. Mercian? Or Saxon? He really needed Cadegan, Illarion, or Blaise here for this. It would be right up their alley.

As it was . . .

He could only vaguely remember their language and pick out a few stray words that made no sense to him.

Not that it mattered. He wasn't here for them and he didn't care about their discussion. Closing his eyes, he used his senses to hone in on what had led him to this dark place. He felt his daughter's presence first.

Her fiery anger that was so similar to her mother's made him smile. Until he understood the source of her fury and why it was so intense at present.

His sight darkened instantly. Wanting blood, he headed straight for the oldest temple a few yards away, where his son and daughter were being held in a large arena that appeared to have been designed for games or events.

That alone would be enough to piss him off. But what set his blood to a boiling heat was what they were doing there. The elder males were fighting his son in an outlawed game of Prine to see who would be the first to sleep with his daughter.

With only a shield and sword for protection, Hadyn stood bleeding and beaten in the center of the arena with one leg held in place by a large chain. Even so, he didn't give up or show his weakness. Rather, he fought them off with a gladiator's courage.

When one of the men rushed his son, Max almost made the mistake of heading him off, and charging in to save his boy. But he was seriously outnumbered.

Not that he needed to worry.

Hadyn caught the bastard with the shield, flipped him to the dirt, and stabbed him before he turned and caught the next one who came at his back. Seraphina had trained their son well. He fought like a champion.

Taking advantage of their distraction as Hadyn cut through them, Max moved quickly to his daughter.

The moment he touched her hands, she tried to fight and attack. "Shh," he breathed in her ear. "I'm here to save you both."

Turning her head to look up at him over her shoulder, she widened her eyes as if she might know who he was.

Max tore apart the chains that held her to the steel post. "Can you ride?" he whispered.

Careful not to alert the others about what Max was doing or that he was there, she nodded in silence as she bravely pulled the gag from her lips.

He took one moment to cup her bruised cheek and admire her courage and beauty, as love, joy, sadness, and grief overwhelmed him. This was his flesh and blood. His child. Something he'd never thought to have. Especially once he'd left

Seraphina behind. He'd relegated himself to living out his life in complete sterile solitude.

Now his beautiful daughter stood before him, all but grown perfection. Not quite a woman, yet definitely not a little girl.

More than anything, he wanted to crush her against him and hold her for the rest of his life. To keep her safe and treasured.

If only he had more time.

But he still had his son to secure. Kissing her lightly on the cheek, he turned and took his dragon's form.

"Get on, child."

As the others screamed and ran for cover and weapons at his sudden appearance in their midst, she jumped onto his neck and secured herself.

Max flew for his son.

Hadyn started to attack him, too, until he saw his sister on his back.

"It's all right, Hade! He's here for us."

Still, he hesitated as he stared up at Max. There was no fear in his eyes, only a healthy appreciation for Max's size and ferocity. With one claw, Max pried up the stake that held the boy in place and lowered his head so that Hadyn could join his sister.

"Don't worry. I'll have you to your mother in a few minutes."

Yet before Max could withdraw, the Arcadians unleashed a full volley of electrified arrows down on him with a frenetic craze.

Well, shit, this is new.

And it wasn't the pain of the arrow wounds that was bad. Not that they felt good . . . particularly. It was the jolts of electricity they sent through his body that forced him to change from dragon to human and back again. Something that felt like the worst kind of muscle spasms imaginable.

His children rolled to the ground and landed near him, out of harm's way. Max stumbled away from them, terrified he might inadvertently crush them while changing. Face it, no one wanted to be caught beneath a nine-ton dragon. The reinforcements the bears had made on the rafters of Sanctuary to support his weight were the stuff of legends.

The Arcadians rushed forward to attack while he was weakened and unable to fight.

Throwing his head back, Max cried out and summoned every bit of magick he could.

And with it, he sent his children to Sanctuary where their mother would be waiting for them. He tried to follow after them, but he didn't have enough strength left for that. Damn it! Electricity was the one thing that was brutal for his kind. It not only played havoc with their physical bodies, it wasn't the nicest friend to their magick either.

Right now . . .

He'd kill for three seconds of control.

Panting and weak, he tried to find shelter. Or roll over on one of those mutant bastards.

It was useless. They were too quick to scurry like the rodent cockroaches they were.

He barely made it ten feet before they had him surrounded.

At least twenty Arcadian dragons and wolves were there. Male and female warriors armed and ready to slay him. Or worse, tie him down.

Even so, he would fight them to the end. He sprayed as much fire as he could in dragon form, but it quickly fizzled as he turned human.

He braced himself for the battle as one of the Drakos who had long dark hair neared him. The man glared his hatred for Max. *Back at you, bitch.*

Yet as they exchanged their mutual disdain and sneers, there was something oddly familiar about the Arcadian. Max cocked his head, trying to place him.

"Do you recognize me, dragon?"

"No," he lied, not wanting to give him any kind of satisfaction.

With a furious shriek, he backhanded Max. "It was my grandfather you murdered!" Stepping back, he jerked his chin at the others gathered around them. "Summon my cousins. Tell Damos that I've finally located the bastard Dragonbane. Tonight we avenge the Kattalakis bloodline! And tomorrow we're going after his children to finish what he started. Sanctuary or no Sanctuary. We will burn them all to the ground!"

9

Seraphina turned at the bright flash, expecting to find Maxis there. The sudden shock of seeing her children . . .

Relief and love poured through her. Tears filled her eyes. Shrieking in gratitude, she ran to them and grabbed them in the tightest hug she could manage even though Hadyn immediately let out a verbal protest that she was hurting him. She shook so badly, she feared her legs would buckle.

Had Hadyn not held her against his chest, she was sure she'd have crumpled at his feet. Not even his bedraggled condition and the fact they needed a bath and fresh clothes took away that they were the most beautiful things she'd ever seen in her life.

"It's all right, Mama," he breathed as he rested his chin against the top of her head. Like his father, he towered over her. "We're fine. It's all good."

She wouldn't go that far. Her poor baby was covered in blood and bruises. His homespun clothes torn and filthy. And that made her want the throats and hearts of whoever had dared touch him. How dare they lay hands on her children!

Her breathing ragged, she pulled back to examine Edena. Like her brother's, her tunic and breeches were torn and covered with filth and blood. Seraphina felt the color drain from her face as an even worse thought went through her.

Edena was the prime age for a mating dragonswan. . . .

I'll kill them. Every one of them with my bare hands and mount their heads to my wall . . . Sanctuary, no Sanctuary.

Mercy be damned.

"Hadyn kept them from me," Edena assured her quickly, as if she could read her mother's thoughts and knew the source of Seraphina's building fury.

"Barely." He staggered back and collapsed to sit cross-legged on the floor. Hard.

Raking a hand through his short auburn hair, he let out an exhausted breath, then winced as he grazed his knuckles against his bruised cheek. He glanced up at her with an adorable frown that was identical to one Max had used when he lived with her and she used to confound him with her strange "Amazon" ways. "Where are we?"

Seraphina didn't answer his raspy question as she stepped over his legs and glanced around, looking for Maxis to join them. He should have been here by now.

How far behind them could he be? What was taking him so long?

Afraid something would tear her babies from her again, she kept her hand on Edena's. "Where's your father?"

"I knew that was him!" Edena smacked at her brother, who grimaced and shoved lightly at her so that she wouldn't hit his shoulder again. "Told you!"

"No you didn't."

Ignoring his ire, Edena met Seraphina's gaze with sadness in her eyes. "They attacked him and he sent us here while he fought them. I don't think he was able to follow."

Blaise cursed.

It was only then that her children realized there were others in the room with them. Edena pulled back as Hadyn rose to his feet to put himself between them and his uncles.

Seraphina smiled at the sweetly protective gesture that was so similar to what Max would have done. Though to be honest, there wasn't much the poor boy could do right now in his wounded condition, except fall down and trip them on their way to attack her. But God love him for trying.

She let go of Edena to gently take Hadyn by the waist and scoot his enormous teen body aside.

Rubbing his back, she smiled proudly at him to let him know

how much she appreciated his sweet thoughtfulness. "Edena, Hadyn . . . meet your uncles. Blaise and Illarion."

"Hi." Blaise gestured toward the wall.

Bemused by that, Hadyn scowled at her and Edena.

Illarion ignored them all. *Screw the pleasantries. We need to get to Max. Where is he?*

Hadyn's frown melted to a mask of shock. "Anyone else think it odd that one uncle can't see and the other can't speak? Is there a reason for that?"

Blaise shot a jolt at him that left him yelping. "Careful, whelp. I don't need my sight in this form to spank your ass. As for the voice, Illarion had his vocal cords cut by moronic humans trying to stop him from breathing fire when he was a kid. Be glad they didn't get their hands on you."

He immediately hung his head. "Sorry. I didn't mean to offend either of you. I'm an insensitive idiot who doesn't always check with my brain before I engage my mouth, especially when I'm hurting. If it makes you feel any better, in the last twenty-four hours, I had three demons try to eat me for dinner, a dozen Arcadians kick the crap out of me, and my sister scream my eardrums to bleeding. Pretty sure I lost some testosterone along the way. Definitely a shit-ton of pride and dignity."

"Hadyn! Watch your mouth!"

"Sorry, Ma."

Shaking her head, Seraphina went and grabbed Maxis's battle sword from the hanger that secured it to his wall near the door. As she started to leave, Illarion caught her. *What are you doing?*

"You and Blaise watch the kids. I'm headed after Maxis."

"That would be a profoundly *bad* idea."

Seraphina glanced over her shoulder to see Fang standing in the now open doorway. "Excuse me?"

He stepped aside to show her the tall, dark-haired Arcadian Sentinel behind him. Only this wasn't his brother Vane. It was another Drakos.

One she'd never met before. Dressed in medieval chain mail and yellow surcoat, and with his hair pulled back in a ponytail, he had an aura of regal refinement and fierce, arrogant warrior. While most Sentinels chose to hide their facial markings with their magick, his were more than apparent.

Fang gestured between them. "Seraphina Drago, meet Sebastian Kattalakis, Prince of Arcadia."

Her jaw went slack as she realized that this was one of the royal princes. A direct descendant of Lycaon, the Arcadian king who'd founded their race.

But before she could bow to him, Illarion snorted disdainfully. *So-fucking-what, Fang? You're a Kattalakis, too.*

Sebastian arched an arrogant brow at his rude dismissal. "Yes, but my grandfather was the king's son. The original Apollite heir born from his queen, Mysene."

Well la-di-da, Mr. Fancy Pants. Aren't you special? You want a hero cookie to go with that title?

Blaise feigned a coughing fit. "Excuse me. I'm having a weird Kerrigan flashback. Should I leave now before lethal things start flying?"

No, I'm the one leaving. My brother needs me and the air in here is suddenly stale.

"Wait!" Sebastian ordered in a tone that left Illarion with a soured expression on his handsome face. One that said Sebastian was about to be in serious pain.

Or in a burn ward.

"I came here to warn Fang about what was happening. A few minutes ago, I received a summons from my cousin to attend a harrowing for the Dragonbane he's captured."

Seraphina gasped at his words.

Why did you come here?

Sebastian shrugged at Illarion's belligerent question. "I thought you might want to get word to Savitar to stop it. As a limani, Fang has the ability to contact him. I don't. And having been harrowed, myself, I don't condone it against another. Ever. I find the whole practice of it distasteful and beneath both our species."

Seraphina couldn't agree more.

Illarion glared at each of them in turn. *What did you people do? Take out ads? For thousands of years, Max stayed hidden and safe.* He pinned that hostile glare on her. *You come back into his life for five minutes and it starts falling apart again. Everyone now knows who he is and they're all attacking him. Why do you have to ruin his life every time you come near it?*

"That's not fair!"

No, it isn't! He never did anything to you, except try to protect you. I wish you'd do him a favor and get out of his life before you kill him.

Blaise gasped. "Illarion . . ."

Don't, brother. It's the truth I speak. We're all thinking it. I just said it. I'm sick to death of watching my brother bleed for her.

Seraphina took a step toward him, intending to make him eat those words, but before she could, a loud thump sounded on the other side of the curtains.

All of them froze.

In unison, they turned toward the unexpected rustling. An exasperated sigh was punctuated by the curtains parting only enough to launch a round object from between them. It shot across the room and landed with another wet, squishy thump on the floor before it rolled a few feet.

Edena shrieked and danced toward her brother as the object came to rest near her and turned out to be a disembodied human head.

An instant later, a huge, spiny dragon poked his head out from between the curtains to offer a lopsided grin. "Sorry, love. Didn't realize anyone was here."

Seraphina gaped at the sight of Maxis lying there as if nothing unusual had happened.

He arched one dragon brow at Sebastian. "Hope that's not a friend of yours. And if it is, tough shit. He was an asshole. Anyone got some extra-large dental floss on them? I've got a chunk of Arcadian dragonslayer stuck in my teeth. Nasty-tasting stuff, that. And Illarion, you're wrong. It does *not* taste like chicken. More like three-day-old rotten ass."

Blaise and Fang burst out laughing. Sebastian looked offended. Hadyn and Edena gaped.

"If I said that, I'd be on restriction forever," Hadyn mumbled to his sister.

"Yes, you would. And don't forget it." Shaking her head, Seraphina closed the distance between them so she could check on Max and make sure he was all right.

That she wasn't hallucinating his sudden appearance.

Max didn't move as he watched his dragonswan walk toward him with a slow saunter. He waited for the condemnation he was sure would follow for his having killed one of her people.

But honestly? He was too tired and in way too much pain to care. Let her hate him. The bastard deserved it. They'd tried to skewer him.

Next time, they should bring more men. Larger spears. And marinate themselves in some soy sauce.

Gah, what kind of piss-poor diet were they on? Rotten cat meat? Cabbage wine?

Yet instead of condemning him, she sank down on her knees by his face and fell against his snout. And when she threw herself, weeping, to hold him close, he wasn't real sure what to think or do. It was so unexpected that for several heartbeats, he was rather certain he was dreaming.

Or dead.

"Sera?" he said from between clenched teeth. The way she had him held, he couldn't open his mouth without harming her.

Still she didn't move. She clung to him with an iron grip as her hot tears fell against his scales. Worried and a lot hornier than he should be given the amount of pain he was in, he forced himself to return to his human body so that he could hold her and not risk damaging her. He took care to conjure a blanket and jeans for himself so that he didn't scar his children or brothers.

He brushed her hair back from her damp cheeks. "What's wrong, Seramia?" he asked, using the endearment he'd made up for her long ago.

She was so upset she couldn't speak. Instead, she rose up on her knees and wrapped her body around his, and held him in a tight embrace with her cheek pressed against his heart. She had one arm draped around his neck and the other beneath his arm, and clutched her hands behind his back so tight, he wasn't sure she'd ever let go.

Completely baffled, he met Illarion's gaze over her shoulder. *Help?*

For the first time, Illarion looked at her with something other than unreasoning hatred. If Max didn't know better, he'd think his brother finally approved of his dragonswan.

Just hold her, Max. She needs to know that you're really here and whole. It's how women are sometimes.

Having been mated to a human female who loved him, Illarion would know better than he. But Max wasn't so sure about the *whole* part. He ached so much that he could barely draw a deep breath. And being in a human body was all kinds of special hell.

Not to mention . . .

"Fang, it won't take the Arcadians long to track me here and demand you turn me over to them." As the Dragonbane, the laws of Sanctuary didn't apply to him. He was the one creature they could legally deny shelter to. It was entirely up to the owners if they wanted the heat of it.

And his personal experience said that no one wanted that kind of misery, and he definitely didn't blame them for not wanting to go against another patria to shelter him. Especially since he wasn't family.

Having lived here for over two centuries, he couldn't ask the Peltiers to go to war for him. They'd already lost enough to this madness of Katagaria versus Arcadian.

"If you'll protect my family for me—they're innocent in all this—I'll make sure I lead the others away from your door. I just need a minute to catch my breath, and collect a couple of things. I promise I won't draw Sanctuary into the cross fire of my mess."

Snorting, Fang tucked his hands into his back pockets. "Boy, don't you dare insult me with that shit. They can kiss my furry wolf ass, which is exactly what Aimee would skin alive if I dared let them have you. I don't give up family." He paused. "Well, they could have Fury. I'm not *that* attached to *him*. But they'd only keep him till he opened his mouth, then launch his ass back to me with a catapult. He's like a bad boomerang that way."

Max laughed at his surly tone, knowing it for the bluster it was. Fang would kill for his brother. "You really don't want this kind of heat. Trust me."

Fang glanced around at the other dragons in the room. "You were one of the first residents the Peltiers took in when they moved here. When Eli and his pack used their witch to set fire to the first bar, you're the one who saved Aimee, Dev, and Cherif from burning alive in it. And you're the only reason that fire didn't spread to Peltier House and trap the others who were sleeping there, including a Dark-Hunter who would have been trapped inside by the daylight. I know the stories, too. Brother, there ain't a shifter in this place who wouldn't fight for you. Now I don't know what happened to cause you to get marked and I don't really care. . . . The one thing I do know is *you*. And if you killed him, he had it coming. So you're free to stay. If they're dumb enough to attack, I know a bar full of hungry Charonte over in the Warehouse District who would love to chomp dragon meat." He glanced over to the head on the floor. "And unlike you, they don't care if it tastes like chicken or not." Then he scratched his chin. "You are picking that up, right? 'Cause I don't want to have to explain it."

Rubbing his forehead, Sebastian let out a slow breath. "I hope you know what you're doing, wolf."

Fang arched a brow. "Have you met me? Of course I have no idea what I'm doing."

Ignoring Fang's surly comment, Max rose to confront Sebastian. "Go to your Regis and tell him that I'm calling hazard on the ones who took and held my dragonets. They want the Dragonbane? I want their throats. Fair combat. In the circle."

"No!" Seraphina gasped.

"No?" Max arched a brow at her.

"I want to kill them."

He smiled at her. That was his dragonswan. Ferocious to the end. "Too late. I called challenge first."

"I birthed them. I should have the honor of avenging them."

"And in the event this goes badly, I'd rather they lose the parent they don't know than the one they're attached to."

"I'd rather not lose either," Edena said. "No offense."

Hadyn nodded his agreement.

"I'm concurring with the kids." Blaise smiled.

Ignoring the comment, Sebastian met Fang's gaze. "If you want me to issue the challenge, I will do so. But watch your back. I have a bad feeling about all this."

Fang sighed. "We will. Give Channon my best."

Sebastian inclined his head to them before he vanished.

"Channon?" Seraphina asked.

"His mate." Fang gestured toward the blood on Max's body. "You guys need me to get Carson?"

Max shook his head. "I just need to rest. I'll be fine." He glanced to Hadyn. "What about you, kid?"

Hadyn glanced to his mother and bit his lip. "Are you good, Matera?"

"How do you mean?"

"About our father?"

She scowled, still not sure what he was talking about.

Edena stepped forward to place a comforting hand on his shoulder. "Tell her, Hadyn. It's time."

Nodding, he bent forward onto all fours as Edena stepped back to give him plenty of room. A second later, Hadyn sprang into a dragon form that was almost indistinguishable from Maxis's.

With a deep, relieved moan, he rolled over onto his back and let his tongue hang out of his mouth. "Thank the gods. I needed this." He panted and groaned his misery. "Ah, gah, it was so hard to stay human!" His tail swished like a happy puppy's.

Seraphina wasn't sure what to make of him or his comments. "Hadyn?"

Laughing at his anguish, Edena moved to rub his belly. "He'll be fine, Mom. He's just a big baby."

"Baby, my ass. That shit hurt!"

"Hadyn!"

"Sorry, Matera. It was brutal!" He draped one claw over his snout.

Stunned, Seraphina tried to make sense of this. "Are you telling me that you're Katagaria?"

Everything went still in the room. As if every one of them waited with bated breath for his response and her reaction.

"Yes," he squeaked.

Seraphina winced at the underlying hesitation in her son's voice. "Oh, Hadyn." Choking on tears, she went to him and nuzzled his snout like she'd done Maxis's earlier. "Precious! How could you think for one moment that I wouldn't love you for this?"

"Oh, I don't know. The fact that you're a dragonslayer who wears boots made from the hides of dragons you've slain?"

"Like father, like son." She held her hand out toward Maxis while she stroked her son's scaly cheek. "I don't care what form you take, boy. You are still the baby I carried inside me. The angel I nursed and protected. How could you think for one second that I could ever hate you for something you can't help?"

Edena slapped his stomach. "Told you."

Hadyn popped her with his tail.

"Mom!"

"Hadyn, stop hitting your sister with your tail."

"She started it."

Seraphina turned to Maxis. "Would you do something?"

"Like what?"

"Talk to them? What did you do when your brothers fought?"

He shrugged. "Let them. They usually stopped once the bleeding got bad."

Hadyn laughed. Edena looked horrified.

Laughing, Max brushed past Sera so that he could finally get a look at his children. It was such a strange feeling to be with strangers that were his. Yet a part of him knew it. Could sense it.

"May I hug you?" he asked Edena.

Tears glistened in her eyes before she threw herself against him. Hadyn returned to being human so that he could launch himself against Max's back and wedge him between them.

Seraphina couldn't breathe as she watched them. In that moment, she truly hated herself for what she'd done. Tears blurred her vision as she watched her children with the father who should never have been a stranger to them.

As if sensing her sadness, Maxis reached his hand out to her and pulled her into their embrace. She took his hand and allowed them to swallow her with their cocoon.

Until Hadyn protested that his ribs hurt. Stepping back, he returned to being a dragon.

Maxis smiled at Edena, then Hadyn, before he turned to Blaise. "Can I ask a favor?"

"Of course."

"The gallu aren't going to stop and neither will the two packs coming for me. This is a blood feud that is centuries old. I need my children where they can't reach them."

"You want me to take them to Avalon?"

"Please. It's the one place I know is beyond their reach."

Hadyn and Edena immediately protested.

Seraphina wanted to argue, too, but she knew Maxis was right. This was the only way to keep them safe. They'd already been punished by the gods for *her* actions. She didn't want them in the line of fire again. "He's right. It's just for a few days. I promise. Go with your uncle and we'll get you soon."

As Blaise started to leave, Max stopped him. "Tell Merlin not to worry. I have not forgotten my oath or my duties. Should I fall, guardianship will go to Falcyn and then to you."

He arched a brow. "Not to Hadyn?"

Max shook his head. "I would never do that to him. The curse of it's too strong."

"So you give it to us. Thanks, brother."

Max laughed. "Getting you both back for all the years of hell you've given me."

Blaise sobered. "I'll tell her. You be careful."

"And you." He kissed Edena's cheek and hugged Hadyn one more time.

It took Seraphina longer to say good-bye. With the exception of Nala taking them, they'd never been separated before. "I will come for you very soon. I love you both."

"Love you." Edena kissed her cheek.

Hadyn hugged and kissed her. "Love you, Matera."

"I love you. Guard your sister."

"I will." And then they were gone.

Alone with Maxis and Illarion, Seraphina felt so strangely empty. She'd been a mother for so long that she'd forgotten what it was like to be by herself. To not have to look over her shoulder to make sure her children were keeping up with her and not falling behind.

Now . . .

"We have to prepare for war."

Maxis nodded.

Illarion went to the disembodied head. *I'll take care of this.* He wrapped it up in a T-shirt. His eyes sad, he locked gazes with Maxis. *I'm so sorry I dragged you into this.* Then he looked at Seraphina. *And I'm sorry I've been so rude to you the entire time you've been here. You're not really the one who fucked my brother's life over and ruined it, my lady. I am. And I swear to you both that I won't take my hatred for myself out on you anymore. Please forgive me.*

10

Max grabbed Illarion's arm as he started to leave. "You have nothing to apologize for where I'm concerned." He cracked a chiding grin. "That being said, you could have been a little kinder to my dragonswan."

The tormented agony in Illarion's gaze was searing. *How can you not hate me? At the very least, blame me or curse me for what I've done to you?*

Max buried his hand in Illarion's long hair

and locked gazes with him so that he could see the sincerity in his heart. "Would my life without you have been better? Really? Let's say that none of this had happened. That I remained a fully blooded drakomas. Where would I be now? In a cave somewhere alone like you were, enduring in Avalon? You're right, Illy. You're a rank, effing bastard to spare me *that* god-awful fate. I should take you outside right now and beat the shit out of you for doing this to me."

Illarion snorted. *I hate you.*

Smiling, he tightened his grip in his brother's hair before he released him. "I hate you, too."

Then Illarion did the one thing he hadn't done since he was a small dragonet. He pulled Max into a tight hug and held him there.

When he finally stepped back, he refused to look him in the eye, as if the action embarrassed him too much to acknowledge. *I'll check on the others. I'm sure the two of you could use a moment to yourselves to catch your breath, and decide what to do about her tribe and the demons out to claim you.*

"Thanks."

Illarion inclined his head to him, then left.

Suddenly alone with Seraphina, Max turned around, unsure of what to say. She'd blown back into his life like an unseen whirlwind and brought all manner of devastation and revelations in her wake. It was almost as swift and startling as Illarion's unexpected return after centuries of absence. Honestly, the two of them had left him reeling and feeling ungrounded and dizzy.

While Illarion's return had required him to reorient his living arrangements—he'd been forced to learn how to share his attic space with another dragon—this . . .

This changed *everything*. The fact that he was a father completely redefined who and what he was, as well as where his loyalties and responsibilities lay.

He had a family now.

His first priority was no longer protecting the Peltier members and the Sa'l Sangue Realle. It was protecting his own progeny and ensuring they lived.

Never before had Max regretted being marked as the Dragonbane. He hadn't even tried to defend himself during the trial. Now . . .

His family needed him to not be hunted. For the first time ever, he regretted that long-ago day and the decision he'd made to throw away his life. What had seemed like a simple solution then, now had lethal, unforeseen consequences.

How do I undo this?

He had no idea.

Seraphina approached Max slowly, unsure of his suddenly somber mood. What to say to ease him. There was a peculiar air about him that she couldn't quite make out. But one thing was obvious . . .

"You're bleeding." She took his arm to lead him back toward his . . . well, she hesitated to call that straw spread out on the floor a bed. Anything else might insult him. "You need to clean your wounds before an infection sets in."

"They'll heal."

She wanted to argue, but he would know better than she. Still . . . "I would feel better if you allowed me to tend them."

Finally, his gaze softened. Some of the rigidity left his limbs.

She brushed her hand against the bloodstain on his shirt and scowled at it. "How are you able to hold human form and be wounded like this?"

He shrugged. "I'm a different beast. With the exception of Illarion and me, the others they caught to form the Were-Hunters were all draconi." Smaller in stature, they were more animal in nature than their larger drakomai cousins. They also lacked the same magical and psionic abilities.

"How did a god not know the difference?"

"I don't think he cared. Or maybe he did and he was trying out the different drako breeds to see which would merge better with Apollite DNA before he mixed our blood with Lycaon's son." He sighed. "In the end, does it really matter?"

Not really. Her heart aching for what they'd done to him and his brother, she pulled the shirt over his head to examine the wounds on his human body. Wounds she knew were probably deeper on his dragon form, yet hidden by his magick—as he often did his mark. He must have fought them ferociously for their children. But then, that was what he did best. Fight and bleed for what he protected. "How did you get away?"

"I fought."

Biting back a smile at his verbal confirmation of her thoughts, she traced the ridges of his hard abdomen. His body had always been among the best of any male. Liberally sprinkled with dark golden hairs, that body had tempted and pleased her to the brink of madness. She'd once spent hours raking her fingernails over the peaks and valleys of his ripped chest and powerful legs. The Greek prince he'd been merged with must have been quite spectacular back in the day. No wonder Lycaon had been so determined to save his son's life.

Maxis caught her hand in his. "Why do you touch me when I know how disgusted you are by my breed?"

Those heartfelt words choked her. "You never disgusted me, Maxis. You only scare me."

"Scare you?"

She nodded as she confessed the one secret she'd always kept from him. It was time to let him know the truth. To let him see her heart and real fears. Why she'd pulled away from him when she should have embraced every part of her dragon lord. "I've fought enough dragons to know how powerful you really are, even though you try to hide it. The very air around you sizzles with the energy you pull. As I said, the fact you can hold your alternate body while in this amount of pain . . . No one else can do that."

"That's no reason to fear me."

She let out a nervous, contradictory laugh. "It's every reason to fear you. You are the Dragonbane. You drew first blood for no reason."

He pulled back as if she'd slapped him. "So that's it, then? You judge me without knowing. You've seen my heart and still you're blind to it?"

"No, now you're the one being unfair."

"How do you figure?"

"If I didn't care, do you think I'd have carried your young while never knowing if they were human or dragon? Every day I was pregnant, I was terrified of what would come out of me."

He snorted dismissively. "Because you feared you wouldn't be able to love a true-born dragonet."

Tears blurred her vision as he spoke her eternal shame out loud. "In part. You're right. I was afraid of that. But every time I thought of purging them from me, I couldn't. Because I remembered the way you held me, protected me. How you endured the mistreatment of my tribe in silence so that you wouldn't hurt my feelings, and it made me determined to keep that part of you, no matter what."

"You saw?"

She nodded. "And I hate myself for saying nothing."

In that moment, as she stared up into his hurt gaze, she saw the same painful memory haunting him that still haunted her.

Seraphina had just ridden back from a particularly dangerous mission. Because they'd been on the brink of war with another Amazon tribe, Nala had stayed behind with a contingency of warriors to defend the village should it come under attack, and sent Seraphina out to lead their forces against the dragons they'd spotted.

Exhausted and wounded after losing half her hunting party to the Katagaria, Seraphina had done nothing but dream of returning home and sleeping for a few hours. Of curling up to Maxis's warm body and having him hold her until she forget the rancid smells of battle.

Instead, Nala had issued an immediate summons for an audience on her return.

Fresh from the kill, Seraphina had gone to her queen and bowed low, thinking the matter had to do with their hunt or the Amazons threatening to invade their lands.

She couldn't have been more wrong.

Nala had risen from her throne—something that was *never* a good sign. "We have had it with that thing you've dragged into our village and forced us to tolerate for years now so that you'd have a playmate."

"Pardon?"

"Your rabid mate! He attacked me!"

Seraphina's jaw had dropped. "Excuse me?"

Nala pointed to the remains of a deep-purple bruise on her arm. "Your animal attacked. Unprovoked. He is disobedient. Disrespectful . . . Dangerous! What if he'd attacked one of the children? Or someone else's mate who couldn't protect himself?"

"Basilinna, please. I'm sure—"

"No! No more of your excuses. He is an animal unleashed that you've left unattended, to walk amongst us without any rules or boundaries. We, *I*, cannot allow him to roam around, unchecked. Not after this. The time has come for you to choose—your sisters or your beast. I will not excuse this!" She gestured at her injured arm.

"Am I being cast out?"

"No. You are to submit him for a harrowing. Only then will I allow him to stay in our village, but only so long as you keep him chained like the wild animal he is. If you disagree, I will have him executed."

Terrified, Seraphina had gulped audibly. Maxis would never tolerate being kept chained down. And she couldn't blame him.

Nala threw a collar at her. "Bring him to me within the hour for his punishment or I'll send a tessera for his head."

Her hands shaking, she'd picked the collar up and slid it into her satchel. A part of her had wanted to beg, desperately, for Nala to change her mind. But she knew it would be useless. Nala was too angry.

And she was queen. Her word was the law they all lived and died by.

Unable to fight Nala's command, Seraphina had headed to her tent, where she found Maxis waiting with his meager handful of clothes already packed.

The instant he saw her face, he'd visibly winced. "I guess you heard."

"That you bruised my basilinna? Of course! What were you thinking?" She would never forget the look on his face. He dared to appear as if she'd slapped him for no reason. And that had only made her angrier.

"I was going to move into my cave, but I didn't want to do so until your return. I thought it rude not to say good-bye and tell you where I was going. I know how upset you get when you don't know where I am. Now that you're back . . . I think it's for the best. No one else here knows where it is."

"That's it, then? *That's* your solution? Aren't you at least going to apologize?"

Total shock filled his eyes and expression. "For what?"

"Embarrassing me? Assaulting the leader of my tribe? Does any of this sound familiar?"

Scowling, he glared at her. "I asked you to leave with me."

"Is that your answer? I didn't abandon my duties and tribe for you, at your command, so it's all right for you to assault them whenever I leave?"

"I didn't say that."

Furious, she'd watched as he picked his pack up and slung it over his back, then his sword and fur cape. A furious tic had worked in his jaw, as if he had some right to be angry after what he'd done to them both. They were lucky Nala wasn't calling for both their lives. "I'll be at the cave whenever you have your cravings for me."

As he started past her, she'd taken his arm to stop him. "Wait, Maxis."

He paused to look down at her with an expression of hopeful expectation that had quickly melted to sad resignation as he realized she wasn't going to stop him from leaving.

Sighing, he leaned down to kiss her cheek.

And as soon as he was about to kiss her, she'd clapped the collar around his neck and turned it on.

His breathing had turned instantly ragged as he dropped everything he held and tried to pull it off. Since she'd never worn a collar, she hadn't known it would be painful. But as he staggered to his knees, panting and desperate to remove it, she realized that it wasn't just prohibiting his magick. It was actually hurting him.

"What have you done to me?" His tone had been filled with utter agony.

"Nala has demanded a harrowing. It's time you learned your place."

His eyes widening, he'd glared at her with such fury that she'd actually stepped back in fear. "Don't do this, Sera. I will not forgive it."

"It's too late for that. I have no choice." Grabbing the collar, she tried to drag him to Nala's tent. Then quickly learned how heavy his stubborn, inert weight was.

With no choice, she'd left him in her tent to tell Nala she had him collared. And as she walked away, his curses for her rang in her ears.

"You do this, Sera, and I will leave you forever! I promise you, I won't take this lying down! You will regret what you've done. What you allow them to do to me!"

In retrospect, she wasn't even sure why she'd done it. Nala had never been *that* good to her. She could blame the humiliation of being called in before her queen on her arrival. Especially given the number of times she'd told Maxis to stay away from the others. Had ordered him to stand down. Her exhaustion on her return . . .

A thousand things that were stupid and poor excuses.

The only thing she could really say in her defense was that she'd had no idea how brutal they would be to him. Normally, a harrowing was a few lashes of the whip—no more than ten for an ill-behaved mate—a few days in the pit, and a few more weeks of shunning.

Then everything went back to normal. Since they already shunned Maxis, and he was stronger than most, she hadn't thought much about his being punished, other than it would appease Nala and prevent any more action from being taken against Maxis.

Yet the instant she told Nala that he was collared and waiting, Nala had led half the village in to drag him out so that they could attack him as if he was solely responsible for every ill a Katagari had ever done an Arcadian. The feral glee in their eyes as they rained down an unimaginable wrath on his body still sent chills over her.

When she'd started forward to protect him, Nala had grabbed her and shoved her back. "You interfere in this and you'll be harrowed next."

"Basilinna—"

"I mean it! No one challenges my authority. And definitely not some piece-of-shit dog."

Seraphina had stepped back, thinking it would be over quickly. But a few minutes later when they showed no signs of stopping, when their jubilant cheers had continued for them to worsen it, and they had yet to do a formal punishment for him, she'd moved in to stop them regardless of Nala's threats.

They'd turned on *her* then. An all-out brawl that had forced her to withdraw or risk losing her unborn children.

By the time their anger was spent and they'd finally dragged, then thrown him into the pit, the damage was done. Maxis had barely been able to breathe or move. His wings broken, he'd lain there, panting in pain like the animal they accused him of being.

"Maxis?"

He'd refused to look at her. Instead, he'd stared at the pit wall, slowly blinking.

Heartbroken and sick, Seraphina had wanted to soothe him. To take everything back. "Maxis, please look at me."

Finally, he'd pinned her with a cold, hate-filled stare.

Time and silence hung between them as she tried to think of something to say to him. But as she saw his condition and the betrayed fury in those golden eyes—anger and rage she fully deserved . . .

No thoughts would come to her mind.

Instead, he'd spoken those quiet words that had haunted her ever since. "I told you when we mated that I would gladly give you my heart, my life, and my love, but that when I did so they came with one condition. Never abuse me. Love is not abuse. And you have harmed me for the last time, my lady. I am done with you. Forever." Then he had closed his eyes and refused to look at her.

Now he stood before her again. And she had a whole new chance to screw up everything.

A new chance to rebuild. If he'd allow it.

Wanting to start over, she reached up and fingered that short hair that reminded her how different he was from the feral dragon she'd been mated to so long ago. "Will you tell me what happened between you and Nala?"

More sadness darkened his eyes. "You don't care. What difference does it make?"

"Because instead of attacking you then, I should have asked

for your side of the story, and I never did. I want to know, now. Please?"

Max hesitated. He still wasn't sure this was a good idea. But really, what difference did it make?

Nodding, he held his hand out. "Let me show you."

She scowled. "Show me, how?"

His eyes took her to task for her hesitation. "You still don't trust me?"

"I didn't say that. Just—"

"You don't trust me not to hurt you." She could deny it all she wanted, but he saw the truth in her hazel gaze. With a heavy sigh, he headed back to his bedroom. "Either join me or not, it's up to you. I really don't care one way or the other." He'd written her and their relationship off centuries ago.

Tired, aching, and honestly pissed off over all of it, he headed for his small pile of furs he sometimes used as a pillow. He'd have already turned into a dragon had it not been for the horror her eyes betrayed every time she saw his true body. But then, he was used to people reacting badly to it.

He was a dragon, after all. They only threw parties for his kind when the dragons were fake ones or had been slaughtered and they were celebrating their deaths.

So he was stunned when she followed after him and lay down by his side.

"Show me."

He opened his arms in invitation.

Seraphina hesitated, unsure of what he would do to her. With no choice, she curled up and allowed him to hold her. Cupping her head, he rested his chin on her hair and cradled her against his body. She could hear his deep, fierce heartbeat under her ear.

"Close your eyes and let me guide you."

She obeyed and was stunned as images . . . no, memories began to play through her mind. Only they weren't her memories, they were his.

Max had gone to bathe and fetch fresh water in expectation of her arrival. For over a fortnight, he'd been forced to endure the excruciating misery of living among the Amazons without her. Because of his promise, he was locked in her village where they wouldn't allow him the most modicum of hospitality.

While she'd known some of it, she hadn't realized that he'd been banned from their meals, too. That whenever she returned home to find food waiting for her, it was something he'd hunted and prepared for her because they wouldn't allow him to take her portions unless she was there and she got it for them.

He wasn't even allowed to draw water from their well lest he contaminate it. Rather, he had to hike to the stream to gather his own and carry it back to their tent.

As he returned to fill their stores, he found Nala in their tent, waiting.

"Where were you?"

Worried by her unexpected presence, he'd set his water down and frowned at her question. "Has Sera been hurt?" It was a natural assumption since that was the only time the queen came to visit someone's mate.

Laughing, she'd circled him. "No. I sent word to them. They won't be back for a few more days."

His stomach had shrunk at the prospect of going even longer without her. "Oh."

"So tell me, dragon, what do you do here while she's gone?"

Shrugging nonchalantly, he refilled their water stores. "I wait."

She'd arched a brow at that. "And?"

Unsure of why she asked that, he'd set the jug aside. It was what his kind did. They weren't a creative bunch. Rather, they checked their perimeter, marked their territory, and guarded whatever fell under their protection. Hobbies served no purpose except to distract them from their duties.

"And what?"

"Don't you get bored waiting?"

"Not really."

She tsked at him. "You know, I could help you with your doldrums."

"How so?"

Nala had stopped in front of him then. Her eyes hungry, she'd reached out and traced a line down the center of his chest that had headed straight for a part of his anatomy that wasn't meant for her.

Max caught her hand just as she went south of his belly button. "I'm mated."

Instead of being daunted, she'd hooked her finger in the waistband of his breeches. "Do you know what I keep thinking about?"

"No idea, my basilinna."

"The night Seraphina brought you in for our inspection."

Heat had suffused his cheeks at the bitter reminder of a night he'd rather forget. To appease her queen and her sister tribeswomen, Sera had "presented" him to them so that they could inspect him and be assured that he was tame enough to reside in their village. Completely naked, he'd been forced to endure their bold scrutiny and rude groping of his body as they made sure he was "man" enough to live among them.

No part of him had been left unexamined.

Or fondled.

By the end of it, he'd been so furious and hurt that he would have left Sera, but she'd apologized and promised him she wouldn't let them treat him like that again. That this was a one-time event, and that she would make it up to him.

Even so, the humiliation and pain had stayed in his heart. Especially since he knew they didn't do that to Arcadian males. The Arcadians were respected and allowed their dignity.

Never him.

The animal.

"What of that night?" he'd asked her, stepping back, out of her reach.

She'd closed the distance between them and reached out to touch the feathers braided into his hair. "You're the most handsome male in our tribe. Did you know that?"

"No, basilinna. I haven't paid much attention to the other men here."

She'd laughed at that. "You know, part of your job in this tribe is to please and serve me."

Those words had sent chills over him. Especially when she reached for the laces on his breeches.

Grabbing her hands, he'd stopped her. "Basilinna, please. I can't do anything. You know the laws of our people."

"And what a waste they are. Still . . . you have other parts that are capable of pleasing me." She'd led his hand to her breast. "Tell me that you haven't been as curious about other women as we are about you."

He'd tried to pull away, but she was relentless.

"Do you know how many times I've seen the two of you rutting like animals? I know exactly how capable a lover you are with your mouth and hands."

Anger and embarrassment made a deadly mix in his heart. "You spied on us?"

"It was human curiosity. Something an animal wouldn't understand."

The insult had stung him. He always hated whenever they said that to him.

"Now as your basilinna, I command you to submit to me. Give me what I want!"

He'd grabbed her more forcefully to keep her hands out of his breeches and off his body. "No."

"No?" Her shocked tone would have been laughable had the situation not been so dire. "You dare deny me?"

He glared at her. "I'm just a dumb animal, incapable of

understanding the complexities of how your society works. In my world, the rules are simple. I have a mate and I belong to her, and no one else."

"And she would be the first to lead you naked to my bed and chain you there if I asked it of her. Are you too stupid to comprehend that?"

Even more furious, he'd started to deny it. But deep down in his heart, he knew Nala was telling the truth. At every turn, Sera had shown him that she would submit to her queen, no matter how ridiculous or mean the command.

How humiliating.

Still, he wasn't going to accept *this*. Not without a fight. "Then get Sera's permission. But without it . . . I won't do this. She is my dragonswan. My loyalty and heart go first to her."

Nala had backhanded him. "And hers go to me, you stupid bastard!" She reached for him again.

This time, Max had grabbed her arm and forced her back, toward the opening of the tent. "I will not fuck you, bitch! I don't care who you are. You are not my Sera and I don't want your human ass in my bed." He'd shoved her away so forcefully that she'd stumbled and fallen through the opening, outside the tent.

Knowing if he stayed, he'd probably kill her, Max had immediately gathered his sword and a few supplies, and left the village to head for his cave to wait for Sera's return. This was the only place he ever felt as if he belonged. Where no one mocked or belittled him.

He'd turned to his dragon form as soon as he could and flew to the safety of his only haven. Sera would be furious over this. He knew it. She never liked it whenever he angered her queen. There would be plenty of screaming to come later.

But he wasn't a whore to be bartered. And while he'd do anything to please his mate, this was where he drew the line. He would deal with Sera's fury. But he was through being treated like an inanimate object with no will of his own.

Yes, his heart was that of an animal. Loyal. Fierce. Protective. He didn't understand the duplicity and lies of her people. Most of all, he didn't understand the betrayal and sneakiness.

Honestly, he wished Sera could understand why he didn't want to stay home without her.

These are my sisters. We take care of each other.

Do I not care for you?

It's not the same, Maxis. You don't understand the bond of sisterhood we share. I have an oath to uphold.

And what of our bond? Your word to your mate?

The Fates forced us together.

The same Fates who put you with your sisters. Your ties to them are no stronger than your ties to me. So no, I don't understand your loyalty to them over that of your own mate. Why will you not come away with me?

I can't leave everything I know to be with you.

Why not? I left my world for you.

It's not the same.

Because I'm not human?

And there the argument always stopped, because it all came

down to that one fact. He was an animal unworthy of her human's heart.

She'd dreamed of finding a man to love. Max would never be anything except a disappointment to her. No matter what he said or did. When she looked into his eyes, she didn't see a man there.

She saw an untamed beast. One who embarrassed her.

Heartbroken over the anger he knew she'd unleash on him when she returned, he'd lumbered into his cave where he'd gathered all the items that fell under his aegis and damned every one of them. With his tail, he whipped at them, hating what he was.

Hating the fact that his dragon's heart loved a human woman who was incapable of loving him.

And that was why he stayed, in spite of the animosity and challenges.

Because deep inside, where he hated it most, was the hope that one day Sera would look past his heart and see his soul that belonged to her. That she would learn not to despise him for something he couldn't help any more than she could help being born into a group of mean-spirited bitches.

But hopes and dreams were for humans.

And so it appeared, was love.

Seraphina pulled away as she came back to her own body. For a full minute, she couldn't move or breathe as she listened to the steady beating of Maxis's heart. As she replayed his memories and felt a blinding rage consume her.

This time, it wasn't at him. It was for the ones who truly deserved it.

"Why didn't you tell me?" she whispered.

"You never listened."

He was right. Pushing herself up, she stared down into those wounded eyes and traced the line of his lips with the tip of her fingertips. "I'm so sorry." For the first time, she saw humanity through his eyes and understood exactly what Aimee had meant.

All her life, she'd focused on the clan of Katagaria that had attacked her village and killed her mother. She still didn't know why they'd done that.

A killing, animal rampage. That was all she'd ever been told. It was what Katagaria did. All they knew. They were wild animals that killed indiscriminately and without conscience.

They didn't care who or what they destroyed. They were incapable of understanding.

But Maxis was right. He'd never shown that side to her.

Well, the rolling head a few minutes ago, notwithstanding. Yet she could excuse that. She'd have done worse had she been there to save her children.

For the first time, she looked at her mate and didn't search for the human inside him.

She saw his animal heart for what it was. Beautiful.

And realized that was what she'd fallen in love with. That it was the animal inside him that she treasured above all else. It was what made him Maxis. What made him different from other men.

Frowning, he brushed his fingers against her cold cheeks. "Why are you crying?"

"Because I hurt you when I shouldn't have. I listened to others when I should have kept counsel with you alone. And most of all because I know I don't deserve the second chance I'm about to ask you for."

Max sucked his breath in sharply at her words. He could sense that she meant them. But she'd "meant" them before and he'd lived to regret trusting her.

"I don't know, Sera. So much has happened between us."

"It has. I know I have no right to ask this of you." She took his hand in hers and kissed his palm. "Can I share a memory with you?"

He hesitated before he nodded. "Just think of it and I'll see it."

She had so many memories she wanted to show him of their children. But there was one in particular he should see.

It was when their twins had first entered puberty. They'd been terrified of their emotions and magick.

Hadyn in particular had been skittish. In retrospect, she realized that he must have suspected that he was changing over from human to Katagari. As such, he'd been even more resistant to his newfound powers than Edena. It also hadn't made it easier that Arcadians frowned on anyone who gave in to their animal nature and transformed.

Her people considered it weak to shapeshift. While other Arcadian patrias had their own laws and customs, hers were expected to maintain their human forms, no matter what.

But her children weren't like the others and she knew that. Most of all, she wanted them to feel closer to the father they'd never met.

To help them come to terms with who and what they were,

Seraphina had taken them to the cave that had belonged to Maxis. Her hopes had been to put them in touch with their noble father.

Hadyn had pulled up short as soon as they reached the entrance. "What's that scent?"

"Your father. This was his lair while he lived with me."

That had changed both their attitudes. They entered the cave and looked around as if seeking some kind of connection to the dragonswain they'd never met.

Edena had scowled at her. "Why did you bring us here?"

"So that you could change into a dragon and not fear what you are."

Hadyn's grimace made a mockery of his sister's. "Ragna says that we should never unleash the beast inside us. Once it's free, it's hard to suppress."

"And they are born Arcadians. You two aren't. Your father was a fierce, proud dragonswain and you should never be ashamed of that part of yourselves. Because you're mixed, I'm thinking you might have special abilities as a dragon that the others lack. You might even be able to hold that form longer. The very least, you should try it and see."

Edena had screwed her face up. "I don't know."

"I'll do it." Hadyn had stepped deeper into the cave, making sure to put plenty of room between them. He flashed them a bright smile. "Watch this!" An instant later, he'd taken his dragon form.

Fear had stolen Sera's breath, but she quickly hid it from her son.

He'd stumbled about, much the same way Max and Illarion had when they'd first been transformed into humans. He couldn't quite seem to get the hang of his huge dragon body. "Oh, this is so weird." Then he'd slapped his tail into the wall. "Ow! Have to watch that." He jerked it back and smacked himself in the head with the barbed end.

Instantly, he'd returned to being human so he could rub the unintended injury he'd done himself. "Oh my God! Is that blood?" He'd held his hand out to his mother. "Look at that. I'm bleeding!"

Trying not to laugh, Sera ran to him while Edena had mocked her brave brother.

"Oh my God! Only my idiot twin could knock himself out with his own tail. How stupid are you?"

"You do it and see how hard that thing is to control. I swear it has a mind of its own."

"No, sugar, that's your front tail."

"Edena!" Seraphina had gasped. "I can't believe you said that to your brother! Where did you even hear that?"

"Good grief, Matera! I'm almost thirty years old. I'm the last of my friends who hasn't had a lover yet. And if that's what concerns you, then you need to talk to your son about where he's been planting that shorter front tail lately."

Growling, Hadyn had rushed at his sister, but Sera had caught him. "Stop! Both of you! And just who have you been courting, young man?"

Before he could answer, Edena spoke for him. "Wouldn't call it courting."

He'd gaped at her.

"Hadyn? Look at me and answer my question. Why didn't you tell me?"

He'd lifted his chin defiantly. "It's not a discussion a man wants to have with his mother."

"And it's not his fault. They crawl all over him whenever you leave us."

"Is this true?"

He'd nodded bashfully. "They say that my father had incredible stamina because he was a dragon and they want to know if I take after him."

Horrified, she'd stared at her son. "And you allow them to test you?"

Unabashed, he'd grinned at her. "Every chance I get."

"You are so grounded. Go on and stand over there, and bleed."

"What?"

"I mean it, Hadyn. Go over there before I do you more harm."

Pouting, he obeyed.

She turned back to her daughter. "All right, Deenie. Your turn."

Edena moved back and shook her arms out to her sides. With a deep breath for courage, she changed forms and immediately smacked her head into the ceiling. "Ow!"

"Hah!" Hadyn had teased in his deep, raspy voice. "Told you!"

"Hush, Hadyn. Or I'll step on you."

"Like to see you try."

Seraphina growled at them. Why did they always have to fight, all the time? It made no sense to her and she wanted to choke them both. "Kids, stop!"

Satisfied they were quelled for a minute, she walked to Edena. "How do you feel?"

"Hadyn was right. It's strange. Did you feel like this the first time you changed?"

Sera had smiled at the question. "Want to know a secret?"

"Yeah."

"I've never shifted."

Both of them had gaped at her.

"Never?" Hadyn gasped.

"Never. My parents didn't believe in it for Arcadians. And since I've never been shocked . . . I've always been human."

Edena had returned to being human. "Then why did you make us do this?"

She'd brushed the hair back from her baby's beautiful eyes that reminded her so much of Maxis's. "Because your father was a beautiful, proud dragon. And I wanted you to share this part of him. No one should take that from you. Don't ever let them."

Frowning, Hadyn had moved closer to them. "You loved our father?"

"I did and I'm sorry I took him from you. But never be afraid of using the gift he left you with. You are drakomai. Hold your heads up in pride of that and never let anyone make you feel inferior."

Max pulled back out of her memory to stare at her. "You really told them that?"

She nodded. "I meant what I said, Maxis."

"Then prove it."

"How?"

"Turn into a dragon."

The color faded from her face. "Pardon?"

Max took a deep breath before he explained his ultimatum. "You say that you want a fresh start? Then open your heart and show me that you're willing to bend. I want you to face the beast inside you. As you made our children shift, I want you to shift. Just once. If you can embrace the dragon inside your own heart, then we might stand a chance."

"And if I can't?"

"Then I know you're lying. If you can't stomach the dragon that lives in your body, how could you ever accept and love the one that is inside me?"

Seraphina knew he was right. But as she stared at him, she doubted she could do this. For too long she'd denied that beast. Had hidden it away. To bring it out now . . .

What if she couldn't go back?

"I mean this, Sera. You gave me an impossible choice once. Now I give you one. Shift for me or lose me forever."

11

"You want me to shift here?" Seraphina asked, looking around the loft that suddenly seemed way too tiny for two full-sized dragons.

A teasing light shone in his eyes. "You'll do it?"

"I don't know . . . I'm scared."

The playful light extinguished immediately. "And that's why I'm insisting. You need to understand the beast inside you. Make peace with that part of yourself. I want you to understand the gift you unknowingly gave our dragonets."

Still, it terrified her. But he was right. She'd made her children do this. In all fairness, she should do it too.

Maxis pulled back from her and rose to his feet. He held his hand out for her. "Come with me, my precious swan. Let me show you what it means to be a ferocious dragon. Trust me."

Against all reason and sanity, she did.

Her hand trembling, she took his and allowed him to pull her to her feet. One moment they were in his New Orleans loft and in the next . . .

"Where are we?"

"Avalon. It's the safest place I know to take you for this. The only place I know we can go and not be disturbed or hunted." His gaze darkened before he gave her a chaste kiss that left her strangely breathless. "Now let yourself go."

She waited for him to put a little distance between them before she took a deep breath and . . .

Dropping her arms to her side, she shook her head. "I can't do this."

He arched a brow as he gave her a stern look and crossed his arms over his chest. "Can't or won't?"

Won't, but she wasn't about to admit that to him. "Why is this so important to you? What does it really matter?"

"Because you fear it and me so much. I want you to understand the beast in your heart. To see for yourself what it means to be a dragon. Just one time in your life, Sera. That's all I ask. Appease me."

In all these centuries, he'd seldom asked her for anything. And as she stood there, shame filled her as she remembered those handful of times.

Whenever she was away from home, he'd asked her to let him stay in his cave where he wasn't ridiculed by her people, and she'd denied him that comfort. He'd asked her to not submit him to her tribe to be inspected like a caged animal.

She'd denied him that, too.

He'd begged her to run away with him, and start their family. To live, just the two of them, in peace. No tribe. No hatred. To start fresh and create, rather than destroy.

And the final thing he'd wanted was for her to spare him Nala's wrath.

Tears filled her eyes again as she realized how unfair she'd been. How cruel. She choked on a sob.

"Sera," he breathed, flashing himself to her side so that he could gather her in his arms. "It's okay. You don't have to do this."

And that succeeded in making her cry like a child. She buried her face against his chest and wept as all the pain and regret poured through her. They should have had a life together. Instead, her fears and pride had divided them for centuries. Had trapped her and her children as stone statues and forced him to live in complete celibate solitude.

Worse, they had hurt the one creature in her life who had never sought to harm her. In all her life, Maxis was the only one who had ever put her first. And in spite of everything, he still did.

Burying her hands in his hair, she pulled his lips to hers and kissed him. She let the taste of her dragon fill her senses as she remembered the way he'd once been. How he'd greeted her and held her. No reservations. No guile. Ever her loyal and precious mate.

Nipping his lips, she stepped back to smile up at him. "I am your dragonswan. Show me." With a ragged breath, she forced herself to leave the shelter of his arms and run toward the open meadow.

Max wasn't sure what to think. Not until he saw her spread her wings, then transform into a beautiful red dragon. Her laughter filled his ears as she ran, carefree, through the meadow.

For about three seconds, then she stumbled and fell flat on her face.

Concerned for her welfare, he ran after her. "Are you all right?"

She tried to right herself and tumbled again . . . and again. Finally, she sat down and let out a frustrated breath of fire. "It's not easy to stand, is it?"

"It is for me." He changed forms to show her. "You have to balance your weight a bit differently. Use your wings to counterbalance."

She tried. And failed. "Curse you for making it look so easy."

With a smile, he helped her to her feet and used his neck and weight to assist her . . . just as he'd done for his siblings when they'd been young. "Better?"

She nodded and smiled as she finally caught her wobbly balance. Extending her yellow wings, she moved forward, then sat down again to stare at him. "You were right. It's not so different as a dragon, is it?"

"No."

"I'm still me."

"Did you think you'd be someone else?"

"No, but . . ."

He arched a dragon brow. "Thought you'd lose I.Q. points?"

No, something worse. "I thought I'd be less . . ."

"Human?"

She nodded.

"As I've said, it's the human and Apollite blood that makes the Katagaria dangerous. Not the dragon. The dragon just makes them bigger."

And apparently top-heavy. "Can you teach me to fly?"

"Best I teach you to hover for now. I don't want you to harm yourself." And so he showed her how to use her wings to lift herself from the ground.

Laughing and smiling, Sera did it after a few minutes of trying. While she still wasn't as accomplished at it or nearly as graceful as he was, she was quite pleased with her efforts. It wasn't bad for a first try.

Max shook his head at her giddy excitement. "I can't believe you've never done this before. Were you never curious?"

It wasn't as simple as that. "I've never been shocked. And . . . I fought the urge to shift anytime it came over me. My aunt, Keria, always said we should never give in to the animal inside us. That we should fear it taking us over and ruling us."

"And now?"

She changed back to being human. "I should never have feared you. I'm sorry, Maxis." Completely naked, she did what she'd never done before. She embraced his dragon form.

Closing his eyes, Max savored the sensation of her warm, feminine flesh against his scales. Damn, it made him so hard that for a moment, he couldn't breathe.

"Um, I do have one question."

He opened his eyes to look down at her. "That is?"

"How do I get my clothes back?"

Laughing, he returned to being a man so that he could gather her into his arms, and press the part of him that was most desperate for her against her hip. "Are you sure you want them?"

Seraphina sucked her breath in sharply as he ran his hands over her bare skin and nibbled the flesh of her neck. "Not if you're going to do that."

And then he stepped away and released her, and started that circling thing he did that always made her so dizzy and hot. It was a combination of his scent and the sizzling way he looked at her. Like he was going to devour her, to savor every inch of her body. Which he invariably did. With a thoroughness that was inhuman and intoxicating.

And that particular combination of wild beast and sexy man was deadly.

"Max . . ."

He dipped down low in front of her and came up for an incredibly sweet, passionate kiss as he lifted her from her feet and held her flush to his hard, muscled body. She wrapped her legs around his waist while he lowered them to the ground so that he could deepen his kiss. Leaning her head back, she moaned at how good his mouth felt on her throat. How incredible it was to have all the hard strength pressing down on her again.

"I've missed you so much," she breathed as she explored the wealth of his satiny skin with her hands.

"And I, you." He cupped her face to stare down at her eyes. "When I heard what Zeus had done to your tribe, I want you to know that I went after you, to free you."

She blinked in disbelief. "What?"

He nodded. "I tried to barter for your release. I'm so sorry I failed you."

How could he apologize to her after what they'd done to him? After what she'd allowed them to do? "Are you the one who placed my stone under a shelter?"

Heat stained his cheeks as he gave her a bashful stare. "Since I couldn't free you, I wanted you protected. Zeus had forbidden that any of the stones be removed from where he'd placed them. He would have splintered you. So I built the shelter over you to keep your stone from harm. I would have done the same for the children, too, had I known."

She stared up at him in wonder. "You can't help it, can you?"

"What?"

"Looking after me."

He took her hand into his and kissed her marked palm. "You are my dragonswan. My Strah Draga. It is my honor to care for you."

"Is that the only reason?"

Shaking his head, he nuzzled her neck. "No." His hot breath

scorched her skin and sent chills over her entire body. "You are my heart, Seraphina. And leaving you was the hardest thing I've ever done."

She sank her hand in his hair and cradled his head against her as love for him flooded her. "I'm so sorry, Max."

He kissed her lips and pulled back to offer her a sad smile. "It's all right. I was born cursed. Even now, I know I won't be able to keep you with me."

"You've said that before, but you never explained it. How were you cursed?"

He ran his fingers through her hair as sadness darkened his eyes. "My mother conceived me to steal from my father. When I refused to allow her to use me, she cursed me for it. It's why Illarion was captured as a young dragon and had his throat cut. It was done to punish me. I'm not allowed to have happiness, as others."

"Oh, akribos . . . it wasn't your mother's curse that separated us. It was *my* stupidity. My selfishness. But I promise, I won't let anything else come between us again."

Max wanted to believe that. He really did. Yet even as she said those words, he knew that some things were much easier said than done.

And no matter the intent or heartfelt emotion, not all promises could be kept. The gods were bitter bitches who often made liars of man and beast. And mercy had never been shown to him or his species.

He'd been so hurt that he couldn't allow himself to believe in anything anymore. He knew better.

But at least he had her for a little while. And he vowed to savor what little time they were granted.

Closing his eyes, he dipped his lips to hers and breathed her in. Her body was so incredibly soft and warm. So sweet. He'd forgotten how good it felt to be held. How much he loved the sensation of her limbs sliding against his as she nipped his lips and chin. She'd always been a woman of incredible appetites. Most men would have been terrified of the way she didn't hold herself back.

He'd always loved that most about her. It was nothing for her to come home and playfully flip him to the ground so that she could straddle him. Sometimes she'd stalked him through the woods whenever he went to bathe. As soon as he'd stripped his clothes, she'd pounced like a predator, raining kisses and caresses all over his body.

Even now, she rolled him to his back so that she could lave and taste his chest and abdomen. She lived to be the more aggressive one in bed. It was as if she had something to prove to them both. And he was man enough to give her the lead and lay back and enjoy her play. To let her have her way with his body.

He hissed as she bit his ribs, then went lower to lick and tease his hip bone while her hand cupped his sac and gently massaged him to the point he could barely restrain himself.

"Sera?" He pulled her hand away as he panted with pleasure. "It's been far too long for you to do that. I fear my control isn't what it used to be."

A small pout tempted him even more. "Then I shall have to

get you back into fighting shape." Her wicked little grin enchanted him until she leaned down to take him into her mouth.

"Oh dear gods," he gasped as everything spun. For a full minute, he was sure he'd explode as her mouth worked its magic on his body. But then just as he was about to lose all control, she gave one long lick to him and crawled up his body until she could smile down at him.

Max sank his hands into the wealth of red curls as they cascaded over her pale shoulders and concealed her plump, full breasts. "My Seramia."

Seraphina cherished the endearment that she'd missed more than she'd realized. "My precious dragon." Leaning forward, she kissed those incredible lips before she slid herself onto him.

They moaned in unison. Biting her lip, she took a moment to savor the large, thick fullness of him inside her. No one had ever felt the way he did. Not because he was a dragon, but because she loved him. And as he slowly lifted his hips to thrust against her, she trembled. "I want you to know that I never broke faith with you, Maxis. Since the day we were mated, I've never taken another lover."

"Why?"

"I just couldn't. No matter how bad it was during my cycle, I didn't want anyone else. I'd look at other men and they weren't you."

The smile on his face warmed her thoroughly. "Thank you."

Taking his hands, she led them to her breasts as she leaned back and rode him the way she'd dreamed of doing every night since he'd been gone. He filled her completely. And there for a minute, she forgot about everything else. About all the years that had divided them.

Max surrendered himself to her completely. But then he'd always done that. She had a way of reaching past any and all defenses he put up. It was why he'd been forced to leave her. Because she was the one thing he couldn't say no to.

Ever.

She was his sanctuary.

And his worst hell. For her, there was nothing he wouldn't do. Even consign himself to death.

When she came in his arms, he held her close and joined her there in that perfect peace. And as they panted, he felt his heartbeat speed up as the thirio rose in his blood. It was an animalistic need to combine his life force with hers so that he wouldn't be forced to live without her again. It was something all unbonded Were-Hunters felt whenever they had sex with their mates.

He'd made the mistake once of asking her to bond with him. And while her words of declination had been kind, the look of absolute horror in her hazel eyes was forever seared in his heart. It had shriveled a part of his soul to see that harsh reaction.

That rejection.

So he held her in his arms and didn't bother repeating that nightmare.

Seraphina listened to the fierce pounding of Max's heart beneath her chin as she traced circles over his chest and around his nipple. Her own heartbeat was trying to synchronize to his. To bond with it. She could even feel her teeth elongate for the ceremony that would fully unite them.

In life and death.

And in her mind, she remembered when Max had first asked her to. It'd been right after they'd been mated. After she'd tossed the knife away and accepted him.

His unexpected request had shocked her.

Now . . .

"Would you bond with me, Maxis?"

He went completely still and turned rigid around her. "Pardon?"

Lifting herself up, she looked down at him. "Can we bond?"

A light scowl drew his brows together as he brushed the hair back from her face. "There is nothing on this earth I'd like more. . . ."

"Then why do I sense a *but* in your tone of voice?"

"You know the *but*. I'm under a death warrant, with pretty much every Were-Hunter in existence gunning for me. And we have two dragonets who need their mother to watch over them. I can't risk the chance that I fall and take you with me to the grave."

"I won't let them have you."

He tightened his arms around her. "And that is the sweetest thing anyone has ever said to me. Thank you. But I can't accept a bond with you right now."

Wishing for things to be different, Seraphina laid her head on his chest and touched the mark on his leg. "How do we stop the demons who want you?"

"That is the question, my lady, that I wish desperately I had an answer for."

Suddenly, a fierce screeching cry sounded from the forest around them.

Sera pulled back. "What is that?"

Max sat up immediately. "It's a Bane-Cry. Illarion's under attack."

12

Max returned to Sanctuary to find all manner of hell breaking loose. Rémi was holed up in Peltier House with his brother Cherif, Carson, and the children and pregnant females, along with the Howlers and a contingency of Arcadians and Katagaria ready to lay down their lives for Aimee and the others.

As he came down the stairs from his attic with Sera behind him, he met Rémi in the hallway outside Aimee's bedroom. No doubt Rémi had taken that post to make sure no one came near his sister and threatened her while she rested.

Max paused in front of him. "What's going on? I heard my brother call."

With his familiar sneer in place, Rémi jerked his chin toward the stairs that led down to the main part of the house. "Illarion's with the others in the bar. We're holding the fort here. The Amazons returned with the Kattalakis Arcadian wolves who want your ass on a platter. You should probably stay here while Dev and the others deal. Personally wish they'd have let me get an ounce of wolf flesh. Since I can't have Fang for taking my sister, I'd settle for his cousins."

In spite of the fact that most shifters and people didn't like Rémi due to his acerbic personality, Max strangely did. They'd always seen eye to eye with their basic philosophy. *When in doubt, kill them all and let the gods sort it out.*

Rémi glanced past Max's shoulder to Sera. "You want me to guard your dragonswan while you see to them?"

Max turned slightly to smile at the perturbed expression on her beautiful face. "Um . . . no." He draped an arm around her shoulders. "I think I'll unleash her on them. She's far more fierce than I am."

Rémi came as close to a smile as the bear could. At least until his nephew Jake came out of the nursery with a small, sleepy toddler in his arms.

"Hey Uncle Rémi, you think it's safe to grab some milk from the kitchen? I don't want to wake my mom and we're out. I tried to get Aubie to go back to sleep without it, but he's not listening to me."

Max didn't miss the familiar deep pain that flashed across Rémi's blue eyes at the sight of Jake and Aubert. They were the sons of his identical twin Quinn and his mate Becca—the bearswan Rémi was still desperately in love with and had wanted to be mated to. But the Fates had been even more unkind to him than they'd been to Max and Sera.

Masking the pain, Rémi brushed his hand over Aubert's dark hair to soothe the fussing boy who wanted his milk. "I'll get it. You two stay here where it's safest."

"Okay. I'll go change him." Jake headed back to the nursery while his little brother whined in protest.

"Aubie want milk!"

As they walked down the stairs and into the kitchen, toward the bar, they could hear the angry shouts that strangely reminded him of Aubert's childish cries.

Rémi bit his lip as he mumbled under his breath at how much he wanted to fight. "Bust some ass for me, Max," he said in a louder tone, before grabbing the milk and heading back toward his nephews.

As Max started for the swinging doors, Sera took his arm. "Run with me?"

He smiled at her unexpected offer. "*Now* you see my way of thinking?"

"I do."

"My lady's timing stinks." Max took a moment to pull her

into his arms and kiss her forehead. "Nothing would mean more to me. But I can't do that to the Peltiers and my brother. Not after everything they've done for me over the years."

"And that's why I love *and* hate you."

Snorting at her strange sense of humor, he released her and slid through the swinging door to see what was happening out in the bar.

Fang, Vane, Dev, Illarion, and the wolves and bears were in the bar, ready to war against every member of Seraphina's tribe. Thankfully, the bar was still closed to humans or this would have been an even worse situation.

"I demand you hand over the Dragonbane! He attacked our patria, killed our members, and—"

"Cry to your mama, bitch, I don't care." Fang flipped the Arcadian wolf off.

"Fang!" Vane put himself between his brother and the other wolf. "Not helping!"

Dev laughed. "Maybe not, but he's highly entertaining and helping lift my mood immensely."

Samia smacked her husband in the stomach. "Stay out of this. If we wanted to blow the bar up, again, we'd have brought Rémi out here."

Sera brushed past Max to address the group. "This isn't about the Dragonbane. It's about Nala's pact with a demon."

"Hold your tongue." Nala glared at her.

"No. Not in this. I won't watch you destroy my mate again."

"Seraphina . . ."

But Sera wasn't having any part of this. "I will renounce my allegiance to the tribe before I allow you to take him." She pulled her sword from its sheath. "You want Maxis . . . you have to come through me."

Illarion moved to stand at her back.

Completely stunned, Max was frozen to the spot. He honestly couldn't believe what he was seeing. Was it even real?

Sera was defending him?

Fang took up the position on the left-hand side of Sera's body. "As you can see, we like our Dragonbane. He goes really well with the furniture."

Sarcastic applause sounded, breaking the tension. "Nice." From the rear of the Arcadians, a demon stepped forward. He wasn't Kessar, but there was something remotely familiar about him. Max tried to remember where he'd seen him before.

Definitely gallu. The stench was unmistakable.

The demon stopped in front of Fang and raked him with a sneer. "However, you're all forgetting something. While you are bound by the laws of your Omegrion, we are not. Do you really want me to unleash my warriors here? How long do you think you and your animals will stand?"

Fang didn't miss a beat. "Long enough to mount your head to my wall."

The demon opened his mouth to speak, then began a strange gurgling noise.

Sera and Illarion stepped back. As did Nala. Max closed the distance between them to protect his family.

Quicker than he could blink, Dev grabbed a mop bucket and had it in front of the demon in time to catch him as he unloaded the contents of his stomach. Grimacing and cursing, he glanced over to Sam. "Yeah, you raise as many nieces and nephews as I have and run a bar, you learn that attractive I-ate-too-much sound, so-grab-a-bucket-uncle-I-gotta-hurl." Making an even worse face, he turned back toward the demon. "You through? 'Cause dude, this is some nasty stuff you got going on. And I really hope this shit ain't contagious."

Instead, the demon fell to his knees in agony. He was in so much pain, he couldn't talk.

Dev set the bucket aside as they all stared at the demon in stunned silence. "Anyone know a demon doctor?"

"What's wrong with him?" Nala asked.

Fury shrugged. "I'm thinking his last victim didn't go down right. Who'd you eat?"

Dev snorted sarcastically. "Judging by the contents of the bucket, I'd say a Muppet. Looks like Kermit."

Sam let out a sound of extreme pain. "Y'all are all so gross."

With an exaggerated gesture, Lia nodded her complete agreement.

And still the demon convulsed and gagged. Wheezed and sputtered.

Then burst apart.

In unison, everyone stepped back from the spot where he'd been as if afraid that, too, was contagious.

"Holy shit," Dev breathed.

Fury took Lia's hand. "My freakin' giddy aunt."

Fang and Vane toed the smoking remains of the demon before they swept their gaze around the room.

"Savitar?" Vane called.

Fang scowled. "Thorn?"

No one answered. His features pale, Fang met Max's gaze. "Have you ever seen or heard of anything like this?"

Before he could answer, Nala gasped in alarm. Then she cried out in pain.

Sera stepped toward her. "Basilinna?"

She held her hand up to show that it was slowly turning gray. "I think I'm returning to stone . . . you?"

Horrified, Seraphina examined her own body. "I don't think so."

Her breathing ragged, Nala shook her head. "What is this?" Shrieking, she vanished, and took her Amazons with her.

Fang and Vane turned to the Arcadians, but without their demon and Amazon warriors, their bluster faded.

"This isn't over," their leader promised. "I, too, am a Kattalakis Lykos and I demand the satisfaction of seeing the one who cursed our race pay for his crimes. I'll be back!"

And with that, they were gone.

Max noticed that Sera was paler than she'd been. "Seramia?"

"I don't feel right, either." She pressed her hand to her forehead. "It's so strange." Her legs buckled.

Max swept her up in his arms and teleported her from the bar, back to Peltier House and into the infirmary. "Carson!"

The Gerakian appeared instantly. "What's wrong?"

"I don't know. She's sick or something."

Max stepped back so that Carson could examine her. Time dragged as he worried his lip and waited anxiously for the doctor to tell them both that she was fine. That it was just exhaustion from the unbelievably long day they'd had.

That was what he expected.

Unfortunately, it wasn't what Carson did.

"This is weird. It's like the spell that Kessar unlocked is reversing itself."

Max's breath caught in his throat as fear went through him. No . . . Carson was wrong. He had to be. "What?"

"She's slowly turning back into stone."

In that moment, he felt as if all the wind had been violently knocked out of his body. "Bullshit! Don't fuck with me, Carson."

He pulled the stethoscope from his neck. "I'm not." Patting Sera gently on the shoulder, he offered her a sad, sympathetic smile. "I'm sorry. I have no idea how to reverse this."

Her eyes glistened as she met Max's gaze, but she managed to blink her tears back. "I should have known the gods wouldn't allow us to go free. We were meant to be punished for riding against them. Let's face it, they're not exactly known for their mercy."

Max sank down on his knees in front of her as a thousand emotions ransacked him at once. But the one that hit him the hardest was fear and anguish. The love that didn't want to lose her again.

"I can't let you go. Not again."

She brushed her hand through his hair. "I'm sorry. I should never have followed Nala in her war against the gods. She was so sure the Sumerians would take over Greece." Laughing bitterly, she winced. "Stupid bitch never backed a winning side in any conflict."

"Why did you ride against them?"

"I don't know. I was angry at the gods for what they'd done to us. What they'd done to our children. I wanted the blood of Apollo and Artemis for creating our races. The heads of the Fates for condemning us. It was a suicide run. Yet it made me feel powerful, as if I had some control over my destiny. How stupid is that?"

"It wasn't stupid. Little arrogant and a lot short-sighted. But not stupid." He laid his head in her lap and held her tight. "I can't go back." He pierced her with a furious glower. "I won't."

"There's nothing we can do."

"Yes, there is."

Seraphina went cold at the tone he used. Foreboding sent chills over her entire body. "What are you thinking?"

Biting his lower lip, he swallowed hard. "Stay here with Carson. I'll be right back."

"Maxis!"

He didn't listen.

As he vanished, she tried to stop him. She jumped off the bed and grabbed for his arm.

It was too late. He was gone without a single trace. Only a slight stir in the air gave any hint that he'd been there at all. Terrified, she met Carson's gaze that mirrored her own concerns. "What is he doing?"

The doctor shook his head. "I have no idea. But I'm thinking it can't be good."

"Yeah. I second that."

.   .   .

Max hesitated as he did something he knew was all kinds of stupid. The kind of stupid that if one of his brothers had done it, he'd have beaten them senseless. Thrown water on them to revive them.

Then beaten them more.

But he couldn't think of any other way to spare his dragon-swan from her fate. And if he didn't move fast, it would be too late.

With a deep breath, he closed his eyes and ignored the pain of his wounds. He summoned every ounce of dragon's breath inside him and teleported from Sanctuary to the Gates of Samo-thraki. While the humans in this time and place saw nothing but the jagged remains of a bygone era, he knew where the opening to a most sacred place lay. Much like the gateways to Avalon and Kalosis, it shimmered only in the faintest heartbeats right at dusk and dawn. So quickly that it was easily missed or dismissed as a trick of the eye.

But this was one of the last places where his brethren slept in the modern world.

And this was one of his last remaining siblings.

"Falcyn?"

Nothing but the evening sea breeze answered him. Max picked his way through the ruins of the ancient temple complex where mankind had once paid tribute to the gods of old. Where they'd once made offerings to his kind, hoping to win their co-operation and affection.

Things today were so different.

"Damn it, Falcyn! If you can hear me, answer!"

"I don't answer to humans. If you want to speak to me, pick the right language."

Max laughed bitterly as he switched over to drakyn. "I don't have time for you to be an asshole. I need you, brother."

Something struck him hard across his chest and knocked him flying. By the pain of it, and the distance he flew before he slammed into the ground, he'd say it must have been Falcyn's barbed tail.

With a pain-filled groan, he pushed himself up. "Feel better?"

"Not really. When I slit you from asshole to appetite, then I should rally emotionally."

This time when he attacked, Max caught the blow. Using his force field, he blocked and sent it back at his older brother. "Please, Falcyn . . . please."

The pressure against him lessened.

Then it vanished. Max relaxed, only to realize too late that it was a trick. Falcyn materialized at his back and caught him in a vicious headlock. He choked him hard as he held Max against his body.

"Behold what is left of my island because of you, *brother*. You brought those Greek bastards here and I hate you for it!"

Yeah, okay, this might have been a massive mistake. He'd hoped a few thousand years would have mellowed his brother's wrath.

Apparently, Falcyn needed a few thousand more.

"I'm sorry. I had nowhere else to go."

"And I have nothing more to say to you."

With no choice, Max turned on him and flipped him. "Listen to me! I don't want to fight you."

But a fight it was. Falcyn came after him like a starving dog in a buffet line that was after the last pork chop. Damn, he'd forgotten how hard his brother could hit. With no choice, he transformed to a dragon. It was the only way to survive and he didn't really want to kill his brother.

Well . . .

Theoretically. However, if Falcyn didn't come to his senses soon, Max might change his mind. He didn't need his brother alive to claim what he was after. Only his conscience required a breathing Falcyn.

Oh dear gods, really? Suddenly, Illarion was between them in his dragon body, pushing them apart. *Stop it! Both of you!*

Falcyn spun around, trying to sting him one more time with his tail.

Max caught it with his talons and bit it so hard, Falcyn yelped.

Illarion glared at him. *Was that necessary?*

Max released his tail. "Little bit."

With an irritable growl, Falcyn shot fire at him.

Illarion froze it with his powers. He glared at Falcyn. *We are down to the last four of our house. Can you please not cull our lineage any more?*

"Then you'd best get him out of my sight."

Falcyn . . .

"I mean it, Illy. I'm not in the mood." He lumbered off toward his gate.

"I need a dragonstone, Falcyn. My children and swan will die without it."

Falcyn froze. "You dare to ask me for that?"

"You're the only one left who has one."

Falcyn turned to pin each of them with a fierce, stern glower. "And I really don't give a fuck. Go home. Both of you. I never want to see you again."

With those cold words spoken, he vanished between the gates.

Stunned, Max stared after him. "Are you serious?"

I'm sorry, Max.

Unable to believe this, he laughed bitterly. "I knew you were selfish and cold, Fal, but this . . . Mom would be proud to know how much you take after her. I wish I'd killed you when I had the chance, you bastard!"

Stop, Max. You know why he feels this way.

Yeah, sure. Like everyone else, he blamed Max for things Max hadn't wanted. For things he couldn't help. That he'd done everything to avoid.

Now Sera and his children would pay for it.

Max ached with the weight of his guilt and pain. It wasn't right. He didn't mind carrying the burden of his punishment. He was used to it. But he couldn't stand for the blowback to hit his family.

Not even Falcyn.

But there was nothing he could do. His heart broken that he'd failed, he led Illarion back to Sanctuary so that he could spend whatever time he had left with his wife before the gods returned her to a cold, dead statue.

Medea hesitated outside her parents' bedroom as a bad feeling went through her at the uncharacteristic silence that greeted her. Not that the sounds she normally heard whenever she ventured here at this hour were comforting, far from it, but . . .

"Mom? Dad?"

The door opened by its own volition.

Even more wary, she slid her hands to her weapons, ready to attack whatever threat might be waiting in the large, candlelit room. With its covers rumpled, the king-sized four-poster bed was empty. On one side, the drapes were pulled away as if it'd been vacated quickly.

Then she heard the faint telltale sound of sickness from the bathroom.

"We're in here," her father called.

Still not sure this wasn't a trick, Medea moved quickly, yet cautiously toward the retching sounds.

When she reached the door that was slightly ajar, she pushed it wider and froze in complete shock.

Barely dressed, her mother was on the floor sick, while her father held her. His short black hair was tousled, and his handsome face contorted by worry. Someone, no doubt her father, had braided her mother's long, blond hair to keep it out of her way while she was ill.

Both of them were pale and shaking.

Terrified, Medea rushed closer to them. "What's going on?"

Stryker swallowed hard before he answered. "I don't know. She woke up gagging. And has been sick for over an hour now." He adjusted the cool cloth on her mother's head.

Since Daimons and their brand of demon couldn't get sick, in theory, or pregnant, this couldn't be good. Medea knelt down beside her mother. "Matera?"

With a greenish cast to her skin, her mother placed a tender hand to Medea's cheek and tried to smile. "I'll be fine, little one. I just need a minute."

But she could tell by the fear in her father's eyes that this was worse than her brave mother was letting on.

"Did you need something?" her father asked.

She let out a frustrated sigh. "I hate to burden you with anything else. . . ."

He arched a brow.

"Kessar's returned to the playing field. My spy at Sanctuary just sent word that he has the Emerald Tablet in hand, and has awakened the Scythian Riders to come for you."

Her mother made a sound of supreme pain. "I hate those bitches. I should have ripped out Nala's throat when I had the chance."

Only her mother could muster that much hatred and venom

in *that* condition. But then, that was what Medea loved best about Zephyra. She was a fighter to the bitter end.

Her father laughed at the threat. "He's coming for me?"

Medea nodded. "And he wants Max."

"The dragon?"

"Yes."

"Why?" her father asked with a frown.

Before she could speak, there was another knock on their door.

Medea rose. "I'll see who it is." She teleported to the door, intending to brush off whoever was there. Yet as soon as she opened it and saw her second-in-command and best friend, Davyn, she knew something was wrong.

He had the same greenish cast to his skin and her handsome, lovely friend looked as ill as her mother. And like her parents, his blond hair was tousled all over his head—something Davyn never allowed to happen.

"What's wrong?"

He braced his hand against the frame as he struggled to breathe. "There's some kind of illness spreading through our ranks." As he started to elaborate, he broke off into a fit of coughing. "It's as if we have a plague."

An even worse feeling went through her at those words. Whenever someone mentioned the words "plague" and "Daimon," only one name came to mind. . . .

Apollo.

And that rat bastard just happened to be in residence.

Terrified she was right, but really, really hoping she wasn't, she moved toward Davyn. "C'mon, baby, let me get you to bed."

He pulled back from her. "Not that I wouldn't appreciate the help, but I don't want you to catch whatever hell this is. Besides, Stryker would gut me if I gave it to you. And you would, too."

She snorted at his sick sense of humor. "Only you could be that funny and that ill simultaneously. Go on with you, before I beat you anyway. Just for good measure."

Offering her a weak smile, he vanished.

Medea took a moment to check on her mom and dad again.

Her giant, muscular father had her mother cradled in his lap like a small child. Zephyra appeared so tiny and frail, two things Medea wouldn't normally apply to a woman who was fierce and strong beyond measure.

He cupped her mother's face with his massive paw of a hand while he rocked her gently and kept her head tucked protectively beneath his chin. His obvious love choked Medea and brought tears to her eyes. For all her father's faults, he did adore her mother.

And her.

Sensing her presence, he caught her gaze. "Who was it?"

"Davyn. I'm going to check on something and then I'll update you."

"I trust you, daughter."

As she started to leave, he stopped her.

"Medea?"

"Yes, Father?"

"Love you."

For a full minute, she couldn't move. While she knew he felt that way, he didn't normally say it. Like her mother, her father was a fierce, violent creature. A ruthless Daimon of action, not affection. The fact that he felt compelled to say that worried her even more.

"Love you, too." And as she withdrew, he heard him doing the last thing she ever expected.

He whispered a prayer to Apollymi to help cure her mother's illness.

Yeah, that was scary.

And ironically, that was where she was headed. If anyone should have a clue about this, surely the ancient Atlantean goddess of destruction might know something.

Medea teleported from their home to the palace on the hill where Apollymi resided with her Charonte guards. Since it was late, she wasn't sure where the goddess might be. During the day, which was as dark as night in this hell realm known as Kalosis, the goddess was normally found in her garden.

Medea wasn't sure if Apollymi slept or what she did at night. Truthfully, she'd never given it much thought. Though now that she did, Apollymi must be lonely. She kept herself apart from the Daimons who worshiped her. Apart from the Charonte demons who guarded her, and there was no cable TV here. The curse that imprisoned her in this realm prevented her from visiting her son, Acheron, or from leaving this place.

What *did* the goddess do?

It definitely wasn't crochet or play Parcheesi.

Medea hesitated in the great hall of the black marble palace. "Hello?" That seemed like the safest way to announce her presence without irritating the dangerous goddess too much.

A tall Charonte female appeared by her side. With long green hair that matched her eyes, she had yellow-orange skin and dark orange horns and wings. "Yes?"

"It's all right, Sabine. I'm sure she's here to ask after a cure for her mother. You're excused for the night. Go see to your wee ones."

Turning, the Charonte gave a slight bow to the ever graceful Atlantean goddess. "Yes, akra."

Like a silent wraith, Apollymi glided out of the shadows. Her long white-blond hair floated around her lithe body, and was a stark contrast for her black gown. Her swirling silver eyes filled with compassion, she approached Medea. "I heard your father's plea. What's going on?"

Medea hesitated. This was the Atlantean Destroyer. A goddess of utter ruthlessness and destruction who had massacred her entire pantheon and family . . .

Not the queen of warm fuzzies.

"Why are you being so . . ." Medea shuddered at using the word in front of the goddess lest she offend her and end up as a stain on the wall or floor, "kind?"

Apollymi laughed evilly. "While your thoughts are correct, child, I would remind you that I killed them all over the fact that they harmed my son." She sobered. "In spite of the fights we've had over the centuries, Stryker is my son as well, and though I did not birth him, he is no less dear to me. And as any mother, I will not and cannot allow one son to harm the other, and that is the only time I've ever stayed Stryker's hand. I won't allow him to attack Apostolos or Styxx. So long as he leaves his brothers and their families in peace, I will not splinter him into pieces. And I would no sooner harm him than I would any of my children."

She cupped Medea's chin in her hand. "And that includes you. Now what do you need from me, child?"

Medea hesitated again. Honestly, she wasn't used to affection from anyone other than her mother, and for a time, until the humans had murdered him, her husband.

Her relationship with her father was a very new one. She'd never had a grandparent of any sort, and this side of Apollymi rather frightened her.

It definitely made her uncomfortable. But for now, she'd go with it.

"There seems to be a plague moving through the Spathi here. Davyn is ill, as is my mother."

Apollymi's swirling silver eyes flashed red as she dropped her hand. An unseen wind swept through the room, whipping her hair around her body.

With a hissing curse, she turned and stalked away.

"Akra?"

"Follow me!"

Medea knew better than to question or disobey that tone of voice. She quickened her steps to catch up to the goddess, who led her down to a lower level of the palace that had once belonged to Misos, the Atlantean god of death and violence. From the looks of this level, she would say that this was where that ancient god had once held his "special" damned guests for punishment in their afterlives.

According to Medea's brother, Urian, those souls had been among the first consumed by the original Daimons Apollymi had brought here and saved from Apollo's curse. The souls of those corrupted damned had fed them for a long time.

But unfortunately, all good things came to an end. And after a time, the Daimons had been forced to leave and prey on humans out in the world to feed and elongate their lives.

Thanks to Apollo and his horrific curse.

As they reached the end of the hallway, Apollymi used her powers to throw open a thick iron door. Chained in a naked heap on the floor was Apollo, the Greek god who had damned them all and brutally gutted Apollymi's son Acheron when he'd been human. That betrayal was what the goddess hated him for most. But it paled in comparison to the thousands of years Apollo had spent torturing Acheron's twin brother, Styxx.

As Apollo's granddaughter, Medea should probably feel bad for the old god. But since his curse had cost her her life and he'd done nothing when the human vermin had slaughtered her husband and young son for no other reason than the fact that Apollo had cursed them to grow fangs and live only by night, she just couldn't find it in her heart to spare him. Rather, she hated him even more than her father did.

Furious, she charged at him.

Apollo pulled back laughing. "I wouldn't, were I you."

She hesitated. "Meaning?"

"I know why you're here and yes, I'm the cause of it all."

Apollymi flung out her hand and pinned him to the wall behind him. "What have you done?"

He laughed even harder. "All of you forgot that I'm the god of plagues. I saved up enough of my strength for one last payback."

Medea went cold. "What do we do, akra?"

The expression on Apollymi's face confirmed her worst fear. There was nothing they could do. One god couldn't undo another god's spell or curse.

Cruelty flashed in Apollymi's eyes. "One bastard turn deserves another."

Apollo actually paled at her words. He'd been here long enough to learn to fear that look, as they all did. "What do you mean?"

Apollymi slid an insidious smile to Medea. "We can't kill Apollo. We can't undo this latest trick. . . . But no one said we couldn't feed him to the gallu and let them turn him into one of their blood bitches as they did Zakar. What do you think?"

Medea laughed evilly. "Oh my Lady Apollymi, how I adore the way your mind works. Shall I summon Kessar for a negotiation?"

"Yes, little one. I think you shall."

Apollo screamed. "You can't do that! Have you any idea what they'll do to the world?"

She raked him with a cold, empty stare. "You forget, dearest Apollo, I am Apollymi the Great Destroyer. You think I care for these mortal fools?" She smiled at Medea. "Summon them."

13

Naked beneath his pile of furs, Max lay on the floor of his loft, holding Sera in his arms. He'd sent Illarion to Blaise to see after the children and return them so that they could visit with her before she returned to stone. But he wanted a few last private moments to say his good-byes.

It seemed that every heartbeat made her body turn colder and stiffer. She was slowly dying in his arms. He was trying everything he could think of to keep her warm and vibrant. How could his powers be so worthless?

She offered him a kind, sad smile as she fingered his lips. "Don't fret so, my dragon lord. It's not so bad. Really. It's not like being dead. . . . Just a long sleep. I don't even know that I'm there."

As if that helped? If anything, it made it worse to know that she existed in a dark, vacant state.

Her eyes glistening, she reached up to brush her hand through his bangs. "I just wish I could have seen your hair the way I remembered it. You look so tame like this. So *human*." She wrinkled her nose playfully.

He laughed as he gently caressed her breasts. "I would have thought you'd prefer my hair short and trim, like the men of your village."

"No. It's your feral dragon ways that have always beguiled me most. It was what first drew me to you, above all others."

"Then close your eyes."

She did, and he used his powers to return his hair to the primitive, barbarian style it'd been when they'd first mated.

Taking her hand, he kissed her palm and led it to his long, thin braids that were laced with feathers.

Sera gasped as she opened her eyes to see it. "How did you do that?"

"I have my drakomas ways."

Laughing, she wound a thin braid around her index finger and played in his long hair with such delight that it actually made him hard again. Though how he could rally given their last heated go-round was beyond him. It was a good thing he didn't have a bed, as he was sure they'd have broken it.

She brushed his braid against her plump lips. "There you are, my wild, feral dragon."

Max leaned over her and kissed her as his heart shattered at the thought of losing her again. He had so many powers. So many trinkets and treasures of the gods. Timeless enchanted objects people had killed throughout history to find and possess. But nothing that could stop or prevent this.

Nothing.

So he held on to her so tightly that she finally protested.

"You're crushing me."

"Sorry. I just want to keep you warm and safe." He teased her earlobe with his tongue.

She sighed in pleasure. "How I wish you could. There is nothing more I wish than to stay with you."

Someone knocked on his door. Max used his powers to put clothes back on them before he called out for their visitor to enter his room.

It was Illarion, with one of Merlin's magical spheres.

Max scowled at him. "Where are the kids?"

They're fine and still in Avalon. Since they're not in the process of reconverting to stone, Merlin kept them there. She thinks whatever is affecting Sera and her tribe here can't break through the barrier to reach them on her side of things. She was afraid that if she sent them back, they'd begin to turn, too.

Sera let out a sound of happiness as she sat up. "They're not changing back?"

Illarion held the crystal ball for her to see into it.

Both of the children were there, in what appeared to be Merlin's castle in Avalon. They looked happy and, best of all, healthy and whole. If not a little concerned and stressed.

Edena bit her lip as she moved her head about like a little bird, trying to focus on her mother's face. "Mom?"

Sera smiled at her as she took the ball into her hands. "Edena? Hadyn? Are you all right?"

Hadyn nodded. "We're fine. You?"

"Wonderful, now that I know you're both okay."

Edena's lips quivered. "Is it true? Are you changing back?"

She nodded. "I want you two to listen to your father and let him take care of you for me. Can you do that?"

They both nodded.

"I love you, Mom," Hadyn said, placing his hand on the orb. "I wish I was there to say it to your face."

"As do I. Just remember that no matter what, I will be close. And Edena, I need you to be kinder to your brother in my absence. Stop trying to clip his wings all the time. Let him learn to fly or crash on his own."

"I shall try. For you."

"I love you both. Please take care of each other and your father and uncles for me."

Edena started crying as Hadyn pulled her into his arms to comfort her.

Max swallowed hard as an idea struck him. "Merlin? Are you there with the children?"

The beautiful white-blond enchantress moved to stand next to them. "I'm here. What do you need?"

"If I brought Seraphina to you in Avalon, do you think you could stop her from turning? That whatever is saving the children could save her, too?"

Merlin hesitated. "It might, but it could also kill her, since she's in the process of changing already. I don't know what type of spell Zeus has her under. You know as well as I do how unreasonable magick can be, and the unforeseen consequences." She glanced to his children. "Plus, she's not your bloodline. While she carried your young and has mixed her blood with yours, it's not the same as being born of the drakomai. There's just no telling what might happen. I'm sorry, Max. I don't want to try something and lose her."

Tears choked him. Merlin was right. With her returned to stone, there was always a chance he could find another way to restore her. To get the Tablet from Kessar and use it to free her again.

But there was no way back from dead. Especially not if Zeus splintered her statue first.

"Thanks, Merlin."

She inclined her head to him before the mist in the orb swallowed them.

Sera cocked her head to stare up at him. "What's with that look? What are you planning?"

Yeah, you're scaring me, too.

He stood up. "I'm going after Kessar and the Tablet."

"Are you out of your mind?"

Max shook his head. "It's the only way. He used it to free you. Then I can use it to keep you here, too." He looked at Illarion. "Right?"

His brother shook his head. *Yeah . . . no, this is a really bad, bad idea. Like trying to blow-dry your hair while showering, or piss into a high wind. Are you out of your mind?*

"No. I'm desperate."

Same thing.

He gave his brother an irritated smirk.

Well, it is.

Sera stood up beside him. "I agree with Illarion. Don't even think about doing this. Are you insane? You can't walk into a colony of demons and Amazons who want you dead, and take the Tablet the head demon covets most. They tend to react badly to such things. Believe me. I've seen it. I do believe Nala wears the claw of the last dragon possessed of such arrogance."

Illarion gestured his agreement at Sera. *How many more challenges are you planning to issue? Sheez, Max. There are far less painful ways to die. Drowning in acid comes to mind.*

Suddenly, a light flashed in the room with them. Max started toward it, but something kept him in place. A strong, unseen force he couldn't break.

Furious, he manifested a fire blast to attack. Until he recognized the source of the power.

Falcyn.

Only this time, he wasn't in dragon form. Dressed in their ancient black war garb, he wore the skins and furs of the slayers who'd made the mistake of coming after him, as trophies and testament to his unsurpassed martial skills. His black hair was short except for one long braid that was wrapped around his throat and adorned with a silver dragon pendant that matched his pale eyes. They flashed like mercury in the dim light.

And they missed no detail at all.

Illarion's eyes widened as he saw him there. He inclined his head in acknowledgment of his older brother's birth order and out of respect.

Returning the gesture to Illarion, Falcyn closed the distance between them with that fierce predatorial walk that was uniquely his.

Without a word, he stopped in front of Seraphina and met Max's gaze. "May I?" It was forbidden for a drakomas to touch another's mate without permission. To do so was a killing offense in their culture.

Max nodded.

Sera frowned at him as she looked back and forth between them. "Max?"

"It's all right, Sera. This is my brother Falcyn. I trust him . . . most days."

Ignoring his teasing barb, Falcyn touched her icy forehead, then her hand. "Who curses her?"

"Zeus."

He scoffed disdainfully. "Then I hope this seriously pisses that bastard by-blow off. You should have told me that originally. I wouldn't have had to soul-search nearly as long before helping you."

With one claw, Falcyn made a small incision on his wrist until he could gather three drops of blood. From his satchel, he pulled a small oblong ball that resembled an egg, then coated it with his blood. He placed it in her hands and cupped them around it while he chanted in their mother's tongue. He used her hands to turn the egg round and round.

After a few seconds, Sera sucked her breath in sharply, but Falcyn held her hands in place around the egg. She hissed. "It's burning."

Max tightened his arms around her. "It'll be all right. He's drawing the poison from you. Give him time to work."

Only then did she relax a degree.

By the time Falcyn finished the ritual, she was even paler, but her breathing was more solid.

Falcyn wiped the stone off on his sleeve, and returned it to his satchel. He glanced about the loft expectantly. "You said you have dragonets?"

"A son and daughter. They're with Blaise. In Avalon."

For the first time, Falcyn's stern features softened. Blaise had always held a special place in his affections. "I'll see them protected and shielded, too."

As he started to leave, Max stopped him. "Thank you, brother. Can I ask why you changed your mind?"

Falcyn turned at the curtains to look back first at Max, then to Sera. "I still think you're an idiot. I still hate and begrudge every breath that fills your lungs. But you are my brother and we are drakomai. It's not my place to take from you your heart. . . . If there is any way to help her, then I am honor bound to do so. You know the code we live and die by. Regardless of my feelings for you, it is my responsibility to protect what you love and preserve our bloodline."

"Again, thank you."

Falcyn didn't respond to that. It was as if a part of him was embarrassed by the gratitude. Instead, he turned toward Illarion. "You still have your dragon's claw I gave you?"

Always.

"Yeah, not what I heard." Falcyn clapped him on the arm. "I heard you loaned it out to an addanc. What the hell's wrong with you? Did I teach you nothing?" He shook his head at Illarion. "An addanc? Really?"

Falcyn made a sound of supreme disgust. "All my brothers are morons. I swear. Now take me to the dragonets before Blaise sucks what little intelligence they have out and leaves them lacking, too."

Illarion rolled his eyes.

After they left, Max laughed.

Sera scowled at him. "What?"

"I just realized why I like Rémi so much. He reminds me of my own asshole brother."

"And you find that funny?"

"I do."

Sera held her arms out to examine them as if waiting to start growing cold and sluggish again. "Will this last?"

"It should. Falcyn is the oldest of our kind, to my knowledge." He wrinkled his nose at her. "He's even older than I am."

"Wow! So why does he hate you, then?"

"I failed him and Hadyn. It's why I won't ever fail anyone else I love." He brushed his hand through her hair before lifting a lock up to rub against his bottom lip.

That single action sent chills over her. Worse, it awakened her hunger for him in a way that was frightening. Before she could stop herself, she cupped his face in her hands and led his lips to hers so that she could ravage his mouth and drink her fill of him.

Max laughed as he picked her up and pressed her against the wall behind her. "How can my swan be starving so soon?"

She nipped at his whiskered chin, wanting to forget about everything else.

If only they could.

"We need to see about Nala."

He nodded. "I need to get the Tablet back and make sure Kessar doesn't use it." He picked her up and slung her over his shoulder.

Sera gasped at the action, especially when he headed for the door. "What are you doing?"

He playfully held her legs against his chest as he continued to carry her. "You keep getting into trouble. I'm not letting you out of my sight."

"I *can* walk, you know."

"Aye, but I'm a dragon. We're known for abducting beautiful maidens and taking them to our lairs."

Giggling, she surrendered to his hold. "I've always wondered about that. Why do dragons take women?"

He tsked playfully. "I'm offended you'd ask that given the ride we just had in my bed."

"That's not a bed. . . . On your straw, you mean."

As they reached the bottom of the stairs, the playfulness faded from his face. His jaw dropping, he slid her from his shoulder and set her on her feet in front of him.

Sera turned to see a new group gathered in the downstairs of Peltier House. The power coming from them was disturbing enough, but it was the two sets of identical twin gods that set her nerves on edge and terrified her.

One set was easy to mistake for each other. They were both tall, dark, and incredibly sexy. The only way to distinguish one from the other was that the one on the left had shorter black hair than the one on the right.

"Sin," Max said, extending his hand to him. "Zakar."

They shook his hand in turn.

The other set was much easier to tell apart. While they both had shoulder-length hair in similar styles, one had his black with a pair of swirling silver eyes. The other was blond with eyes of vibrant blue.

"Styxx," Max greeted the blond. "Acheron." He stepped back to introduce her. "My mate, Seraphina."

Acheron inclined his head to her. "Wish we were meeting under better circumstances. Especially since I'm here to ask your mate if it's okay if we feed him to the gallu."

Sin clapped Max on the back and put a firm hand on his shoulder. "Actually, it's not a request. Buckle up, Buttercup. We're throwing you under the bus."

Max gaped. "Pardon?"

"Yeah," Styxx agreed as they surrounded Max. "And knowing them, they're planning to back up over you, too." He flashed a grin at Max. "Like the new hair, by the way. It goes well with the whole dragon sacrifice we're about to make to the gods. Good times."

14

"Dragon sacrifice?" Sera repeated with a gasp. "That is a joke. Right?"

"Sure. We'll call it that."

Gaping, she looked from Styxx to Max. "I don't think I like him very much."

Max cleared his throat. "That's all right. Some days, I don't like him either. And I'm thinking today is definitely going to be one of them. All of you do know that at this point I'm going on about thirty hours with no sleep, right?"

Acheron laughed. "Welcome to my world, *adelphos*. I think I remember sleep . . . once upon a grand time ago. Or maybe that was a hallucination brought on by extreme sleep dep. Hard to tell, at this point."

Max rubbed at his eyebrow with his middle finger. "So you're planning to feed me to the gallu. Any other votes taken while I was away that I need to know about?"

Zakar let out an evil laugh. "You're remarkably calm for a dragon about to be sacrificed."

"Yeah, well, we don't go down easy. You don't know what indigestion is until you try to eat a dragon. We tend to bite back. And hard."

Dev cried out in pain. "And that's more about your sex life than *any* of us need to know."

Max playfully shot a blast of fire at him.

"Hey! Do you mind?" Fang stepped between them and extinguished it. "No burning down the bar! Damn it, children, there are some things I shouldn't have to say, and that is really at the top of my list. Stop playing with fire indoors . . . around the wooden bar and flammable alcohol!"

"Anyway . . ." Sin ignored Fang's outburst. "Do you know where they're hiding?"

"Irkalla."

"Oh," Sin said in a tone so dry it could be used to dehydrate oceans. "That's awesome. Irkalla . . . Why?"

Max bent his head as if imparting a huge secret. "Well, I'm no . . . oh wait. Yeah, that's right, I am an expert. So I'm going to assume he's there because *you* can't go get him, and drag him out by his ears, screaming. Or kill him."

"He's right." Zakar let out an aggravated breath. "I wish we could go back in time and kick the ass of every family member we had who took a hand in unleashing these bastards on us."

Sera frowned. "Wait. . . . Didn't Ishtar descend into Irkalla and return? Doesn't that mean you can, too?"

Grief darkened Sin's eyes. "Different time and place. And I'm sadly not the god my daughter was." He stepped back as he reconsidered their course of action.

"You may not have to be. . . ."

They looked at Max with an arched brow.

Max rubbed his bottom lip with his thumb as he considered their resources. "Sera gave me an idea. I actually have what Asushunamir used to restore Ishtar to life."

Zakar gaped at him with a look of total disbelief. "You're the Koru-Nin?"

"Yeah." Max met Fang's equally slack-jawed stare. "The real reason why I've never left Sanctuary before now. I couldn't care less about the Dragonbane mark. Anyone wants to try and kill me, bring it with friends, and shovels to mark your graves. Rather it's what I protect that keeps me hidden. I can't afford for it to fall into the wrong hands. And should I ever happen to go down . . . only my brothers Falcyn or Blaise have the ability to take over its stewardship. Not even Illarion could handle its power."

Seraphina had known the Sa'l Sangue Realle was important,

but it wasn't until she saw their faces now that she fully understood her mate's duties. Just how important Max was to the universe as a whole.

And how incredibly powerful and deadly an object it was. No wonder the demons were after it.

Zakar narrowed his gaze on Max as if trying to understand him. "Have *you* ever used it?"

"It's not my place. Nor does it tempt me."

"Hence why he's the guardian for it. Anyone else, we'd all be paying tribute to as our grand and evil overlord."

Max snorted at Acheron's dry tone. "Bow down before me, Atlantean scum."

"Exactly."

His eyes haunted, Max laced his fingers in Sera's hair while he talked to the others. It was the tenderest expression of care anyone had ever given her and it touched her a lot more than she wanted to admit to. "Considering all that, there's no reason we can't reclaim the Tablet from Kessar and the others. Even in Irkalla."

Sin knuckle-bumped him. "Let's salt the sands of Irkalla with their blood."

"No." Acheron shook his head at Sin's offer. "I think that's a profoundly bad idea, since Katra would have both our asses if you went in and we couldn't get you back for whatever reason. She's not going to let you go there without her. You willing to risk her life?"

"Hell no!"

Acheron winked at him. "Good answer."

"Who's Katra?" Sera asked Max.

"Sin's wife and Acheron's daughter. As his wife, she's technically part of the Sumerian pantheon and could descend into Irkalla with us, should she choose to do so, and as Ash said, she would do it to protect Sin. But she's also the daughter of Artemis. With that lineage and those ties to that many competing pantheons, who knows what could happen to her if she went in there. While most of the gods should be sleeping, we don't know for certain if that's true of all of them. Our luck, and my personal experience, says prepare for a nasty surprise." Max sighed heavily. "To be safe, we have to do this independent of outside pantheons. With the exception of Illarion, whose father is Ares, the drakomai can go without a problem."

"What about a Hellchaser wolf?"

Max inclined his head to Fang. "You are welcome, brother."

"Amazons?" Sam asked.

"Are you a demigod?"

She hedged a bit. "Granddaughter of Ares. Does that count?"

"Closer than we should chance, especially given the disgruntled look on Dev's face."

"Yeah," Dev said irritably. "Back to the Katra thing. You go. I go. Don't turn me into a demon, Sam. I'd look bad with serrated teeth."

She groaned at her mate.

"That also leaves Chi out, and me," Acheron said. "We better not chance it either."

"But I'm still in."

Sera scowled at Styxx. "How can you be in if your twin isn't?"

Styxx let out an evil laugh. "That's a long story. The shortest version is he was hidden in my mother's womb as a fetus to keep his pantheon from killing him. While his mother is a goddess, my mother was a human queen. So even though we look alike—another trick of his mother's to hide and disguise him—I'm a Chthonian. He's a god. Clears me for active duty in nether realms ruled by ancient pantheons that bar his participation."

Fang checked his phone before he spoke again. "And that's my boss. Thorn's got his own major situation exploding that's requiring his full attention. In fact, he wanted me to help with it, then decided he'd call in Cadegan and Varyk instead, and leave me to deal with this."

Sera crossed her arms over her chest. "So we're a handful against a horde?"

A playful light darkened Styxx's eyes. "Typical odds for me."

Max jerked his chin toward Styxx. "Styxx was the commander of the Stygian Omada."

It was her turn to have her jaw drop at the name of one of the most successful and famous armies in history. It ranked up there with Achilles and his Myrmidons. In the Greco-Apollon wars, the Stygian Omada had been invincible. "That was *you*? But you're just a baby."

Styxx laughed at her unintentional insult. "So was Alexander the Great. It's amazing what people can do when they're highly motivated and there's an enemy army about to swarm over your carcass, should you fall."

"Very, very true."

Now it was Acheron's phone that rang. He stepped away to answer.

"Blood moon," Dev said, feigning an evil accent. "What we live for."

Cherif scoffed. "I can handle that. It's the dying for it that terrifies me."

Fang nodded in agreement as he went over their latest plan in greater detail. Though to be honest, Seraphina still wasn't happy with it. Something was nagging in the back of her mind.

After a few seconds, Acheron returned, his features pale and drawn. "That was Artemis. The gallu are attacking Olympus."

"Mia!" Sin vanished immediately.

Sera scowled at his terrified reaction.

"Mia's his daughter," Max explained. "She must be with her grandmother."

"Oh crap."

Max met Acheron's gaze. "Lead us in."

"Thank you."

They stood back as Acheron teleported them to Olympus. Because it belonged to the Greek pantheon, only the gods, or those they permitted, could access it. Obviously, both Acheron and Sin had permission to visit.

At least Artemis's temple, if not the rest of the buildings on the mountain, since that was where they appeared a few seconds later.

Max had never liked going into battle with family. He liked it even less with Sera by his side. But he knew that this was who and what she was.

A fierce Amazon warrior.

It would be the worst of insults to ask her to stay home and sit this out. So he did the only thing he could. He manifested her helmet and sword and handed them to her.

She frowned at him as she took them, and put the helm on her head. With an adorable smile that did awkward things to his body, she unsheathed her sword. "How did you do that?"

"I'm the one who gave the sword to you, remember?"

Seraphina narrowed her gaze suspiciously on him before she examined the hilt of her sword as if seeing it for the first time. "It's enchanted, isn't it?"

The blush on his face and bashful tilt to his head answered her question.

"This was never a wedding present. It was your way of protecting me in battle."

"I didn't want you hurt." He bit his lip in the most adorable fashion. "It's the Sword of Peleus. Achilles sent it to me to watch over and protect."

Tears choked her. She'd noticed that her battle skills had improved after her mating to Maxis. And she had thought it odd that she'd ceased being wounded in battle. Not even a scratch. She'd attributed it to her own need to stay whole and an improvement to her skills.

Now . . .

She kissed him as a depth of appreciation for her mate over-

whelmed her and flooded her heart with warmth. He was ador-
ably precious. "I love you."

Max couldn't breathe as those words struck him like a blow.
She'd never said that to him before.

Not once.

Honestly, there had been times when he was rather sure she
hated his guts. Times when he'd have sworn she wanted to take
that sword and run him through with it. Or cut off a part of his
body he was rather fond of.

Teasingly, she placed her hand to his chin so that she could
work his gaping mouth for him. "I love you, too, Seraphina,"
she said in a feigned masculine voice.

He laughed and kissed her marked palm. "That I definitely
do. You just caught me off guard with your reaction."

Gathering her in his arms, he held her as Artemis's hand-
maidens threw open a door and ran screaming into their room
with demons chasing after them.

Yeah, this was even worse than they'd expected. How the
gallu had gotten here, he couldn't imagine. They shouldn't have
had any access to Olympus.

Yet here they were.

Acheron ignored the maidens and rushed to a room on their
left. Max led Sera after him while the others went to help Artemis's servants and the other gods.

Seraphina had never seen anything like this. It was worse
than any dragon attack she'd ever been in. The gods were fighting, yet the gallu were fierce.

As soon as Acheron opened the door on their right, they

saw that Artemis had been locked in her bedroom with her granddaughter, who had Sin's coloring, but was the spitting image of a micro Artemis. Remarkably, the girl was fiercely calm as she held on to her grandmother. It was as if she knew Artemis would never allow any harm to come to her.

But the most shocking sight was the Malachai demon who protected them both. In full demon glory, he wore his black battle armor and had his wings spread wide to provide a barrier between them and anyone or anything that came through the doors after Artemis or Mia. His red and black skin swirled over a handsome face and perfect body. But for his demonic appearance and bright red eyes, he'd have been exquisite.

At Sin's entrance, he allowed the Sumerian god to run behind him to see to his daughter, who released Artemis to fall into her father's arms. When they followed after Sin, the demon faced them with his sword, ready to battle.

Until he saw Acheron.

Acheron drew up short as if waiting for the demon to attack him.

Instead, the Malachai inclined his head. "We tried to teleport Mia out when it started, but they have the whole place locked down. I'm amazed any of you got in."

Acheron manifested his staff. "I don't use the standard channels. I have my own access point."

"Glad to hear it. Can you get Artemis and the baby out?"

Sin cupped Mia's head with his hand. "Nick's right. I can't teleport out of here with her. We're locked in."

"Great," the Malachai mumbled before he narrowed his eyes

on Max. "Hey dragon, want to help a brother out? I think together we can route them out of here."

"Right behind you, kid." Max turned into his dragon form. He hesitated. "You want to join us or stay?"

Seraphina frowned at the question until she realized that Max had a saddle on his back. While she'd heard of war dragons and their riders, she'd never seen one. "Are you sure?"

"There's no place I'd rather you be."

The thought of riding a dragon terrified her. But she knew Max would never harm her, and her curiosity rose up. How different could it be than riding a horse into battle? Just a little larger horse, really.

Okay, a much larger horse. Still . . .

Swallowing her fear, she forced herself to climb up his wing and into the saddle.

"You ready?"

She secured herself to the saddle and braced herself for flight. "Ready."

The force of his lift stole her breath. No wonder the saddle had such a high back to it. Winds whipped at her as he followed after the Malachai and into the battle. His massive wings were swift and he could seriously maneuver in spite of his gigantic size.

As could the Malachai.

Together, they rained down blasts of fire onto the gallu. The fighting out here was ferocious. Between the gods and the demons. For her life, she couldn't understand why the gallu were attacking the Greek pantheon. And as they battled, she began to realize why Maxis had placed her on his back.

From up here, she couldn't reach anything. Nothing and no one could get near her. A part of her was irritated. The other was charmed by it.

Until he banked hard to the left. She grasped the saddle to see what had caused it.

Artemis had come out of her temple and was firing fierce and fast at the demons with her bow and arrows.

The Malachai laughed at her fury. "I think someone's a little upset they dared to threaten her granddaughter."

Max nodded. "But it gives me a thought."

"What?" Sera asked as he flew away from the Malachai, toward the main temple on the hill.

He skimmed over the demonic horde. "Look at the number of demons here."

"There are a lot of them. Your point?"

Max hovered just out of the battle frenzy. "Want to do some recon?"

"Depends. If we have to fight, are you going to let me touch the ground?"

He turned his massive dragon's head around to look at her over his shoulder. "You caught that, did you?"

She lifted her legs that were a mile or so above the ground. "Hard to miss."

He flashed her an unrepentant grin. "Fine. If there's fighting, I'll put you down for it."

"Very well, then. Lead the way, my dragon lord. Obviously I will go wherever you take me."

Maxis pulled out of the fighting and attempted to leave

Olympus. At first, he couldn't. Something had him blocked. But his mother's heritage allowed him to bypass the gallu magick and find a back way through it in spite of whatever they'd put over the place to keep the others from coming in or leaving.

Determined to get to his brother's Tablet, he carried her down to Irkalla. While he hadn't seen Kessar among the attackers on Olympus, he knew that the majority of the gallu demons had to be there and not in their hidden realm where they'd been earlier.

Which meant he had a shot at getting the Tablet while the gallu fought against the Greek gods and others.

He hated to back out of the fighting, but this was much more important. The Emerald Tablet was as much a threat to their safety, if not more so, than the demons they were battling. This was their best chance to get it back.

At the entrance to the ancient nether realm, Max stopped and allowed Sera to dismount. He manifested his own armor and weapons. He paused as he caught the curious frown on her face while she watched him. "Hard to sneak about in caverns in a dragon's body."

"True. You do take up a lot of room." There was an impish light in her hazel eyes that was so incredibly beguiling. He remembered now why it'd been so hard to leave her. Why he'd carried her to a private room that night they'd first met, instead of sending her on her way.

He'd always been so discriminating about the swans in his life. Never had he taken a human lover. Humans had never appealed to him in any way. He'd been so selective and sparse in his lovers that his brothers had often mocked him for it.

But the night Seraphina had come into that ancient drinking den with her sister tribeswomen, he hadn't cared what she was. Her bold touch had electrified him and her lips had awakened a part of him that he hadn't known existed. That alone should have warned him that they were destined to be together.

That the Fates had decreed her as his.

Now . . .

He dipped his head beneath the crest of her helm so that he could capture her plump lips and drink her in. As always, she answered his passion with enough heat that it made him curse this mission and the fact that they didn't have a single minute for him to strip that armor from her lush body and savor her the way he wanted to.

But later, he would make damn sure that she knew exactly how much he still craved her. Deepening his kiss for one last taste, he pulled back with an irritated groan and forced himself to attend to the most pressing matter.

Which unfortunately wasn't the aching need in his swollen groin.

Seraphina felt the absence of his body heat like a physical blow. Her senses were still reeling and unfocused from that incredible kiss. And as she watched him walk in front of her, she had a hard time staying focused on anything other than how undeniably sexy he was. It was much easier to fight with him as a dragon.

No man should look *that* fine in the flesh.

Biting her lip, she used the pain to focus her thoughts on something other than the way his armor clung to his muscles. The way he moved like a lethal warrior.

Stop it!

She shook her head to clear it. *Have you any idea where we're going?* She sent her thoughts to him.

Yes and no. I'm tracking the Tablet. But no, I don't know the layout here.

You fake it well.

He laughed silently.

She didn't know why she allowed him to charm her so. He was completely irresistible. And she remained quiet as they snuck through the nether realm, so as not to distract him from his task. It was incredibly dark here. Eerily quiet. No wonder the Sumerians had always described this place as drab and bland.

The dead here decayed into nothing just as they did in their graves. And the only good thing she could say was that they didn't punish their dead. But neither did they reward them for a life well lived. They merely existed here until they faded away.

How completely tragic. What a dreary, awful place to be sent to for eternity.

Suddenly, Max paused.

Sera tried to peer over his shoulder to see what had his attention, but he was too tall for that.

Wait here.

She wanted to argue, but knew better than to try, so she nodded and stayed put. It was probably for the best. This way she could watch the darkness for someone sneaking up on them. Not that she could see them in the darkness.

But maybe they'd be heavy breathers. Make her job easy.

Not have bathed for a few days . . .

A few extremely long minutes later that felt like an eternity in hell, she felt a presence behind her. She jerked around, intending to punch the culprit and run.

"It's me," Max whispered in her ear. "I got the Tablet."

"Don't do that!" She lightly flicked her fingers against his stomach to let him know how little she appreciated his startling a hundred or so years from her life.

He opened his mouth to speak, then went completely still as a voice cut through the darkness with an eerie, deep resonance.

"Well, well. I knew if you thought our numbers were down you'd come. And here Nala thought I was a fool for telling her that."

Gasping, Seraphina flinched as someone lit a torch in the darkness. Then she wished they hadn't.

Oh dear gods.

They were surrounded by gallu.

15

Max cursed under his breath as he saw Kessar in the blinding torchlight. An effing trap . . . and he'd walked right into it. He should have known the Tablet wouldn't be so easy to find and grab.

How stupid am I?

Well, that didn't bear thinking about right now. Worse, he'd known the demon wasn't an idiot. That he'd only have one shot at this and that would be it.

And I blew it.

Good going, jackass.

Not only had he killed himself, he'd killed Sera, too. Yet he refused to be a part of her death. One way or another, he would get her out of this, at least.

Praying for a miracle, he swung around on Sera and gently pushed her into the shadows, hoping this worked, since he was the bigger target they were after. Then he ran, drawing the others away from her location. Okay, not the brightest plan ever, but luckily they were pretty stupid and ran after him with everything they had.

What he didn't expect was for Sera to run after him, too. And when she turned into a dragon and picked him up to fly him above the demons chasing them, he couldn't have been more stunned.

At first, he hadn't even believed it was her. But as he looked over her beautiful red scales and the talons that held him, there was no doubt.

His dragonswan had saved him . . . as the dragon she hated.

Unfortunately, she couldn't travel far in that form. The walls of the cavern narrowed so much that she had to set him down and return to being human or risk losing or breaking her wings.

"Impressive," he said in an awed tone.

She flexed her arm as if assuring herself that she was "normal" again. "And what you did was wildly stupid. How have you managed to survive for so long?"

"No real idea." He checked to make sure he still had the Tablet with him, then felt along the glassy walls, trying to pick a way through the domain toward an exit or at least some light. Not even his powers could detect anything. It was so frustrating to be this completely blind.

"Do you still have the Tablet?"

"Yeah. Not that it seems to be doing us any good. And if Kessar captures and bleeds me, it'll be a lot worse. For everyone . . . especially me."

Sera considered that. "He used the Tablet to awaken my tribe. Can you use it to do the same?"

Max hesitated. "How do you mean?"

"Can you reverse whatever he's done to my tribe and free them again?"

He wasn't sure he liked where her thoughts were going with this. "Yes, but I fail to see how that could be helpful." Especially since the Amazons and Katagaria wanted him even more dead than the demons did.

"If you free them, we can drive back the demons, and I'm thinking Nala will know some way out of here."

"Even if she does, I doubt she'll help you and I know she won't help me. I'm the dragon whose head she wants to mount on her wall."

"I think I can persuade her."

"I'm not sure I want to bet my life on this."

"You have a better idea?"

"Fight our way out."

She scoffed at what he considered an almost legitimate, if not sane, plan. "You think that'll work?"

"Did I throw logic at you? No. Why do you want to be mean to me like that?"

She laughed at his teasing tone. "I'm serious, Maxis. I can get them to help us and fight them."

"And if you're wrong?"

"I'll build you a nice funeral pyre."

He let out a short laugh. "You are all kinds of not funny."

"Do you have a better option?"

"Sadly, no. At least nothing that wouldn't get me slapped for proposing it." He let out a long sigh as he heard the demons closing in on them. They had to decide and move fast or they'd be captured again. "All right. We'll try this your way with your tribe. But if I get eaten or speared to death . . . I will not be happy."

She took a step, then paused. "Any idea where the demons might have taken my tribe?"

He groaned at her question. "None."

Before she could speak, he pulled her behind him and began hammering the demons with fire again. It terrified her how close they'd come to them while she'd plotted an escape. Had he not been paying attention, the demons would have had them. As it was, they screamed from Max's attack and fell back, into the darkness.

Max pressed her forward, deeper into the nether realm he wasn't completely unfamiliar with, wishing he had another way out. Worse, the smell and sight of the damp cavern dredged up long-buried memories he didn't want or need at this particular time.

In the back of his mind, he saw Dagon as the ancient god walked between their cages, trying to decide who to use next in his inhumane experiments. The young dark-haired prince who took after his father and not his Apollite mother trailed after him.

"I want to be a dragon! You have to make me one! You promised!"

Dagon had glared at the prince. "Stop whining, Linus. I'm doing the best I can. You saw what happened. The last Apollite I merged with a dragon exploded into gory pieces. You really want to risk that?"

Linus had expelled a frustrated breath and stomped his foot like a petulant child. "It's not fair! I'm a prince. Second in line to the throne. I should have my choice of animals I want to merge with!"

Dagon had passed an irritated glare at the younger man. "You're lucky your father's half sister is a goddess whose devoted husband is willing to do this shit for you. So instead of bothering me with your insipid complaining, you should be saying, 'Thank you, Uncle Dagon, for doing everything you can to save my life and for not merging me with a hyena or a donkey.'"

"You wouldn't dare!"

Dagon turned on him with an evil smirk. "I'm a god of black magick and possessed with a wicked sense of irony and hostility, you really want to push my patience, boy?"

Linus had wisely backed down and left Dagon to pull a lion from its cage toward the room where he performed his grotesque experiments.

Alone, the prince had drifted to Max and Illarion. His gaze tinged by insanity, he'd stared in at them. "You can understand me, can't you? I know you can. I want to be a dragon, too. Like you. To have your power and strength. Imagine what we could do together . . . the power of a dragon and the bloodline of a divine prince. We could rule this earth and all the kingdoms and peoples. Then we'd show my father and brother who the real heir should have been. . . ."

As he wandered off, Illarion had glanced over to Max. *Are you going to tell the god what his nephew thinks?*

No. Let Dagon merge him with one of us. The best thing that can happen for this world is that Prince Linus explodes and dies. Preferably in a great deal of pain.

Maxis! You can't do that. We're supposed to protect human life.

He's not human, Illy. He's Apollite and he's insane.

Even so, I think we need to tell Dagon.

And I think we should stay out of it. No good has ever come from drakomai meddling in the affairs of gods or man. They dragged us into this, and we need to extricate ourselves as quickly and cleanly as possible.

But true to his most irritating nature, Illarion hadn't listened. He'd told Dagon of the prince's illustrious plans. And to protect his nephew from them, Dagon had lied and told Linus and his father that he didn't want to risk merging the prince with the dragons. Rather, Linus's elder brother, Eumon, had been crossed with them, and Linus with the wolves.

An even more dangerous concoction and not the safer alternative Dagon had imagined. Since the merging heightened the essence of both species, it'd taken the ambition of the Apollite prince and crossed it with the extraordinary cunning and bloodthirsty ruthlessness that marked the wolves.

By trying to save his sons, Lycaon had damned them all.

Thus proving that even the gods and kings could be stupidly blind when it came to family and wanting to do their best for them. Feelings forever got in the way of common sense and blinded the most intelligent of beings.

And because of that, Max and Sera were about to be eaten by gallu.

Max groaned in frustration. His entire life had been screwed by the gods messing with things they should have left alone. And that included his mother and her fascination with his father. But for one horny afternoon, he wouldn't have even been conceived.

Right now, Max would have been deeply grateful had his father kept it in his pants and not gone dallying with the bitch who spawned him. How much alcohol had his mother plied him with, anyway?

Irritated about it, Max gently grabbed Sera back from the way they were headed, and pulled her down an offshoot. He had no idea where this led. But it seemed a bit safer than the way they'd been going.

All the powers he had and not a one could help them out of this. What then was the use?

"It'll be all right, Max."

He hesitated at her encouraging tone. "I'm glad you still have your optimism. Mine slammed into a wall a while back. I think it now has a concussion."

"I have faith in you."

"Since when?"

"Always." She placed her hand on his arm. "Do you know why I chose you that night in the drinking den?"

"I was the only sober male in the room?"

She laughed. "No. In that room full of warriors, you stood out as the most fierce. While they clumped together for protection and safety, you stood alone. Fearless. Defiant. It was the sexiest thing I've ever seen. You were everything I'd always wanted to be, but never had the courage for."

Max paused as her words struck a tender place in his heart that left him feeling strangely vulnerable. No one had ever said anything so kind to him. Oddly enough, he'd never felt particularly heroic. Most days, he just felt lost and adrift. He barely got through them.

But he wanted to be a hero for her.

"Oh Seramia . . . you are far braver than I."

"How do you figure?"

"Your biggest fear has always been the dragons who killed your family. Of them coming back to slaughter what you love. Instead of hiding and running, you taught yourself to fight them and confront them. Any time the call went out for battle, you were the first one saddled and ready. And when the Fates tied your life to the very thing you despised most, you accepted it and allowed me into your home, all the while you waited for my betrayal."

"That wasn't courage. What I did to you was so wrong. I blamed you for what other dragons did. Instead of judging you by your actions and heart, I judged you by theirs and by my own fear."

"You were human. And there's nothing wrong with that."

Seraphina swallowed against the tears choking her. She still didn't know how he could accept her for who and what she was. Maybe that was the dragon heart inside him. It enabled him to see the world so differently at times. Clearer. More concisely.

She envied him that ability. To her, everyone and everything was viewed through a veil of hazy suspicion. And he was right. Trust had never come easily to her. There had been too many women in her tribe who'd tried to pull her down and lie about her to Nala so that they could replace her as champion. Even Nala, lying about Max to hurt them both.

Sera had never known who to trust, except herself.

Until now.

In all her life, he was the only one she could have faith in. Her dragon had never sought to betray her.

"So how do we get out of this, Max?"

Max paused as a radical idea hit him. *Really* radical. The kind that would either save them or damn the entire world. Too bad he didn't know which and wouldn't be able to tell until he pulled the switch.

Then it would be too late.

But then that was life. Sometimes you had to take that leap and pray.

Skidding to a stop, he pulled Sera against him. Just in case the worst happened. If he had to die, he wanted it to be with her in his arms. He just hoped she didn't pay for one of his stupid mistakes.

"Max?"

He didn't respond, rather he used his powers to access the Tablet and speak an ancient language he hadn't used since the day he'd slain his mother for her last betrayal.

Seraphina could barely breathe as Maxis formed a tight wall of protective muscle around her. She knew he was doing this to keep her safe, but at the moment she just wanted to draw an unencumbered breath. His heartbeat pounded beneath her cheek as a strange light began to illuminate around them.

She had no idea what he was doing until white smoke began billowing out of the floor and walls. Iridescent and translucent, it was beautiful, and swayed as if it were dancing. The gallu drew up short as if mesmerized by the rhythmic movements. The mist began to spiral and form larger shapes.

Pausing, Namtar cursed at the demons. Then he urged them to disperse. "Run! It's the liliti!"

But it was too late. The liliti descended on them with a hungry vengeance, like piranha who hadn't eaten in decades.

When they came toward Max, he let out a burst of fire that drove them back. Moving in the opposite direction, he pulled Sera after him.

"That was horrifying!"

"I know. Let's hope they have no way out of here. But it was all I could think of. After what you said about waking your sisters, I remembered that my mother would be here in Ikalla, sleeping, too. As her son, I have the ability to summon them."

"That is even more terrifying."

"And one of the very few benefits that come with being my mother's son, and having been suckled by her sisters."

She scowled at his words. "But I thought you told me you weren't suckled."

He gave her a bitter smile. "It's not the same way human mothers nurse their young. Believe me, it's much more harsh and uncomfortable."

That was all he needed to say. She definitely didn't want more information than that, given what she knew of him and his people. "I'm sorry, Maxis."

"For what?"

"Everything that's been done to you. And for the fact that you look so tired right now. I wish I could find a safe place for you to sleep for a little while."

He kissed her cheek. "It's all good."

Still, she felt guilty over it. She'd brought them to his door and led them straight to him. Instead of feeding him to the demons, she should have protected him with the same resolve and integrity he would have shown.

Never again will I be so selfish.

But then motherhood had taught her that. How to put someone else and their needs before hers. To value another being more than herself. Strange how Max, the animal, had been born with that sense of how he was part of a larger whole and his life wasn't as important as the continuation of others. Or maybe it was his being male. She wasn't sure. All she knew was that it'd taken the birth of her children before she'd understood it.

How she wished she could have loved him back in their past the way she could now.

It's not too late.

At least she hoped that was true.

Yet as they made their way through the dark nether world, she wondered.

All of a sudden, Max froze in front of her so quickly that she slammed into his back. He remained completely ramrod stiff and still.

She opened her mouth to ask him what was wrong when she saw.

There in front of her was Nala and the rest of her Amazon tribe. Only they weren't stone, or in the process of returning to stone.

They appeared completely normal. As if nothing had happened or that demons weren't out to kill or eat them.

Confused, Seraphina stepped around her mate and approached Nala, who wore a peculiar welcoming smile on her face. "Basilinna?"

Nala let out a relieved breath. "There you are! We thought we'd have to send out a patrol to find you."

That weird feeling of trepidation worsened. Something definitely wasn't right. "We came to free you, Max and I."

She laughed again as if Sera was insane. "That was never the bargain, child. The bargain was that Kessar would overthrow the Greek gods from Olympus and surrender it to me, and in turn, I would give him your mate. He just fulfilled his part. Now I'm going to fulfill mine."

16

Max couldn't breathe as he heard those harsh words and was instantly taken back to the day when Sera had surrendered him to her tribe for his harrowing. He still remembered the cold resignation on her face as they hauled him out to beat him.

The way she'd just stood there . . .

Like he deserved it. As if she didn't care at all what they did to him.

A part of him had died that day. The biggest being his heart that had never completely healed.

Now, she was going to do it to him again. Only this time, Kessar would kill him. He knew it with every part of himself. There was no chance of survival.

Had this been her plan all along? Was that why she'd been so desperate to find her sisters while they were here?

You're such a fool. When are you going to learn that you'll never come first with your mate?

Seraphina saw the expression on Maxis's face. In that moment, she knew what he thought and it slapped her hard. Not that he doubted her.

The fact that she deserved his doubt.

Reaching up, she cupped his face in her hands. "I made you a promise, baby. I intend to keep it."

With those words spoken, she did what she'd never done before. She stepped back, turned toward her queen, and let loose a burst of fire at them all.

"And I'm fulfilling mine, Nala. Anyone wants a piece of my mate has to come through me. You want to fight? You better arm up, bitches." She let loose one more shot before she grabbed Max about his waist and pulled him back the way they'd come.

He stumbled and almost fell as they ran. "You just attacked your tribe."

"No. I just defended my mate."

"You shot fire at them."

She paused to glance at him. "Are we really going to waste time reliving it?"

"We're definitely doing something." He cracked an adorable grin. "Arm up, bitches?"

"You left me alone too long with Fury."

He laughed at the same time her tribe was closing in and gaining ground faster than she cared for. Arrows shot past them. "Arm up, Strah Draga."

With those words, he turned into his dragon form. She jumped into her saddle and held on tight.

Max rose up on his hind legs and used his wings to create a massive wind that sent them tumbling back on their asses.

In that moment, she loved him even more. "You don't have to take mercy on them for me. They wanted to tilt the dragon. Let them tilt."

"Are you sure?"

She leaned down over his neck and kissed it. "Positive. In this battle, you're the only one who matters to me."

"In that case . . ." Max threw his head back and let loose his Bane-Cry.

It was something no drakomas did lightly and was reserved for only when their lives were under dire threat, and they had no way out. In all the centuries he'd lived, he'd never made the cry. He'd only answered them.

Mostly because he'd never cared whether or not he survived a fight.

For the first time, he wanted to live. And he fought the Amazons and gallu with everything he had. They came at him with spears and claws, and he unleashed his fire and magick at them, while he whipped at them with his tail.

He banged at the ground, causing the stalactites to fall down on top of them. Several screamed as they were impaled.

Still they kept coming.

Max couldn't teleport out. The gallu wouldn't release the nether gates. Which meant none of his drakomai brethren could get in.

But it didn't stop his demonic aunts from helping. They circled and ran at the gallu and Amazons, doing their best to protect him and Sera.

He kept inching back into the darkness, trying to find some way out of this mess and dark realm.

As he went back, he lost his footing and fell, and tumbled down the side of a ravine.

Sera's gasp echoed in his ears.

For a moment, his heart stopped beating as he feared he'd lost her. Then, he felt her hands on his scales, near her saddle, clutching at his body. "I'm still here," she breathed.

Reassured, he extended his wings and caught the light breeze so that they could ride it through the unseen black. The very edge of his talons scraped against the sides of the walls, but it seemed large enough to hold him. "Can you see anything?"

"No. You?"

"Nothing."

Suddenly, he heard Kessar screaming out. "If you want me to release you, dragon, give us the Tablet and Bowl."

Max let out a tired sigh at a demand he knew he could never meet. There was no way he could surrender either of those objects to a creature like Kessar. He would be too destructive with them.

"Looks like a nice vacation home. What do you think?"

"Sure," Sera said in the same playful tone. "Put up some curtains. A little color. Shrunken heads. We can make do. Particularly if we nail Kessar's hide to the wall. That would be a lovely decoration. Don't you agree?"

"Throw in Nala's scalp and . . . aye. Quite homey."

Seraphina laughed. Only her dragon could manage to be so amusing when things were this serious and frightening.

"What's your answer, dragon?" Kessar demanded again.

Max sped up.

And slammed into a net.

Terrified he'd crush or hurt Sera, he immediately changed forms and caught her against him. Unfortunately, when he did so, she'd already pulled out her knife to try and cut the ropes. A knife that went deep into his very human stomach.

Sera's features paled. "Max?"

Unable to breathe from the unexpected pain and depth of the cut, he fell back and used every bit of magick he could to hold his human form. He had to. There wasn't enough room in the net for the two of them if he were a dragon.

He'd kill her.

Seraphina shook as she saw how much blood was pouring out his side. "What have I done?"

His breathing ragged, he gave her a sad smile. "You have to run, Sera." He handed her the small Tablet and placed it in her hand. "Don't let them catch you."

"I can't leave you like this."

"You have to. Think of your children. They need you." His hand trembling, he kissed her. "I love you, Seramia." And with that, he cut through the net with his claw. "Use your dragon form and fly."

Sera fell through the rough hemp cord, and changed, but she didn't go far. She couldn't. Especially not when she looked back to see him lying inert in the net, waiting to die.

Alone.

And all because of her.

Refusing to let it end like this, she went back for him.

The instant he saw her hovering dragon body, he glared at her. "Sera! What are you doing?"

"We got into this together and we're getting out that way." As carefully as she could, she cradled him with her dragon arms to her chest, and gained a whole new appreciation for his restraint. He made it appear so easy to use his dragon body like a human's, but it wasn't. It required a whole different kind of dexterity and skills.

And as she flew, she prayed for a miracle.

One she knew wouldn't come as his breathing grew fainter and fainter, and the demons came closer and closer.

"Don't leave me, Maxis. Please . . ."

Just as she thought she might have slipped past their enemies, a bright flash in front of them blinded her.

And more enemies surrounded them.

17

Max came awake to a strange mechanical humming noise. Like a vaporizer or something. It blended in with the faint sound of zydeco and laughter. Cars passing by on the street outside.

Of a crowded bar and metal music from next door . . .

"Don't move!"

Blinking open his eyes, he found Sera sitting on the floor by his side, stroking his snout. But the most shocking part was the fact that his dragon's head was cradled in her lap.

And her breasts were pressed against his cheek.

Um, yeah . . .

He had no desire whatsoever to move from this position. Especially since she held his head at an angle that allowed him to see straight down her shirt, and the fact that she didn't have on a bra. Something that made his mouth water and his heart race.

In spite of the pain, he went rock hard. Thankfully, he was lying on his stomach so that the only one who knew about this uncomfortable situation was him. And the floor beneath him, which probably wasn't any happier about it than he was.

"Am I dead?"

She frowned at him. "Why do you ask that?"

"This doesn't feel real. My room . . . You." Dead or dreaming seemed the two most logic conclusions, and if it was a dream, he'd like to think he'd already be naked with her.

"It's real. As is the accidental stabbing I gave you when we were caught."

Damn, that hadn't been a dream. No wonder his side hurt so much. At least now he knew his memory was whole.

"You sure it was an accident?"

"Ah, now who's being mean?"

"Still you."

She snorted at him. "Yeah well, that's my story and I'm sticking to it."

If he wasn't in so much pain, he might have joined her laughter, but he still wasn't convinced she hadn't done it intentionally.

Is he awake?

Max started at the sound of Illarion's voice in his head. Before he could move, his brother came forward to stand in his field of vision. Alongside Falcyn, who knelt beside Sera.

Yeah, he was back to fearing death again, especially with Falcyn here to check in on him. Hell must have frozen over and a few other catastrophes for that to happen.

Falcyn picked up his ear and coldly let it flop back over his eyes. "You took a nasty wound and spill. If not for your swan, you'd have never survived."

Sera visibly cringed. "If not for me, he wouldn't have been injured."

"Well . . ." Falcyn wrinkled his nose. "Win some. Lose some. Besides, we've all wanted to stab him at times. You're just lucky you got to do it first."

Max laughed, then groaned. Leave it to his brother, the asshole. Ignoring Falcyn, he looked back at Sera. "So what happened, anyway? How did we get out of there?"

"They answered your Bane-Cry. It just took them a little while to break through the shields that were holding them out and preventing them from helping."

"And your sisters?"

She lifted her chin as a cold ruthlessness darkened her eyes. "My sisters died beside my mother when I was a girl. The Amazon tribe I was tied to is still serving the gallu, for who knows what purposes. That's their choice."

"We routed the gallu out of Olympus," Falcyn said, sitting back on his haunches. "But it was a bad day for Zeus and crew. They're not happy with the damage that was wrought."

Sin least of all, since his wife insisted that Artemis stay with them until things settle down. And Apollo is captured again since he is now working with the gallu against his father and the rest of his former pantheon.

Max sucked his breath in sharply at that. Sin and Artemis had a bad history together. No doubt Sin was extremely unhappy to have his mother-in-law camping out in his casino since he could barely tolerate Artemis's presence. Even though he had plenty of room, he wouldn't welcome her there.

Falcyn brought his attention back to him. "I have Hadyn's Tablet. We decided it would be safer to break it apart from what you carry. And keep them in separate locations."

"Thank you."

Falcyn inclined his head to him. "Still doesn't mean I like you, though."

"Hate you, too, brother."

There was a timid knock on the door before it was pushed open to show Edena and Hadyn entering. They came in with food and drink that they set down on the floor, beside their mother.

"We'll give you space," Falcyn said before he led Illarion and Blaise from the room.

Alone with his mate and children, Max wasn't sure what to say. It was extremely surreal to have them here in his solitary loft. Or rather *their* loft. As a family, they'd be sharing it from now on. Yeah, that really did a number on his head.

Edena sat down next to her mother. "How do you feel?"

"Good."

She smiled. "Glad to hear it." Even so, there was a hesitancy that blemished her smile and feigned cheerful words.

Max manifested a blanket, then turned himself human. "Better?"

She blushed profusely. "Um . . . it doesn't matter to me. I'm used to Hadyn as a dragon."

"Deenie's the one who tends to me whenever I'm sick or . . . stuck. Did you ever get trapped in one form or the other and not be able to change? It really sucks."

Max grinned as he remembered those days, and he welcomed his son's friendliness. Unlike his sister, Hadyn had no reservation in his form, tone, or manner. "It's been a while, but yeah. It sucks."

Hadyn came forward more slowly. "We know you need to rest some more. We just wanted to make sure you were all right. You haven't moved in three whole days. All of us have been scared about that."

Max choked at his revelation. "Three days? Are you serious?"

Edena nodded. "The demons are so unhappy. Zakar, Thorn, and Fang have put up seals and mirrors all over Peltier House and Sanctuary so that they can't get in again. So far, it's working."

"What about the Amazons?"

"They tried," Hadyn answered. "Mom and Samia, along

with the Peltier females and a Dark-Huntress named Chi kicked their butts so hard that I doubt they'll be back for a while."

"Good."

Edena leaned forward to kiss his cheek. "We'll be back later to bother you. Get some more rest." She got up to leave.

Hadyn moved forward. "I'm really glad Mom didn't kill you." And with that, the twins were gone.

Max wasn't sure what to make of his kids. They were a bit odd, but he loved them. And speaking of things that made him uncomfortable . . .

He gently pushed the blanket back and shifted.

Sera immediately gasped. "What are you doing?"

"It's been three days. I need to go to the bathroom."

Sera's face exploded with color. "Oh. Sorry." She let go of his arm so that he could stand up. "You need me to help?"

Her offer charmed him. But . . . "There are some things I prefer to do alone. This is one of them."

"Okay."

Seraphina leaned back on her arms while Max went to attend his needs. It'd been a strange few days while they'd acclimated to their new lives. This world was so different than the one they'd known.

Luckily, Hadyn and Edena seemed to be adjusting easier than she was. Of course it helped that the Peltiers had children close to their age who'd taken them under their bear claws and were teaching them idioms and culture.

Max's brothers were still quite suspicious of her. As were Fang and the others.

There was nothing she could do about that. So she did her best to ignore it and not let it bother her.

When Max returned a short time later, he had a black towel wrapped around his lean hips and his long blond hair and feathers were wet.

"You showered?"

Nodding, he headed back to his pallet on the floor.

He'd also shaved. The fresh, clean scent of soap and dragonswain set her head reeling. But the sight of his stitches across his abdomen, where Carson had tended him, reminded her that he was in no condition for what her hormones wanted.

Too bad, that.

As he lay down, she was overwhelmed by the sheer size of him in his human body. While he wasn't as large like this as he was as a dragon, he was still a good-sized creature. Still ferocious and delicious.

"You keep looking at me like that and you're going to have to fulfill that silent promise in your eyes."

She scowled. "What promise?"

"To climb on top of me and ride me like a giddy kid on the mechanical horse outside of Piggly Wiggly with a sack full of quarters."

Her jaw dropped. "I'm not completely sure what that analogy means, but—"

He interrupted her words with a scorching kiss that left her breathless and dizzy. "I think you know exactly what I mean." And to prove his point, he pressed her hand against the bulge under his towel.

"I don't want to hurt you."

Laughing, he nipped at her lips and then her chin. "You're worth the pain."

"Maxis!"

"It's true." He slid his hand under her shirt to cup her breast and tease her hardened nipple with his thumb. "Make love to me, Sera. I've lived too long away from you."

"And I, you." She reached down between them to remove his towel. Her breath caught as she stared at his unadorned beauty. He was unbelievably handsome and fierce.

Best of all, he was hers.

And he watched her with a hunger that was its own form of foreplay. One that made her want to please and tease him until he was as giddy as the child he'd described with the sack full of quarters.

Rising to her feet, she slowly stripped for him like she used to, delighting in the murmurs of pleasure that escaped his lips as he watched her peeling her clothes off. When she was finally naked, he reached for her and pulled her close enough that he could lave her breast while his hands gently stroked and caressed her body.

Her heart pounded as she savored his touch and did her own exploration of his long, hard, muscled flesh. She'd always loved spreading her hands over the massive planes of his back. Feeling the texture of it and the flexing of his muscles as he moved.

"You are exquisite," she breathed.

"And you are beautiful." He tongued her ear until chills sprang all over her arms. Laughing, he slowly slid his fingers up her thigh, to the center of her body where she craved his touch most. She groaned out loud at how good his touch felt while he gently played and teased until she was so hot and breathless that she was on the verge of coming.

But this wasn't how she wanted it to end. And definitely not this soon. Pushing him back, she straddled him and gently impaled herself on his body.

Gasping, Max gripped her hips and thrust against her, driving himself in even deeper.

Afraid he'd hurt himself, she adjusted her weight until he was forced to surrender all control over to her.

The smile on his face made her heart beat faster. "I see what you're doing. I'm all yours, my lady dragon. Have your wicked way with me until your heart's content."

She buried her hands in his damp hair and slowly rode him until they came in unison. Only then did she slide off him and lay by his side as she listened to his ragged breathing.

Closing his eyes, Max held her as he savored the familiar New Orleans and Sanctuary sounds blending with her precious breaths.

So familiar and so alien. Nothing would ever be the same again.

"Where do we go from here, Sera?"

"What do you mean?"

He was so afraid of her answer, but he'd never been a coward and he had to know. "What are your plans for our future?"

Seraphina froze at his emotionless tone. "Do you want me to leave?"

"Gods no. I just . . . I know how you feel about this time period. About . . ."—he barely bit back the word *"me"*—"dragons. So I was curious where you saw this going."

"What do you want?"

"You."

"And?"

He tilted his head to look at her. "I've always been a dragon of simple means. You know that. But we've stirred a hornets' nest with everything that's happened since your arrival. One I'm not sure we can walk away from. The gallu will be able to follow us. And it's not just us we have to think about. I am still the Dragonbane."

Seraphina swallowed hard at something they couldn't escape. That would be with them forever. "Why did you kill him, Max?"

"Does it matter?"

"No. I love you, regardless. But I would like to hear your side of it."

With her head tucked beneath his chin, he toyed with her hair. "Would you believe my truth should I give it?"

"I have learned to trust you. Whatever you say, I will believe."

Still, he hesitated before he answered. "It was an accident. He wasn't the one who was supposed to die. Rather it was his brother."

Gaping, she rose up to stare down at him. "And that makes it all better?"

"Had you met his brother, yes. He was an asshole."

"Max!"

Before he could respond, another knock sounded on his door. By the scent, he knew it was Alain Peltier. The eldest of the bears. "Yes?"

Alain didn't open the door, rather he spoke through it. "I hate to disturb you, dragon. But we have a bad situation. Savitar has called the Omegrion and you've been summoned. By law, we have to take you in. However, we've taken a vote and we're standing in solidarity by your side."

"No!" Sera shook her head. "You can't go. I won't allow you to face them. I don't care what Savitar says or how many stand with you. This is suicide!"

Max didn't respond to her upset outburst. "How long do I have?"

"We need to leave immediately."

18

After the quickest shower of her life, Seraphina dressed in a pair of jeans and a shirt, and walked with Max down to the parlor of Peltier House, where their children and basically every adult resident under the roof waited for him. As well as every Dark-Hunter, former and current, in New Orleans, along with Acheron, Sin, Zakar, and Styxx.

"This is utter bullshit!" Dev snarled, unaware

of their presence behind him. "I say we tell Savitar where to shove it."

Acheron laughed as he glanced past Dev to meet Max's gaze. "I dare you."

Max stopped next to Dev and put his hand on his shoulder. "It's all right, bear. I'm not afraid."

Seraphina laced her fingers with his. "For the record, I am."

With a stern frown, Aimee caressed her stomach. "Can't we do something? Max is here under our protection. I thought our laws protected him, so long as he doesn't leave."

Styxx sighed heavily. "They did. But the other dragons are calling for his ass. He attacked and they have the right to demand a hearing for his new crime . . . and the old when he appears for it."

Vane nodded. "That's why we're all going. As Kattalakises, we're character witnesses. Our family started this against you and we're going to do our damnedest to stop it."

Hadyn's scowl matched Aimee's. "And if you can't?"

Dev cracked a wicked grin. "I'm tossing the dragon over my shoulder and running for the door. You gonna cover my retreat, kid?"

Sighing heavily, Samia pressed her gloved hands to her nose. "I wish he was joking with that threat. Instead, I have this awful vision in my head and an ulcer in my stomach."

Dev kissed her cheek. "I promised you that living with me would never be boring."

She let out a tired breath. "That you did. You are definitely a bear of your word."

As they started to leave, Illarion stepped forward to go with them to the Omegrion.

"No!" Max roared, pushing him back toward his brothers. "Blaise, keep him here."

The stunned look on Illarion's face would have been hysterical if Max's life didn't hang in the balance. *You can't leave me out of this.*

"I can and I will."

Illarion shook his head in denial. He tried to step around Max, but Max wasn't having any of that.

Max caught his brother and pushed him back again. "I mean it. You go and I'll run." He looked to Falcyn, then Blaise. "He's not allowed to go. You have to keep him here. No matter what."

A chill went down Seraphina's spine. Illarion knew something about all this. Something Max didn't want spoken out loud. And given what she knew about her mate, it would incriminate Illarion in the murder and free Max.

There was no other reason for him to act this way. To be so angry and insistent. No other reason to bar Illarion's presence from the hearing. Not unless he was afraid his brother would speak up and condemn himself in order to protect Max from harm.

She met Illarion's grief-stricken, tormented gaze and in that moment, she knew exactly what had happened. "You killed the prince, didn't you? It wasn't Maxis. It was *you*."

"Sera," Max growled. "Stay out of this."

But she couldn't. Not if it meant saving her mate. Releasing

Max, she went to Illarion and forced him to meet her gaze. "Tell me what happened."

"It doesn't matter." Max swallowed hard. "I bear the mark and I'm the Dragonbane, not Illarion. Leave him alone." He glared at his brothers. "Do not let him leave here."

And before she could say another word, Max vanished.

"No!" Yet it was too late. The irritating beast was already gone.

Terrified and shaking, she turned on Illarion. "Tell me the truth. What happened?"

It was an accident.

She met Acheron's gaze. "We've got to get the others to listen. Somehow."

Vane agreed. "Don't worry, Sera. They can't start the council yet. Four of the members are still here."

She arched a brow at the number. "Four?"

"Me, Fury, Alain's mate—Tanya, and Wren Tigarian behind you."

Tanya Peltier she'd met while tending Max's wound. Quiet and shy, the tall, dark-haired Katagari bear worked as one of the cooks in the kitchen of Peltier House who oversaw caring for the residents there, and not in the public Sanctuary bar. She made the menus for their children and families, and was the Ursulan Regis for the Katagaria branch since the death of the Peltier matriarch, Nicolette.

And while Tanya was mated to the eldest Peltier bearswain and had three sons with him, Seraphina couldn't help noticing the way the bearswan's face lit up whenever the lead singer of the Howlers came near her. Tanya positively glowed at Angel, who did his best to avoid being around her.

That too said a lot about their relationship, since Angel was extremely friendly and easygoing.

Not wanting to think about that, Seraphina turned to find the other council member, watching her from the back corner of the room. A part of the group and yet apart from them.

Like Max, Wren held that same disturbing aura of quiet predator that said he was eyeing you like prey. Sizing up your every movement to detect the weakness he was about to use to bring you down for a kill. The most disturbing thing was the way his eyes that changed color depending on the way the light hit them. They went from a light gray to a vibrant turquoise.

Highly disturbing.

Until he unleashed a friendly grin at her that made him appear boyish and shy, and around the same age as Hadyn. "Sorry. My wife Maggie is always getting on to me for making people uncomfortable. Although she seems to enjoy my doing it at her father's cocktail parties. Sometimes she even puts me up to it, but it's a bitch at the playground. I've sent three of my daughter's playmate's nannies in to therapy."

Unsure what to think, she let out a nervous laugh.

He held his hand out to her. "Wren. Nice to meet you."

She shook his hand and by the mark on his palm, she knew he was a rare tigard. His scent told her he was a Katagari snow leopard and tiger. . . . What a peculiar mixture.

"Sera. Thank you for coming."

He tucked his hands into his pockets and stepped back. "My

pleasure. I had a similar unpleasant experience with the Omegrion a few years back. Let's hope this turns out as well, shall we?"

Tanya moved closer and rubbed Seraphina's arms comfortingly. "Don't worry. We won't let them take your Max, any more than we let them hurt Wren. We always watch after our own."

But as they arrived in the Omegrion council room on the mysterious Neratiti island home of Savitar, Sera felt her hope dwindle quickly. The large circular chamber was decorated in burgundy and gold. Through the open windows that spanned from the black marble floor to the gilded ceiling, she could see and hear the ocean on all sides of the room. Oddly enough, the entire room reminded her of an ancient sultan's tent. Lavishly decorated, it had an enormous round table in the center that made her curious as to what the rest of the palace might look like. But one look at the angry grimace on Savitar's handsome face and she knew she wasn't about to ask him for a tour.

He was still dressed in a black wetsuit, his hair damp and his arms crossed as he sat on his throne that was set to the side of the room so that he could watch over the council members— most of whom were already there, and so silent you could hear the wood drying on the walls.

That, too, said it all about Savitar's somber mood.

Composed of one representative from each breed of Were-Hunter, and from the Arcadian and Katagaria branches, the Omegrion council that made the laws to govern their races should have had twenty-four members.

But one chair at the table remained forever empty. An eerie warning and reminder.

Back in the day, it'd belonged to the Arcadian Balios or jaguar patria. Legend had it that centuries ago, the Regis of that group had run so afoul of Savitar's temper that he'd single-handedly destroyed every member of their species.

Total extinction.

Which said it all about the power and temperament of the disgruntled Chthonian sitting in judgment of her mate.

His long dark hair brushed back from his face, Savitar glared at the group who'd arrived with her. "How nice of you to join us. I trust all of you had a nice nap after I summoned you?"

Acheron had the audacity to laugh. "Miss a gnarly, awesome wave, Big Kahuna?"

"Don't start, Grom. Not in the mood." Savitar sat back on his throne to glare at the large crowd. But it was the collection of Arcadian and Katagaria dragons and the Arcadian Kattalakis wolves on his right-hand side that set his jaw ticcing.

Savitar let out a long, exasperated breath. "Hear ye, hear ye . . . ah, fuck it. We're here today for bullshit and we all know it. So let's dispense with the usual formality and get on with this witch hunt before I lose what little grip I still have on my patience." He ran his thumb along his goatee. "So, Dare Kattalakis, state your case and demands to the council. And do it fast, with as few words as possible."

A wolf who bore a striking resemblance to Fang and Vane stepped forward. Sera wasn't sure if he was born of the same litter or not, but from appearances she would say he had to be of close kinship.

Clearing his throat, he moved to stand in the center of the round table to plead his case. "First, I want to restate what a travesty it is that my family's seat is taken by—"

"Wah, wah, wah . . . quit crying at the tit," Savitar snarled. "Your brother Vane is the head of the Arcadians and Fury leads the Katagaria. Seek a therapist who gives a shit, or if you'd like to challenge either of them for their position, we can do with some entertainment. Hell, I'll make popcorn for the show. Otherwise, bitch, get on with it."

Wow, he was in a particularly nasty mood. Sera was so glad he wasn't angry at her.

Dare lifted his chin, but wisely kept his gaze away from the surly ancient. "Fine. We all know why we're here. Maxis Drago as the Dragonbane is the cause of the war between the Arcadians and the Katagaria. Because of his actions alone, all of us have lost family and been scarred and cursed into perpetual war. Now he's unleashed the gallu and Apollo on us! He's—"

"That's not true!" The words were out before Seraphina could stop them.

Every eye in the room turned to her. That would have been bad enough, but when she came under the vicious scrutiny of Savitar's lavender gaze, she wanted to run screaming for the door. And it didn't help that Illarion and his brothers picked that moment to show up and garner an even more fierce glare from Max.

But at least Savitar's features finally softened as if he approved of both occurrences. "The dragonswan speaks."

"She's his whore!"

Savitar slung his hand out and caught the Kattalakis dragon who'd insulted her with an unseen force that lifted him up and pinned him to the wall between two of the open windows. "Only I'm allowed to be an insulting asshole in this room. Understood?"

The dragon nodded.

Savitar dropped him straight to the floor, where he landed with a pain-filled groan and in an unceremonious lump, before the ancient returned his attention to Sera. When he spoke, it was in a kind, fatherly tone. "You were saying, dear?"

Yeah, his kindness was even scarier than his nastiness. And it left her terrified. She'd never liked public speaking and this . . . this was worse than facing a herd of angry dragons out to feast on her entrails.

"It's okay, Sera," Max said kindly. "You don't have to speak up for me."

Those words gave her the courage she needed. "No, but someone does. I don't know who released the gallu—"

"That would be us," Zakar said, raising his hand. "Oops. Sorry about that."

Savitar rolled his eyes. "Sit your punk ass down and shut up. You and I will talk later."

Zakar laughed good-naturedly. "Hope you take your Abilify first, old man."

Savitar started to wag his finger at Zakar, then gave up and waved him away. "Shut up." He returned his attention to Sera. "You were saying?"

"Just that my mate is innocent. The gallu came after him first. And neither of us have a clue about Apollo. We don't even know what you're talking about." She tucked her marked hand into Max's.

He winced before he laced his fingers with hers and clutched her hand tightly in his.

Savitar watched that single gesture closely for several heartbeats without comment.

"I demand he pay for his crimes!" Ermon Kattalakis—one of the Arcadian dragons—demanded. "It was the blood of my grandfather he spilled!"

A strange look passed between Savitar and Acheron, then him and Styxx, before he rose to his feet.

Without a word, Savitar closed the distance between him and Max. "It occurs to me, Maxis, that with our historian, Nicolette Peltier, gone, there's no one here who knows the history of this council. She died before she could pass the origins along to her only daughter." He turned toward Tanya. "I suppose you should inherit that part of her job as well, no?"

Tanya looked as frightened to be under that fierce scrutiny as Sera had been. "It would be my honor to record it, my lord."

An odd half smile played at the edges of Savitar's lips while he continued to stroke his goatee with his thumb. He glanced back to Max. "What do you say, drakomas? Have I your permission to break our pact?"

She saw the indecision in Max's golden eyes as he debated. He glanced from her to Illarion, then to their children.

It's time. Illarion inclined his head to him. *Tell the truth, brother. Let them decide for themselves.*

With an audible gulp, Max nodded. "Although, I would remind you both that when the truth was told last time, it didn't help. No one cared."

Ignoring that, Savitar stepped back then so that he could walk a circle around the table. "Some of you have been coming here for centuries. You occupy seats you inherited from your family or won through combat. All of you know what an honor it is to sit here and represent your independent species. Both those who hold human-Apollite hearts and those born with animal hearts. Two halves of a single whole. Both sentient, and forever condemned by the gods to war against each other for no real reason, other than the fact that the gods are assholes. Everyone knows that part of the story. What none of you know is why you answer to me. Why you answer to this council . . ."

Savitar gestured to Max. "You blame the Dragonbane for the war that divides your two branches of the same species, but he didn't do this to you. That belongs to the three bitches who cursed your race in the beginning. To Zeus and Apollo and their childish tantrums that made them cry to the Fates to do something because they felt cheated that you were spared the Apollite curse that would have required all of you to die horribly at age twenty-seven over an event you had no part in. But as with all history, that is only one tiny, bit part that you've been told, which was colored by those seeking to sway your opinion and make you hate for no real reason. To keep you divided by your inconsequential differences when you should be whole and focused on the real tragedies you have in common. The ones that unite you as a single, sentient species. Follow me, children, and let me show you what you've never seen, but what you need to know."

And with that he threw his hands out. The doors crashed closed and darkness fell into the room so completely that for a moment, Sera felt like they were in Irkalla again.

The sudden, unexpected nothingness was oppressive and terrifying. But for Max's pressure on her hand and presence by her side, she'd have run for a door.

And just when she thought she couldn't take it anymore, a light came up to show a much younger Max and Illarion. While she'd known how much Hadyn favored his father, it wasn't until now that she realized just how much they shared in face, form, and mannerisms.

But what struck her most was the starved and ragged, filthy condition Illarion and Max had been left in. The two of them were in human form, kept there by their collars, and locked inside a cage where another man stared in on them. This one was impeccably dressed in royal princely garb.

Sera's jaw went slack as she saw the last thing she'd expected. Maxis wasn't the Greek prince.

Illarion was.

Meanwhile, Max stared through the bars of their cage at the prince and his elegant clothes, and the dark-haired lady beside him. He'd seen the prince numerous times since they'd brought them here, but the woman was a new addition to their drab, dingy home.

"Eumon?" she whined, trying to pull the prince away by his

arm. "Why did you bring me here? Don't you grow weary of looking at them all the time? It's so creepy!"

Max didn't appreciate being called creepy when the only real oddities in the room were the ones who needed his species to continue living past their twenty-seventh birthdays. There was nothing *creepy* about being a dragon.

Human-Apollite bodies?

That was the stuff of nightmares. They smelled and had all manner of weirdness to them he'd rather not suffer.

The prince smiled at his beautiful, petite wife, but his gaze never wavered from the two inside the cage. "Look at them, Helena. But for the fact that he doesn't speak, you'd never know he wasn't me. And the other . . . he is the very image of Pherus. It's as if I'm still looking my brother in the eye."

She wrinkled her nose in distaste. "Pherus was never your brother. He was the son of a slave."

"Slave or not, he was my brother through my father. And I loved him as such." Eumon licked his lips. "Do you think they can understand us?"

"No. They're animals and you're lucky you survived the merging your uncle did to you. Now, can we go? I don't like it here. It smells." She pressed her dainty hand to her nose to illustrate her point.

Instead of leaving, Eumon knelt down and held his hand out to Illarion. "Here, boy . . . come to me."

Curling his lip, Illarion scooted closer to Max.

Eumon lowered his hand and sighed. "It seems like we should be able to train them. Doesn't it?"

Max bit back a scoff. As if.

"Maybe so as not to wet the rugs or their beds, but I wouldn't hold out hope for any more than that. As I said, they're stupid animals, incapable of thought or civilization."

Oh yeah, *they* were the problem in this equation. . . .

"You are terrible, Helena!" he teased.

All of a sudden, a large number of guards stormed into the dungeon. Max tensed at the sight of them. Something that never boded well for those kept in cages. Anytime that many came in like that . . .

One of the prisoners got seriously hurt.

Or seriously dead.

Prince Eumon shot to his feet to confront the stone-faced soldiers. "What's the meaning of this?"

"Orders from the king, Highness. We're to destroy all the experiments to placate the gods."

The prince's face went white as Max's stomach shrank. "What?"

The guard nodded. "The dictate came from the head priest this afternoon. The gods are demanding that all the abominations be put down. Otherwise, they'll kill your father and you, and your brother."

Illarion exchanged a panicked look with Max.

Never fear, brother. I won't let them take you, Max promised, hoping he wasn't lying as he spoke those words.

But there was nothing save doubt in Illarion's eyes. Something that cut to Max's bone. How could his brother think for one minute that he'd allow them to hurt him?

Never. Even if it meant his life, he'd keep Illarion safe from them and get him out of this mess.

With a mighty roar, Max rushed at the bars.

The prince stumbled back with a fierce gasp, dragging his wife with him.

Screaming, she fell to the floor. "I told you! He's an animal! Kill him! Kill him now!"

Fury tore through Max with such ferocity that he lost complete control of his magick, even with the collar on to control it. All he knew was that he refused to go down like this. He refused to watch them kill his brother.

The howls and screams of the others filled his ears as the soldiers set about carrying out their orders.

This was utter bullshit! Max threw himself against the bars, over and over. When that wasn't enough, he summoned every bit of magick he could and held his concentration. Then he sent it out into the air around them.

Like a thermal shock, it rolled out of him and sent a pulsating wave through the air. One that shattered the cage and sent the guards, prince, and princess tumbling.

Weak, but determined, Max grabbed Illarion. "Free the others. Be damned if those bitches are going to take their lives for this!"

It's not our place!

"I don't answer to the Greek gods. They can kiss my scaly ass." Max grabbed the keys from the guard who was closest to him. Baring his fangs, he took the man's sword, then moved to free the Arcadians and Katagaria. His brother still stood there. "Illarion! Move! Save everyone you can!"

Finally, Illarion began to cooperate.

As soon as they had the doors open and had started to leave, the guards moved to stop them.

"We have to talk to the king, first. No one can leave here."

To his complete shock, Eumon stepped forward. "Let them pass."

"Highness—"

"Do it!"

Reluctantly, the guard stepped aside and ordered his men to stand down.

Grateful to the prince who was allowing them to leave without war and bloodshed, Max inclined his head to him. "Can you show us the way out?"

The prince narrowed an evil glare at him. "I knew you could speak! I need you to show that to my father."

"And we need a guide before your father learns of this and kills us. . . . Please. My brother and I have always been overtaken whenever we've tried to escape. I know there's a way to the forest, but we haven't been able to locate it."

Without hesitation, he nodded. "Follow me."

"Eumon!" his wife breathed. "You can't do this. If the gods have spoken—"

"They're sentient, Helena. Look at them." He gestured at Max and Illarion. "Half of them are Apollite. I can't condemn them to die and especially not by execution in a cage after everything else we've done. It would be wrong. I'm their prince. It's my place to protect them."

"And what of your son I carry? Who will protect him when the gods kill you for this hubris?"

He kissed her lightly on the forehead. "Relax, precious wife. No one's going to kill me." Pulling away, he led Illarion and the others through the dark cavern. "Follow me and I'll see you to your freedom."

She glared at Max as they started filing out of the dungeon. "I have a bad feeling about this."

Max ignored her and the indigestion he thought was a bad feeling, too, as he sought to get the others out as quickly as possible. He didn't trust the guards not to attack them, in spite of what the prince had ordered.

As the last Apollite animal filed past them, he began to breathe a little easier. They were almost out of here.

True to his word, Eumon helped them relocate to a small campground in the forest, where Max and Illarion made sure everyone had a place to sleep and something to eat.

"Thank you," Max said to the prince before he went to tend his brother.

Eumon stopped him. "All these weeks and you've said nothing. You've pretended to be mute. Why?"

"There was nothing to say. Your uncle ripped us from our homes and lives for you. Both Apollite and animal. No regard for what we thought or wanted. And then we were turned into this?" He gestured angrily at his human body. "You may have desired the dragon in you, Highness, but I promise neither Illarion nor I wanted this. Nor did any of the others. Now that you have some of my brother's genetics in your heart, you should know exactly how we think."

"You have a fierce code of honor and kinship. That's where this comes from?"

Max inclined his head. "And now you tell me that your gods have decreed our death for *your* deeds. How do you think that makes me feel?"

"I will talk to my father. He's a reasonable man."

Max arched a brow at his lie.

"He loves us."

Which was true, but . . . "That makes him highly unreasonable."

The prince nodded. "If you and your brother come with me. . . . Let my father see that you're capable of rational thought and speech. It will change everything. I promise. Come and help me to set this right."

Still, Max was skeptical. It wasn't as easy as the prince made it sound. He knew that. Yet as he looked among the desolate, fear-filled faces, he knew he had to try.

For them.

Illarion wended his way through the others to approach Max. *Surely you don't believe his lies.*

"We have to try."

Shaking his head, Illarion didn't want to participate, but he loved his brother too much to let him go about his stupidity alone.

So together, they headed back toward the palace, with Eumon in the lead.

For the first time, they emerged out of the dungeon and into the palace grounds that led to where the royal family lived.

They had just reached the gardens when a man who appeared eerily similar to Vane approached them.

"What is this?"

"We're going to see Father."

The newcomer scowled with fierce disapproval. "What have you done?"

The prince let out a tired sigh. "Linus, please. I have to speak to him and I don't have time."

"You heard what the priest told Father. We've angered the gods. If you don't return them for execution right now, they'll demand our heads, too! Do you want to die?"

"And what's to stop them from doing that anyway after the others are gone? The gods are capricious. You know that. I don't trust them."

Linus gestured at Max and then Illarion. "But you would trust an animal?"

"They're not just animals. They can speak."

Linus scoffed. "Now you're being ridiculous. Did you perchance eat a bad lotus batch?"

"He's not wrong."

Linus's gaze had widened at the sound of Max's voice. "You can think and talk?"

"Of course."

His eyes darkened dangerously as he moved to confront Max. "Are *you* the reason Dagon did this to me?"

"Did what?"

In response to his brother's question, Linus turned on Eumon. "Or did *you* do it?"

"Do what?" Eumon repeated.

Linus raked him with a scathing glare. "You were always Father's favored son. Had your life not been threatened, I'm sure he'd have let me die, as he did our mother."

Eumon let out a tired sigh. "I don't have time for your insecurities. Move aside."

"Oh right. You *never* have time, do you?" Linus sneered at Helena. "You took the bride that was meant for me and now you took my true animal form. *I* should have been the dragon. Not you!"

"What madness do you speak?"

"Helena was my bride!"

She lifted her chin defiantly. "I refused your hand after I met you. There's a cruelty in you, Linus, that scares me. Treaty or not, I would never have married into this family had I not met Eumon and seen for myself that, unlike you, he has a soul."

Shrieking in anger, he lunged at her, but Max caught him and forced him back. "Stop it. We have dire business to attend to here."

Linus's jaw went slack. "So, it's true. You do speak. You could have convinced Dagon to give me the form I wanted, but instead you chose to remain silent? Did you kill your own to keep me from being like you, too? You did, didn't you?"

"What?"

Linus shoved Max away. "You all disgust me. You never let me have what I want."

He's mad, brother. We should leave.

Max couldn't agree more. *Protect the princess.*

As Illarion moved in to comply, Linus pulled out a knife and attacked. "Don't you turn your back on me, Eumon! I will not be disregarded!"

Eumon shoved him aside as he lunged for Illarion. "Are you stupid? He's the animal, you moron! I'm the prince. How can you not tell us apart?"

Those words had slapped Max hard. Especially since the only way to tell them apart was by the finery one wore and the filth on his brother. In his opinion, it said more for Linus that he hadn't noticed their difference in dress.

Linus wrested his hand and weapon free from his brother. "I should have been heir! I'm far more worthy!"

Eumon had laughed in his face. "You were never worthy." With that, he disarmed him and kicked him back.

Horrified, Max had helped Illarion to his feet. Then placed his body between Illarion and the princes to protect him.

Rolling his eyes, Eumon threw the knife down. "Ignore him." He chucked Max on the arm and then Illarion. "Follow me and we'll settle this."

As they started away, Max caught the movement from the corner of his eye. He turned to disarm Linus, but he still hadn't mastered his human body. Before he could do anything to stop it, Linus stabbed him, then turned on the others.

Furious, Illarion attacked.

"Stop!" Eumon growled, trying to get between them.

Max knew the prince would be hurt if he didn't remove him

from the conflict. "Highness?" He pulled him back at the same time Illarion and Linus staggered together, fighting for control of the knife.

They slammed hard into Max and Eumon, knocking them off balance and sending them reeling.

In a huge clump, the four of them fell to the ground.

As Max went to stand, he realized they were covered in a lot more blood than they should have been. Stunned, it took him several seconds to realize it was Eumon whose artery had been sliced open in their fall.

Panting for air, he met Max's gaze. "Protect my wife."

His eyes haunted, Linus pushed himself to his feet and staggered back. Dropping the knife, he pressed his blood-soaked hand to his lips.

"Highness?"

Screaming in agony, Helena had rushed forward to weep by her husband's side. "Don't leave me, Eumon! Stay with me!" She applied pressure to his wound, but it was too late.

As his last act, Eumon reached up and removed Max's collar so that he could shapeshift freely. "Protect them all." And with that he expelled his final breath.

Helena had thrown her head back and shrieked like a harpy. "You beast! You killed my husband!"

"No . . ." Linus backed up in terror. "You saw for yourself. It was an accident."

Shaking her head, she sobbed and sobbed.

Max glanced to Illarion, who watched them with an equally horrified gaze. *What do we do?*

He had no idea. Linus was insane and he'd never tell the truth and implicate himself in this. His fear of being blamed for his brother's death wouldn't allow that. The gods had decreed them all to die. . . .

But one look at Illarion's face and he knew he'd never stand back and let that happen.

I have to get them to safety.

There was only one place he could think that would be safe from the reach of the gods. One place where the king couldn't demand Illarion's head. Gathering his brother and the weeping princess, he shifted to his dragon form and took flight with them.

Her terrified shrieks filled his ears as she insulted him and tried to break free. Illarion fought against his grip. *Remove my collar so that I can fly, too!*

Not yet. He wasn't sure what reception they'd have when they reached his destination. It could be welcoming.

Experience said it wouldn't.

Even so, Max closed his eyes and prayed for this to work. When he finally reached the southern beach, he laid his brother and the princess down on the white sands, then landed. His stomach knotted, he gazed out over the perfect waves and did something he hadn't done in centuries.

He summoned the demon Chthonian. The one being who was given protection and charge over their kind.

Granted, no one had seen the bastard in centuries and all kinds of speculations abounded. Some said he'd finally died of the wounds he'd sustained during the great Chthonian war.

Others that the Greek god Mache had cursed him in retaliation for being bound and imprisoned.

Another said that the goddess Apollymi had drowned him when she sank Atlantis. There was even a rumor that Artemis had captured him and was keeping him as her pet on Olympus.

Max didn't know if any of that was true.

All he knew was that he needed a miracle and that the only creature who *might* help them was the Chthonian who'd once led Max's mother's people to freedom.

Throwing his head back, he let out a summoning cry for the beast.

The princess shrank away from him as the waves rolled in and out on the beach.

"What is he doing?" she asked, throwing her hands over her ears to mute the sounds of his call.

Max ignored her as he continued to summon Savitar.

And as time moved slowly and no one responded to his summons, he realized that the Chthonian must be dead.

Or that he didn't care.

Heartsick, he turned away from the beach, toward his brother. His jaw went slack as he saw the tall, muscular man approaching them.

Savitar.

His lavender eyes glowed as he paused by Illarion's side and swept his gaze over the blood-soaked gown on the cringing princess. "Seems I missed an impressive party. Care to enlighten me, dragon?"

Max quickly told him what had been done to them, and

what had happened to Eumon and Illarion. "I need your help, Chthonian."

Savitar had scoffed. "I'm done helping others. Last time I did that . . . it turned out badly for everyone. Especially me, and I rather like me, most days."

"They'll kill us."

"Everyone dies sometime."

"That's it, then? You're literally washing your hands of us?"

Savitar shrugged. "You have a new life. You should enjoy it."

"Until the Fates have us killed, you mean."

Savitar had gone stock-still. "Come again?"

"The Greek Fates? Because of Apollo and Zeus, they've ordered all of us to be put down."

"You should have led with that, little brother."

"Meaning?"

Savitar smiled. "Meaning there isn't much I wouldn't do to make those three bitches scream in agony. Take me to your camp."

By the time they returned, most of the Apollite-animal hybrids were dead. While Max had been gone, the guards had found their camp and slaughtered them down to a meager handful before they'd driven them off.

Disgusted by the cruel horror, Max had walked around the other newly made shapeshifters, assuring them as best he could.

"What are we to do?"

He met Savitar's gaze.

Finally he saw the spark there that lived in his heart.

Savitar stepped forward. "As a new species, I offer you my

protection. I will make it known that the Chthonians are aware of you and that no one, especially the gods, are to prey on you without repercussions."

While Savitar dealt with the new species, Max had finally removed Illarion's collar.

About time.

"I know. I'm sorry."

Why did you wait?

"In case we were taken, you could have passed as the prince and escaped. So long as you remained in a human body."

Illarion shook his head as he scanned the others. *We are an abomination. Are you sure we should have survived? Perhaps it would have been kinder to consign us to death.*

"Perhaps. But then life isn't kind. All we have to get through it is each other. I couldn't stand by and watch them die."

Illarion let out a tired sigh. *Your Arel blood seriously screws you at times. What is this innate need you have to protect?*

"I don't know, but you should be glad I have it. A sane dragon would have left you behind."

As they rounded them up, Lycaon and his army rode in to finish their slaughter.

Until the king saw Savitar. "What is the meaning of this?"

Savitar faced the king without fear. "I'm here to take them to their own lands to live."

"You can't do that."

Savitar arched a brow. "You want to cross me?"

"The gods have decreed—"

"And I, as a Chthonian sworn to protect mortal life from the gods, overturn that decree."

Lycaon shook his head. "You can't do that! They'll kill my children in retaliation."

"It's done."

While they argued, Helena grabbed Max's arm. "You can't let me return to the palace. Not after what's happened."

Confused, he scowled at her. "You want to travel with us, the animals?"

"Please. I'm afraid of what Linus will do to me and my children. While he might keep me alive and claim me as his, he will never suffer my children to live. Not so long as they are heirs to their father's throne. You saw him. His ambitions are ruthless and he will stop at nothing. Worse, we know he killed Eumon. So long as any of us are alive, he'll view us as a threat and want us removed. Understood?"

Illarion had shaken his head. *Max . . . I know that look on your face. You're the one who's always telling me to stay out of things.*

Max had nudged the princess closer to Illarion. "Keep an eye on her, for a minute."

Not quite sure what he was doing, he closed the distance between Savitar and the king. The moment Linus saw him, he did just as his sister-in-law predicted.

He ordered Max arrested for the murder of his brother, and demanded the return of Helena.

She was right. Linus would never suffer her to live and birth those children. He would kill them and remove them from the line of succession.

"He and his brother slaughtered mine, and I demand their heads for it!"

"Illarion is innocent. I, alone, am responsible."

Savitar faced him with a stern glower. "Do you understand what you're doing?"

Hell, no. But it seemed to be the only option.

He met Savitar's furious stare. "I only understand what will happen if I don't."

Sighing in disgust, Savitar pressed his fingers to the bridge of his nose as if he had a brain tumor forming. As the guards came to retake Max, Savitar stopped them.

"No! The Arcadians you've created are a separate race and shouldn't be subjected to the laws of man." Savitar glared at Linus and his father. "They are a sentient group and should make their own laws to govern them. If Maxis is to face judgment, it will be by a jury of his own hybrid peers and not handed down from a scheming brother and grieving father. If travesty is to be done, it should be impartial."

" 'Cause that makes it all so much better," Max muttered.

Savitar narrowed a threatening glower at him. "Don't lip me, dragon, or I'll turn you over to them."

"And what of this jury?" Lycaon demanded. "Who's to oversee it?"

"I will personally guarantee it. You have my word."

Fury, and the promise that this wasn't over, glared out from the king's eyes. "Fine. I'll hold you to it. But I want that dragon's head mounted to my wall for what he's done! I will be expecting you to bring it to me when this is over. Otherwise, I'll be declaring war on this new breed." And with that, the king led his army away.

Illarion finally approached them. *I'm glad that's settled. Not even a little.*

Savitar laughed bitterly. "You're right. Nothing's over. This is just the beginning. Wait until Zeus and Apollo hear of it." He glanced around at the faces and animals. . . .

Apollites, lions, eagles, falcons, hawks, tigers, wolves, bears, panthers, jackals, leopards, snow leopards, jaguars, cheetahs, and dragons.

"What the hell was Dagon thinking?"

Max let out his own exhausted breath. "That his wife was grieving for her brother and that he had the magick to make it better."

"You consider *this* better?"

Max shrugged at Savitar's question. "Better than death? Aye. Barely."

"And you, dragon, are an idiot."

"I've been called worse." He glanced to Illarion. "And that was just a few hours ago."

Savitar shook his head as he met the gaze of the princess. "Those are the first of their kind you're carrying, you know that, right?"

Her face had gone pale. "What?"

"You conceived them after your husband had been transformed. The good news is, they won't die of the Apollite curse that comes with Eumon's bloodline. The bad news is, the gods won't be happy that your prince thwarted said curse." Savitar growled in aggravation. "There's only so much mitigating I can do. Knowing the gods and those bitches in particular, I can tell you this isn't over. They will have something new in store for us all. And it won't be merciful."

And he'd been right. In spite of the evidence, and Helena's testimony over what had happened, Max had been found guilty during that first Omegrion meeting. When Illarion went to testify, Max had kept him out of it, lest he implicate himself and come under fire.

Better one should be marked than both. He'd pressed upon Illarion the necessity of keeping Helena safe and fulfilling their promise to Eumon. Something they couldn't do if they were both being hunted.

So he'd been marked while Illarion had been left as a Katagari guard for the first Arcadian princes born to a human mother.

But for Max and Illarion, there would have been no Were-Hunters spared the sword.

Only Linus and Eumon.

Lycaon would have gladly slaughtered the rest to spare his two sons from the wrath of the Olympian gods.

One wolf and one dragon.

Seraphina stared in awe of her mate. She'd had no idea of the sacrifices he'd made for their people.

No one had. True to his Arel birth and blood, Max had borne his duties in silence. The only time he'd struck out against them was when his brothers were threatened.

When she and their children were under fire.

The worst irony was that neither he nor his brother even held a seat at the very council that had been started because of them. Rather Helena and another Drakos born from an earlier experiment between an Apollite slave and dragon had taken the first Regis positions. Helena as the Arcadian Regis, until her eldest son, Pharell, had been old enough to inherit it, and Cromus, who ceded his place to Helena's Katagari son, Portheus, when he'd come of age.

Linus had been left to found the same wolf bloodline that had led to Vane, Fang, and Fury. Ever bitter over being forced into his wolf status, he had gladly waged blood feuds against the Katagaria and other species. And it had been his powerful testimony and leadership that had condemned Max.

His ruthless need to put down all the others and rule them that had forced Savitar to create the limanis so that the Were-Hunters would have some refuge from the gods and others out to slaughter them needlessly.

Now, Savitar pulled back and lightened the room. One by one, he met the gaze of those seated at the council table. "There you have it. Yes, Max technically drew first Were-Hunter blood, but he did so in protection of you all. Are you really going to be as the first council and condemn him again, knowing that?"

Damos Kattalakis, the descendent of Eumon and Helena who currently held the Arcadian Drakos seat, rose. His looks reminded Sera a great deal of Vane's and he closely resembled his brother Sebastian, whom she'd met earlier.

Slowly, cautiously, he approached Max and Illarion.

His face unreadable, he removed the feathered mask that covered his Sentinel marks. Running his hand over the scales and delicate workmanship, he studied the mask before he spoke. "It is the custom of my patria to make these out of the remains of the Katagaria we've slain. It's done to remind us that while they are animals, we are not. That we are civilized and descended from the blood of princes. In particular, Eumon Kattalakis."

He dropped the mask to the floor and met Max's gaze, then Illarion's. "I don't know why my great-grandmother failed to tell us of you, but I promise that if I should be fortunate enough to have dragonets one day, they will know the truth and what we owe our Katagaria cousins." Striking his shoulder with his fist, he saluted Max. "Thank you for saving my family. As the head of the Kattalakis Drakos, I swear that should we ever hear the Bane-Cry of you, or your mates or children, every member of our patria will answer. On our honor."

Max inclined his head and saluted him back. "Thank you."

Smiling, Damos drew him in for a hug, then Illarion. "My father rolls in his grave." He turned back at Savitar and scowled. "Is this why you've always hated me?"

Savitar nodded. "Sins of the father, brother. Sins of the father. But today, you took the right step. And I saw it."

Snorting, Damos appeared less than amused as he turned toward Dare Kattalakis. "What of you, cousin?"

"They can kiss my furry ass. We're still at war."

19

"You should have eaten the wolves, little brother."

Everyone in the room turned to look at Falcyn for his dry, emotionless, and very callous words.

He stared back, completely unrepentant. "Just saying. They're crispy when fried. Lean meat. Low gristle. It would have saved everyone the migraine of dealing with them now."

Fury choked. "Speaking as one of the wolves, I'm extremely offended by that."

"Good," Falcyn said without a hint of remorse or apology in his tone. "I've offended wolves and Were-Hunters alike. All I need to do now is feed on a cute, cuddly baby and my work for the day is done."

Blaise smacked Falcyn on the chest. "Don't worry, he's part Charonte. Hand him some barbecue sauce and he's happy."

Falcyn passed such an irritable scowl at Blaise that even though he was blind, Blaise felt it and shrank back—not in fear, but from common sense.

"He's not Charonte," Max said drily. "That would be too easy an excuse for him, and there really isn't one. He's just an irritable bastard. . . . Much like Savitar."

Savitar arched his brow. "I save your ass and you take a swipe at me? Really?"

"I'd apologize, but you hate insincerity more than you do insults."

"Yeah, I do." Savitar eyed the council members. "Well, we know where the dragons stand and where the wolves are officially. . . ." He looked at Vane for confirmation on their stance.

Vane cut a vicious glare at his litter mate, Dare. "Officially, the Kattalakis Lykos, both Arcadian and Katagaria, consider Max a brother. We have no issue with him and vote that the mark be stricken."

"I second that," Fury concurred. "And I hope you choke on it, Dare. It *and* my furry ass."

Dare took a step forward, but his sister caught him and kept him from doing something profoundly stupid. Like attacking his brothers in front of the Omegrion and Savitar.

Savitar turned his attention to the other Kattalakis Drakos, who was standing with Dare and Star. Tall and dark, the Katagari Regis favored Fang more than the others.

His ebony eyes flashed as he considered his response. After a few seconds, he pulled the silver dragon pendant from his neck and looked down at it resting in his palm. "I grew up with stories about the Dragonbane and how he killed the first Arcadian in cold, vicious blood, and started our war of species. My father impressed upon me that we were never to be such animals. That we should strive to find the human in us, even when it seemed buried and lost." He glanced to Dare and Star. "I'm thinking that my father was wrong. We should have embraced the Drakos more than that so-called humanity."

Darion came forward to lay his pendant in Illarion's hand. "I vote to remove the mark and I cede my seat at the council to the rightful heir. You are the one made from Prince Eumon's blood, not my family. It's only right that you should be the one making the laws for our people."

Illarion shook his head. *I can't take this.*

Darion held his hands up and stepped back. "You are Regis, Stra Drago. I refuse my seat. I have no right to it."

Savitar glanced around to the rest of the Omegrion members. "For the sake of brevity, I'm assuming the rest of you concur. Is there anyone who objects?"

Dante Pontis, the Katagaria panther Regis, held his hand up. With long dark hair he wore in a ponytail, he was the epitome of a disgruntled predator. "I'm not protesting, but I have a question." He turned toward Maxis. "Why were you marked originally?"

Max shrugged with a nonchalance he really didn't feel. "I'm an asshole."

Dante grinned. "While, as a fellow asshole myself, I can respect that, care to elaborate?"

"The council mood back then was a lot different. They were still raw and pissed off from being held in a cage and experimented on. They'd just been told about the curse the Fates had handed down, that we couldn't choose our mates. They'd be assigned to us, whether we wanted them or not, and that the Fates had decreed eternal war between our species."

And human rationale was new to the animals, Illarion inserted. *They were angry and lashing out at everyone, especially my brother and I.*

Max nodded. "When they started to attack me, I reacted as any drakomas would. I told them to fuck themselves and attacked back."

Savitar snorted disdainfully. "Talk about putting lipstick on a pig. . . . You are allowed to say that you reacted badly."

"All right, I reacted badly."

"Yeah, that's an exaggeration," Savitar said under his breath.

Max feigned indignation. "I don't know what you're talking about. It's been a million years since I last exaggerated about anything."

Savitar rolled his eyes.

"Anyway," Max continued. "I lost my temper over their accusations and . . ." He pointed up at the ceiling. "You can still see some of the marks where the fighting broke out and we almost burned down the building."

"That's where I reacted badly." Savitar flashed a fake smile. "As a result, Max was condemned and I was in no mood to refute or acquit their unanimous decision. We all had a very bad day."

"And I've had a few more," Max whispered loudly.

"Yeah. Sorry about that." Savitar crossed his arms over his chest.

"Wow," Dante said in a sarcastic tone. "Sounds like the mood I was in when I mounted my brother's hide to the wall of my club."

Savitar nodded. "Basically . . . So, we are all in accord?"

"Yes." Fury flashed a devilish grin. "Dare is an asshole and nobody likes him, at all."

Dare started for him.

Fury bared his teeth. "Bring it, you little punk bastard! Let's go! C'mon, you and me. Here and now! I'm ready to pick your fur out of my teeth! C'mon!"

Vane caught Fury and pushed him back toward Max. "Did you by chance bring a leash? Or a muzzle?"

"No, but I'm thinking I should have."

Just as Dare broke loose to run at Fury, who was still taunting him and questioning his parentage, a bright flash lit the room, causing him to pull up short. All movement stopped as Cadegan and Thorn appeared near Savitar. Both bleeding and in bad physical shape. Barely alive they lay in a tangled heap at Savitar's feet.

Thorn had his arms around Cadegan as if he'd barely gotten them out of a nasty situation right before they'd been torn apart. The paleness of his bruised features added further testimony to that assumption.

Stunned, Max didn't move. As the sons of a powerful demon, they were both seasoned warriors and had once been medieval knights. Thorn was actually even older than that and had been born an ancient warlord, and had thousands of years of heavy combat experience against the damned and cruel.

One thing those two knew how to do . . .

Fight. Especially anything fanged, clawed, winged, and preternatural.

His breathing ragged, Thorn cupped Cadegan's face in a strangely tender gesture. "You still with me, little brother?"

"Ach, aye, boyo, but only because me Jo would kick me arse if I came home dead to her."

Analise Romano, who was the Arcadian Regis for the snow leopards and a doctor, rushed from her seat to Cadegan to check on him.

Thorn carefully ceded his brother's care over to her before he stood and wiped the blood from his lips. He looked first to Fang, then Savitar. "Remember that situation I mentioned?"

"Blew up a bit?" Savitar asked sarcastically.

"Like your temper on Olympus during a full moon party. Needless to say, we have a massive problem. And our names are engraved all over that apple of fun." Thorn moved to drape one arm over Styxx's shoulder and the other over Acheron's. "Checked on Mom lately?"

Acheron visibly cringed. "Ah God, what's she done now?"

"Well," Thorn tightened his arm around both their necks, "I've just *got* to know . . . whose bright idea was it to surrender Apollo's custody to her?"

Styxx made the same grimace Acheron had worn a moment ago. "That idiot would be me. Why? What did I do?"

Thorn released Acheron to playfully slap Styxx on the face and squish his cheeks together. "Mama Apollymi found him a new playmate," he said in the same falsetto people used when talking to small children. "She fed his ass to Kessar, and aren't we happy he has a new friend, boys and girls?"

"Oh dear gods." Zakar repeated Acheron's words and stumbled back. "Please tell me she didn't."

With a sarcastic, hysterical laugh, Thorn released Styxx, stepped back, and clapped his hands together. "No, wait! It gets so much better! You haven't even heard the good part yet. No! Yeah . . . she decided it would be a great idea to turn Apollo into a blood-bitch like you were, Z. Yes . . . yes, she did."

Groaning, Zakar covered his face.

Thorn nodded and clapped the Sumerian god on the back. "At least you see the train wreck coming."

Acheron glared at him. "Enlighten those of us who don't."

Thorn stepped away to continue. "Long story short, Kessar fed from the god, and they made a pact to combine their fun-loving natures and kind spirits. As a result, Apollo attacked Olympus."

"No." Acheron shook his head. "I was there. That was Kessar who attacked Olympus."

"No, punkin.' *That* was Apollo leading those demons. It's

how they got in. Three guesses what he wanted. And world peace is definitely not one of them."

"Revenge."

Thorn shook his head at Dante and made a sarcastic buzzer sound. "Too easy, and a given. Guess again."

Sick to his stomach, Max exchanged a panicked stare with Illarion.

Thorn applauded. "Oh look, I think the dragons got it. And why shouldn't they? Illarion, being the son of Ares, ought to know exactly what he wants."

He's after the Spartoi.

"Yes. Yes, he is."

Fury scowled. "What's the Spartoi? Is that like a plastic model of the *300* characters? Gods, someone, please tell me that it's an action figure and not what I fear it might be. . . ."

Seraphina grimaced. "No. It's your fear, I'm sure. They're a rather nasty and invincible branch of Ares's army. It's said that when a Drakone of Ares sows them into the earth, they sprout full-grown, ready to battle and destroy at the command of whoever planted them."

"And guess who has custody of those little darlings right now?" Thorn pointed to Illarion. "How do *I* know this? Your father squealed like a thirteen-year-old girl at a Shawn Mendes sighting."

"Aye, he did indeed," Cadegan agreed as he rose on shaky legs, holding his ribs. "For a god of war, Ares is a bit of a wanker. He ain't no Aeron, that's for sure."

"And speaking of our favorite Celtic war god, he's still fighting them and I need to get back and help before they make a gallu of him and we all go down in a ball of sarcastic Aeron fire. They convert him and I'm out. I don't want no part of that fight. Ever." Thorn glanced at Savitar. "Yes, I am that big a coward, for I have fought the evil that is Aeron, had my ass handed to me on a platter with applesauce and garnishings, and yeah . . . no, thank you. Nothing is worth an ass-kicking that severe."

Max stepped forward. "We'll settle this with you."

"We?"

"The drakomai."

Sera nodded. "And the Drakos."

Wide-eyed and furious, Max gaped. She passed a chiding smile at him. "Don't give me that look, Lord Dragon. I don't want you fighting, either."

Edena and Hadyn moved forward to join them.

"Oh hell no!" Max snapped. "I might not have a say in what Sera does, but you two I do!"

When they started to protest, Seraphina shook her head. "Your father's right. Neither of you is ready for this. And if you roll those eyes at me, young lady, I'll ground you till the sun explodes, and your brother, too, just because he taught you to do it when you were little."

Edena huffed and crossed her arms over her chest. "I liked it better when they didn't talk or get along."

Hadyn nodded his agreement, but wisely remained silent.

As Thorn moved back to leave, four Were-Hunters fell to the floor for no reason.

Dead.

Silence echoed as everyone knew exactly what it meant. Those were bonded mates whose spouses had been killed somewhere else. Three council members and one of the Arcadian wolves who'd come in with Star and Dare. For that to happen simultaneously, there was only one cause.

War.

"What the fuck?" Dante breathed.

Thorn and Savitar went pale.

As did Acheron. "They're dividing and attacking our families to thin our defenses and hit our morale."

"It's working," Fury said in a panicked tone.

Savitar motioned for Zakar, Sin, and Styxx. "We'll see to Apollymi in Kalosis and make sure she's secure."

Thorn jerked his chin at the Peltiers and the Kattalakis brothers. "We'll take Sanctuary. Sera, you better join us. Nala's with them. I can feel it."

Cadegan and Blaise exchanged a determined look. "We'll stay here to guard your young. No fears there for you."

Acheron looked to the drakomai. "We'll return to Olympus, and finish it. Once and for all."

Illarion and Max nodded.

Seraphina hesitated. Strange, she'd never minded riding into battle alone.

Now she did. The last thing she wanted was to be without Max by her side. But this they had to do for each other and for their people.

"Remember, Maxis," Sera reminded him. "There is no *I* in team."

He winked at her. "True, but there is in 'win,' 'fight,' and 'die.'"

She growled at him, tempted to beat him into submission. "And you'd best not do the latter."

"Or you. Don't make me go to Hades and beat that bastard down to get you back." Kissing her, he took a moment to savor her scent and the sensation of her body pressing against his. "I love you, Seramia. Don't break my heart."

She sank her hand deep in his long hair and clenched her fist. "For you alone, I breathe."

Max ground his teeth at those words. For her people, they were the deepest avowal of love, and it made it almost impossible to leave her.

But he had no choice. With one last kiss, he glanced past her to their children. "Don't forget your sword, my lady dragon."

She winked at him. "Never."

Inclining his head, he turned and joined Acheron and his brothers. It'd been centuries since he'd gone to real war with Falcyn and Illarion. Yet it seemed like no time at all as they changed forms and fell into formation.

As eldest, Falcyn took lead. The Katagaria Drakos came to fight with them on Olympus while the Arcadians went with Sera and the others to protect Sanctuary.

By the time they arrived, it was much different than earlier. Apollo and Kessar had virtually torched every building, and most of the gods had withdrawn from the conflict. Only a brave handful remained to try and salvage what they could. Demon and his twin, Phobos. Most of the Dream-Hunters, including

Arik and Delphine, as well as Lydia, Solin, and Xypher, who must have been summoned by the others when the fighting started.

Only Apollo's temple remained standing perfectly intact. But that wasn't their target or destination.

Ares's temple was what drew their attention. The iron structure had the front doors ripped open. And the perches that were usually manned by Insidia and Nefas stood empty. Bodies of demons smoldered on the steps.

It was easy to find where the Malachai was still embroiled in a bitter fight against the demons and Apollo.

Max smiled at the sight. Nick had always been stubborn in a brawl. That boy never knew when to give up or surrender. It was one of the things he liked best about the kid, and it was what had kept Nick from turning evil.

So far.

Even though Nick had been born cursed and destined to be one of the creatures who ultimately destroyed the earth, he battled an inner war every day to keep himself from crossing over and becoming what his father had been.

Cherise Gautier would be proud of her son. Especially to see him getting his Cajun ass kicked in defense of a pantheon that didn't care about him. But the ones Nick cared about were bound to Olympus, and to save them, he fought on against overwhelming odds.

Yeah, he was still a good kid.

As they circled, Max caught sight of Illarion and saw the grief in his brother's eyes. Unlike him and Falcyn, Illarion had been born and trained to fight as a team. Every time his brother went into war without his Edilyn, he felt her loss with every part of his being.

And the fact that Illarion would ride for Sera's defense meant everything to Max. It was his brother's unselfishness that he treasured most.

In every garden grows one single rose so perfect that once the frost takes it, no other can ever grow there again. My rose is and will ever be my Edilyn. And I shall never stop mourning her.

Those were the words Illarion had tattooed on his arm with a rose for his fallen wife.

Whenever he was alone, Illarion would idly caress the words as if he touched his wife. She had left a part of him shattered that Max wasn't sure would ever be whole again.

If I could have one wish, it would be to take away your pain, brother.

But the Fates had never been kind to dragons.

"Incoming!"

Max moved to engage the winged demons first, in an effort to protect his brothers. Illarion and Falcyn stayed at his back, covering his flank.

Sin had been right. The gallu were vicious in their skills.

"Don't let them scratch you!" Acheron warned, unaware of the fact that they were immune.

Max spewed fire and swept the ground, razing as much of it as he could. He and his brothers fell in beside Zarek and Jericho while they tried to route a group of demons out of the Hall of the Gods. It took a while, but they eventually had them on the run, headed up the hill toward Apollo's temple.

Winged himself, Jericho shot up between the dragons. "Thanks for the assist."

Falcyn inclined his head to him. "What are they after?"

"Apollo showed up, telling Zeus to abdicate. You know how that went. Even though he's just a figurehead these days, Zeus tossed a few lightning bolts at him and it was on."

Zarek grabbed a demon that tried to bite him and slung it so hard, it flew up and almost hit Max.

"Hey!"

"Duck," Zarek said, a little late.

Max flipped the surly god off.

For once, Zarek ignored the insult as he headed off after another group. At least someone enjoyed the fighting.

A weird flash distracted Max as he started to turn. He glanced over his shoulder to see Illarion losing altitude. Afraid something was wrong or that Illarion had been wounded, he went after his brother.

Without a word, Illarion tucked his wings and landed near his father's temple.

"Is something wrong?"

Do you hear that?

"Hear what?" Only the sounds of the battle filled his ears. That and the fierce beating of his racing heart.

Illarion cocked his head. *It's Cercamon.*

"Who?"

A twelfth-century troubadour. Edilyn was forever making me take her to see him play.

Max heard it then. Light and subtle. Barely audible and yet distinct.

Bel m'es quant ilh m'enfolhetis
E·m fai badar e·n vau muzan!
De leis m'es bel si m'escarnis
O·m gaba dereir'o denan,
Qu'apres lo mal me venra bes
Be leu, s'a lieys ven a plazer.

What the hell? Why would that be playing in the background? It seemed a strange choice for a Greek god of war.

Metallica, Pantera . . . that would make sense. Death metal, definitely. But medieval love poetry?

Nah, it just didn't fit.

Illarion turned human so that he could sneak inside for a peek. Max followed suit only to find that it wasn't Ares who was playing and singing in the middle of battle.

It was Apollo. Which kind of made sense, he supposed, since Apollo was the god of music and poetry, and rather passive. *Sure, why not?* Him and Nero. Fiddling while Rome, or in this case, Olympus burned.

The god probably needed the light from the fires to read with his old eyes.

As if sensing their presence, Apollo stopped playing and narrowed his gaze angrily on the shadows that concealed them.

"Little dragons, all in a row. Tell the big Greek god, how deep is your sorrow flow?"

A chill went down Max's spine. He grabbed Illarion's arm and tried to pull him back, but his brother wouldn't obey. It was as if he was being drawn forward by some unseen, mystical force. Like the music lured him against his will.

Apollo rose to his feet, while he continued to pluck at his lyre. "I know you're there, son of Ares. I can feel you. Come and give your uncle a hug . . . sing with me."

Illarion actually took a step forward.

Max sank his claws into his brother's arm, hoping the pain might get through to him since nothing else was working, and shook his head no. *It's a trick!*

Pressing his lips together, Illarion finally hesitated.

"Ahh," Apollo said in a petulant tone. He plucked a sour note. "Don't you trust me? You do know that's why Dagon chose you for his experiments all those centuries ago, don't you? Because you were my nephew, he thought to use you to spare the Apollites my curse. He knew my love for you, as your uncle, would sway my mercy. It's why I begged Zeus and the Fates to spare you from the slaughter."

Apollo tsked. "Your jealous half brother Max didn't tell you that, did he? That I never wanted *you* harmed. You and Lycaon's sons were to be excluded from the cleansing. Your brother lied to you, Illarion, to save his own ass, and to win you to his cause. It's what he's been doing since the very beginning. Why do you think he left you trapped all those centuries in Le Terre Derrière le Voile?"

Max gaped furiously at that accusation. How dare he! *Bullshit! You know better, Illy. You were there. You heard them, same as I. That's not the way it happened! And I never knew you were trapped. I would have come for you, had I known.*

The sudden doubt in Illarion's eyes cut him soul deep. How could he believe Apollo for even an instant over him? Especially after everything they'd been through together.

"You aren't born of Arel blood, little nephew. You have no loyalty to anyone save our pantheon. Join us and I'll give you what you want most."

"Illarion," Max spoke out loud, trying to reach his brother through whatever spell the god was weaving with his lyre and words. "Don't listen to him. He's lying. You know he's lying!"

His brother took a step back and grabbed on to Max's arm to steady himself.

Relieved beyond belief that his brother had chosen wisely, Max wrapped his arms around him and held him close. He could feel Illarion trembling against him.

Until a light, musical voice called out with the cadence of a perfect angel.

"Illarion?"

His breathing ragged, Illarion pulled back and looked up with wide eyes. *Edilyn?*

"I'm here, my precious dearling. I've missed you so much!"

Apollo laughed. "All you have to do is join me, nephew. Help me take back what was stolen and I'll see you reunited with your Edilyn."

Max shook his head and held on tight to Illarion's arm. "You can't do this! Illarion! It's a trick!"

His eyes haunted, Illarion met his gaze with a longing insanity he'd never forget. *And if it were Seraphina? What choice would you make, brother?*

Damn it! The truth of that statement burned like fire in his gut. He knew what choice he'd make.

The same one Illarion did as his brother shoved him back and ran to Apollo.

In that moment, Max knew he couldn't stay. If he did, he'd be forced to fight the last creature on this planet he'd ever harm.

The brother he'd spent a lifetime protecting.

Worse, he knew that wasn't Edilyn. It couldn't be. It was an illusion of some kind. But Illarion was so desperate to have her back that he didn't care. He was past listening to reason.

Distracted, Max glanced back into the temple to check on Illarion as he embraced whatever demon or creature wore the skin of his brother's wife. His thoughts and emotions were so scattered and raw that for a moment, he forgot he was still in a human body.

Forgot he was in the middle of a war and a battle.

But he was reminded fast when a demon materialized in front of him and ran him completely through his heart with a sword, and kicked him to the ground, leaving him there to die.

20

Savitar went into Kalosis expecting a war zone. But the absolute silence of Apollymi's dark palace was even more terrifying. Nothing seemed out of the ordinary.

Nothing.

It was so quiet that only the sound of his own heartbeat filled his ears. The dark was oppressive and sterile. Unsettling. Downright terrifying in its own right. Yeah, this had all the markings of a Creature Feature film and was exactly the type of home you'd expect for a woman termed *The Great Destroyer.*

Zakar scowled at him as Savitar turned around, looking for the body count that should have been here. "Is it supposed to be empty like this?"

Styxx shook his head. "I don't think so," he said slowly, stretching the words out. "It's a little too . . ."

"Normal?" Zakar asked.

"Yeah."

Savitar couldn't agree more. "I could have sworn there'd be more . . ."

"Blood?" This time it was Sin who weighed in. As the grandson-in-law of the Destroyer, he was well versed in her more vicious mood swings and bloodbath parties.

Zakar nodded. "And violence. Definitely expected blood on the walls and violence."

"Violence? You dare barge into my home without an invitation? Oh, violence I can definitely give you, Sumerian dog."

They turned to find Apollymi standing in all her regal glory on the stairs of her palace, glaring at them. Her black gown spread out around her ethereal figure and contrasted sharply to her snow-white hair.

Her swirling silver eyes glittered like ice. "Why are you here? How dare you barge into my home." To be barely more than a whisper, those words carried more threat than any shout.

Savitar cleared his throat. "We thought the demons would be attacking you."

"So . . . what? You were going to ride in on your white surfboard, and save helpless little me from the big bad demon horde of my enemies? How vulgarly heroic of you, Savitar. But as you can plainly see, I've no need of rescue. Everything's fine and normal here."

"Were you not attacked?"

Apollymi laughed. "Oh yes. I was attacked, and I unleashed my tidal and formidable wrath upon the vermin who dared such." She shivered as if in the throes of ultimate pleasure. "It was exhilarating. Positively divine and delightful. If you have any more demonic issues that plague you on the surface, please, please send them here for my enjoyment. I've so missed the thrill of the kill. The taste of blood and orgasmic screaming they do just before they expel that final breath where they uselessly cling to life but ultimately must surrender to death. Such sweet, precious harmony." She expelled a breath of supreme satisfaction and smiled in complete ecstasy. "That is what I live for."

Zakar looked at his brother and snorted. "I'm thinking she needs some private time."

Savitar slapped him on the chest. Hard. "Be nice. Be polite. Or I'll unleash her on you." He left them to climb the stairs where she stood above him, the epitome of utter icy perfection. "Are you sure you're all right?"

She passed him a droll stare. "I would show you the bodies, but my Charonte are having a feast with them. If you hurry, you might find a few remaining scraps. Maybe a fingernail or tooth they have yet to consume." She arched a brow. "Were you truly concerned?"

"Of course. As was Acheron."

Her features softened. She glanced past him to see Styxx at the bottom of the stairs. For him, she smiled warmly. "My beautiful boys. You may rest assured that it will take much more than Sumerian gutter rats to threaten me. However, there is a matter of concern."

She returned her attention to Savitar. "It would seem Apollo unleashed a nasty disease among the Apollites here. We've already lost a number of them to it. Many more are sick. The only ones who appear immune are Medea and Stryker, no doubt because they're his children. Even Zephyra is ill. I've tried everything I know to offer a cure, but I'm not a goddess of healing."

"Is it a curse or a plague?"

"The Greek bastard called it a plague. An illness, I presume. Can you help them? Please."

Those were words he could never ignore when she uttered them. For her, there was nothing he wouldn't do. "Absolutely. I'll do everything I can."

She swept her gaze over his clothing and sighed in total irritation. Shaking her head, she grasped the edge of his wetsuit where he'd unzipped it and pulled it closed. "Will you ever learn to dress as a human?"

He snorted at her condescending tone. "Will you ever cease to nag me for my wardrobe?"

"No . . . and you reek of sea and sunshine. It's a revolting combination." She shivered and curled her lip. "Smacks of happiness and good times. Disgusting things, that." She gave him a light, dainty push.

By that alone, he knew he didn't irritate as much as she

claimed. If he did, she'd have thrown him down the stairs or blasted him through her walls.

She jerked her chin toward the Sumerian gods. "Get on with you, now. See to curing my Daimons. They need you."

As they started to leave, she called Styxx to her side.

Styxx was bashful as he climbed the stairs and stopped in front of her. "You're not thinking of throwing me down them, are you?"

Smiling as if she savored that thought, or maybe his playful cheekiness, she ruffled his hair. "You dress as poorly as Savitar. I swear, you and your brother. You ever seek to vex me." She took a moment to straighten his clothes. "I expect a visit soon from your Bethany and the babies. I rely on you to care for your brother and Tory and their sons in my absence."

"You know I do."

She nodded warmly. "I do. It's why you live." Kissing his cheek, she gave him a hug. But the way she held on to him, it was obvious that it wasn't Styxx she imagined holding.

It was Acheron.

Apollymi cupped his head in her hand before she released him. Her gaze went to Savitar and turned to absolute granite. "Keep them all safe, Chthonian. I will not forgive you for the death of another child I love."

"I will never fail you again."

This time, she did blast him through the wall before she turned and vanished.

. . .

Seraphina held the line at the kitchen door. Their instructions were to keep Nala and her warriors in the club and to not allow the fighting to spill into the street where the humans might see them, or into Peltier House where the children, human or animal, could be harmed.

Nala kicked her back, into the wall. "You dare to call yourself an Arcadian and side with the Katagaria? I knew the day you brought that animal home with you that you'd turn on us one day, Katagari whore!"

"Better a Katagari whore than a demon's bitch. You must have swallowed his nectar whole for him to let you live."

Shrieking in outrage, Nala swung at her head.

Seraphina used her sword to deflect the stroke and kneed her hard.

Nala stumbled backward with a groan of pain. Sera gave her no mercy. She advanced on her, raining blows as fast and controlled as she could. This wasn't just about her. It was about protecting her family and what she loved most.

"Apollo will return us to stone if we don't follow his orders. Is that what you want?"

Sera struck out at her. "I won't live my life afraid. That is not part of our Amazonian code and it's definitely not drakonian." Furious, she swept Nala's feet out from beneath her and disarmed her. "And it damn sure isn't becoming of a basilinna! Hem me never," she said, repeating their code of honor. She angled her sword at Nala's throat. "Now cede your crown or lose your head."

Suddenly, the fighting slowed and stopped as those around

them became aware of the fact that Nala was no longer in the battle. That she was on her backside, crawling away from Seraphina's blade.

Nala stopped moving as soon as she realized everyone was staring at her. Only then did she push herself to her feet and stand with her former haughty glower.

Sera cut off her retreat. "Cede the tribe, or I'll call for a vote." Which, after this pathetically weak display, Nala would lose.

And that would be even more humiliating.

"Fine. I'll cede my position as basilinna, but not to a Katagari whore."

Growling, Sera started for her, but Samia caught her and stopped her from taking the bitch's head in cold blood.

"She's not worth your honor, Seraphina. Besides, we all know the truth. She gave up her honor attempting to take Max's and he, a simple Katagari, upheld his vow to you."

Sam raked a scathing glare over Nala's body. "The only shame in this room belongs to her. Let her live knowing that. Let it haunt her every night when she attempts to sleep and it echoes in her head with the voice of the Furies until it drives her mad with the truth." She glanced around to the rest of Sera's tribe. "As the basilinna for the Thurian Riders, I call a vote from the Scythians. Who do you want to lead your nation? A coward, or do you choose someone worthy?"

Tisiphone stepped forward and sheathed her sword. "Honestly? We just want to go home to what we knew. Scythians are done with the politics of the gods. They have brought us nothing save misery. Our only wish now is to return to our time period at the next moon. None of us are happy here. And while we would be honored to have Seraphina as our leader, we respect the fact that she will want to stay here with her mate and children. She has more than earned her peace. None of us will ever judge her for that."

Sera lowered her sword from Nala. "Is that truly how all of you feel?"

One by one, they nodded.

"Then it is with great sadness that I lose my sisters. But I won't stop you. I know what it's like to live without what you need to be happy. And I wish that on no one."

Seraphina narrowed her eyes on Nala. "Not even you." But in spite of those words, bitter hatred rose up inside her and she had one thing she needed to know. "I put my faith in you. I trusted you over even my own mate. Why did you lie to me about him?"

"Because I hate you!" Tears glistened in Nera's eyes as she pulled off her leather gauntlet and showed her palm to Seraphina. A palm that bore a Katagari mating mark. "Like you, I was given to a Katagari bastard. But I held my dragonslayer's oath sacred and refused to seal the mating." She glared at the rest of their tribe. "They lied to us. The mark *never* fades. It stays as a forever reminder that I am sterile, and that the bastard who did this to me still lives. My only comfort is that he's impotent." She raked a vicious sneer over Seraphina's body. "It's not fair that you should have your Katagari mate and I, the basilinna of my sister tribe, should be without his comfort. Should be without children."

While Sera felt bad for her queen, it didn't justify her cruelty to them. "You had no right to blame either me or Maxis for your cowardice. It wasn't your oath that kept you from mating. It was your own fear."

Nala screamed and ran toward her, but Dev caught her and forced her back. "You need a time-out, woman." He glanced to Sam. "I'm putting this one on ice. I'll leave you ladies to attend the others."

Sam swept them with a gaze. "It's up to you, my sisters. Behave and we'll allow you freedom here until the next moon. Start shit and you can sit in a cage with Nala to wait it out."

The Amazons sheathed their swords and stood down.

Fang sighed in relief. "Good. Now all of you can help us clean up the mess you made."

Grateful to have it over and done with, Seraphina had moved forward to help him when someone touched her on the shoulder. She gasped, thinking it was another attack, then relaxed as she saw Falcyn behind her. She glanced past him, looking for her mate. "Where's Max?"

The expression on his face made her stomach tighten.

"What?" she gasped.

When he didn't respond right away, she felt all the air get sucked out of her lungs as if she'd been punched.

"No . . . he's coming." Her tone brooked no argument. Max would be here. He'd promised and he never broke his word.

Tears glistened in Falcyn's eyes as he gently took her hand and teleported her from the bar into the attic with Carson and a redheaded woman she didn't know.

In his dragon form and on his side, Max lay on the ground with blood pooling around him. Carson and the woman were trying to stop the bleeding, but nothing was slowing it down. It ran everywhere and coated Max's beautiful scales.

When Carson saw her, he winced. "I'm sorry, Sera. There's nothing we can do. He took a wound straight to his heart. Honestly? I don't know how he made it back alive and is still breathing."

"No . . . no!" She ran to Max's large head and threw herself against his neck. His faint labored breaths rattled ominously in his chest and throat. "Maxis? Can you hear me?"

I hear you, Seramia.

He was too weak to even speak. And even the voice in her head was nothing more than the faintest of whispers.

Tears blinded her as she clutched at him. "You can't leave me! Not now. You promised me you wouldn't break my heart."

I'm sorry. He slid one bloodied, taloned paw toward her so that he could touch her hip.

Sobbing, Sera thought about all the times she'd slaughtered dragons in her past and had taken so much pride in it. Had stupidly worn their hides and scales as trophies. Was this her payback for that cruelty?

She brushed her hand against his scaly ear and the prickly spined ridges along the back of his skull. "Please don't leave me, Max. I don't want to live without you. I love you . . . I've only ever loved you, my dragon lord."

And then she felt it. That last expulsion of breath as he died in her arms. His entire body went limp.

Throwing her head back, she screamed out in misery. It wasn't fair. It wasn't right.

Damn you, Fates!

"Sera?"

She ignored Falcyn as she cradled Max's head and continued to cry against his beautiful scales, wishing she could have one more day with him. Wishing she'd never allowed him to leave. Why had she ever chosen her tribe over him?

Why hadn't she left with him when he'd asked her? This was all her fault. They could have been happy together.

I'm such an idiot!

"Seraphina? Look at me."

It took everything she had to force herself to draw a ragged breath and lift her head to meet Falcyn's gaze. She realized that Carson and the woman had left them alone in the attic.

And Falcyn held something in his hand. "If you love him, *really* love him, we can bring him back."

"W-w-what?"

He swallowed hard and licked his lips before he spoke again. "What I'm about to do is forbidden. It's the darkest of magick. But I can do it, only if you mean what you say. Because if you don't . . . you'll consign both my brother and me to someplace I don't want to be and to the cruelest of fates."

Her vision swam. "Please bring him back to me. Whatever it takes. If there's a price for this, I'll pay it."

"Then close your eyes. Think of your fondest memory of my brother and hold it dear. Whatever you do, don't look until I tell you. Understood?"

"Yes." She clenched her eyes tight and held on to Max as she thought back to the night they'd first met. To the sight of him stripping her clothes from her body as he kissed and caressed her in a wild frenzy.

She could still hear his deep, infectious laughter in her ear at the way she jerked his clothes from him to uncover more and more of his incredible flesh.

"Eager, are you?" he'd asked with a grin.

"Don't waste your tongue with words. I've much better uses for it."

Laughing again, he'd obliged her with a searing kiss that had left her breathless and weak. She'd barely loosened his pants before he was deep inside her, filling her to capacity and thrusting against her hips while he held her against the closed door.

With her legs wrapped around his lean waist, she'd met him stroke for stroke, growling and urging him on. She'd raked her hands through his hair, delighting in the sensual way it felt sliding between her fingers as he sated the ache inside her. Then she'd run her hands over his strong, broad shoulders and down his back so that she could savor the sensation of his muscles rippling while he pleased her even more.

It hadn't taken any time at all for her to come, screaming as pleasure ripped through her body.

Then, in the tenderest of actions, Max had cupped her cheek and kissed her while slowing his strokes until he came, too. Still inside her, he'd shuffled backward along the floor, finally stepping out of the breeches that had been pooled at his ankles, until he reached the bed and then, laughing, had fallen onto it with her on top of him.

There his golden eyes had darkened as he slowly, carefully cupped her breasts in his hands and licked his lips. Her eyes had widened as she felt him growing hard inside her again.

"Still hungry?"

He'd expelled a deep, sexy sigh. "For you? Famished. Gods, woman, your breasts are ample and supple enough to shame any woman I've ever seen."

"Then lay back, my lord. I intend to make sure you are well sated this night."

For years, she'd considered him her one knight stand that had seriously skidded off the rails. Now . . .

"Open your eyes, Sera."

Hoping and praying for a miracle, she obeyed Falcyn.

Max still wasn't moving. And now there was a grayish cast to his scales.

Worse? Falcyn was now as pale as Blaise. His hair had gone snow-white.

Concerned, she dropped her gaze from his face to the small bowl he held in his hand that contained blood. "Are you all right?"

Sweat beaded on his forehead and upper lip. "Tell me what do you love most about my brother."

"The way he makes me feel."

"And that is?"

She swallowed hard. "Like I can fly. Even when I'm in this body without wings, he makes me feel like I'm in the clouds, looking down on the world."

"Then breathe into him. Let your breath be his."

"I don't understand."

"Embrace the dragon, Seraphina. Breathe into him."

Cupping Max's snout, she did what Falcyn said. Then waited . . .

And waited.

Her heart clenched tight as Max remained still and pale. "Nothing's happening."

His hair darkening, Falcyn touched Max's body and the moment he did, a deep, dark crimson light shot through his cells, illuminating them like a flashlight through skin on the darkest night. Translucent and bright.

Before she could move, Max drew a deep breath and opened his eyes.

Sera gasped. "Max?"

He blinked slowly. "What happened?"

"Do you remember anything?"

Groaning, he laid his head back, then cursed. "Falcyn . . ." He immediately shifted to his human body to stare up at his brother. "You broke your oath."

His gaze went from Max to Sera. "Sometimes it's worth it. We are brothers, after all."

And with that, Max knew that Falcyn had finally forgiven him. "Thank you."

Falcyn inclined his head to him. "Remember the cost I've

paid for your life today. Don't ever waste it and don't make me regret it."

Max held his hand out to him. "Never."

Falcyn tucked his hand into his and shook it, not as a man, but as a drakomas. Then he cupped Seraphina's cheek in his hand and kissed her forehead. "May peace and happiness be with you, only."

As he withdrew, she caught his arm. "You're not leaving after this, are you?"

"Drakomai are creatures of solitude."

She glanced to Max before she turned back to Falcyn and smiled. "But they can learn another way. And I'd like to get to know my brother-in-law."

He met Max's gaze with an arched brow.

"You are always welcomed at my nest. Especially since we've lost Illarion."

"What?" Sera gasped.

Falcyn sighed wearily. "Not lost entirely. Temporarily adrift." He inclined his head to Max. "I shall stay, but only to help you knock sense into Illarion. I won't let those bastards take him. Not after everything else they've stolen from all of us. Now rest. We'll have more fights to come and you have a beautiful swan to soothe."

And with that he was gone.

Sera turned back to Max. She still couldn't believe he was alive again. Laughing, she threw herself against him and kissed his cheeks and lips and neck and forehead.

He laughed, too. "Careful, love. Else I'll think you missed me."

"Don't you ever die on me again!"

"I didn't mean to this time."

Her amusement fading, she pressed her marked palm to his as she moved to straddle him. "As soon as you heal, I want us to bond."

"Sera—"

"No arguments. Our dragonets are grown. They will find their own mates soon. But the one thing I learned today is what the dragonbane really means."

"And that is?"

"Living without your heart, and my heart is *you*, Lord Dragon."

"Then come, Strah Draga. Bond with me. For I know that without you I don't live. I only survive, and that is the bleakest and longest winter of my life."

EPILOGUE

Max snorted as he caught Falcyn staring hungrily at Tisiphone's posterior while she leaned over the pool table where Colt and Rémi were teaching her to play billiards. "I think you used me as an excuse to stay, brother."

Falcyn slid an unamused glare at him. "I don't know what you're talking about."

Shaking his head, Max handed him a drink before he started breaking down the soda dispensers. Fang had just closed the bar to the humans. It'd been almost three weeks since that fateful night when Sera had crashed back into his life.

And he cherished every minute of it.

Mostly because he knew war was here and a battle was coming. Blaise and Merlin were working on a Daimon cure, but so far nothing had helped them. Apollo was still after all the Olympians and the Were-Hunters.

With Kessar leading the charge.

They were on the cusp of the full moon and with it a bad feeling that Max couldn't shake. While his mate and children were safe upstairs with Aimee, he knew Illarion was out there, working with Apollo against them.

The countdown had begun.

And the Fates hated them all.

Max reached for a cloth, and when he did, he accidentally knocked a glass from the counter. Cursing, he moved to pick it up. The moment he did, an arrow shot past his head.

One that would have hit him had he not moved just then.

Furious, he and those around him looked for its source. But it'd come out of nowhere.

Falcyn met Fang's angry glower. "We need Acheron and Thorn to tighten the shields on this place."

He pulled the phone from his pocket. "On it already."

While Fang made the call, Max yanked the arrow out of the wood and saw the note wrapped around the shaft. He unscrolled and read the ancient Sumerian writing before he handed it to Fang, who screwed his face up at it.

"Hieroglyphs?"

"Cuneiform." Max handed it to Falcyn.

"What's it say?" Fang asked.

Falcyn answered for Max. "It's a full-on declaration of war. They are coming for us and they intend to mount our hides to the wall."

AUTHOR'S NOTE

Bel m'es quant ilh
m'enfolhetis

It pleases me when she mad-
dens me

E·m fai badar e·n vau
muzan!

When she makes me stand
gaping and staring!

De leis m'es bel si m'escarnis
O·m gaba dereir'o denan,

It pleases me when she
laughs at me and makes fun
of me, behind my back or to
my face,

Qu'apres lo mal me venra
bes Be leu, s'a lieys ven a
plazer.

For after the ill, the good
will come very quickly, if
such is her pleasure.

~Cercamon

343